Black and Blue

Lee-Ann Khoh

Cover Design by Luke Buxton | www.lukebuxton.com

To DC
who said I had to live to tell my stories.

Chapter One

I knew something was wrong with me when I found out Samson Otto was dead and all I could feel was dull envy.

I didn't feel much of anything most days. Just went through the motions. For the past ten weeks, I'd been coming in for work experience at the Create Tomorrow Foundation, and that's where I was when I heard about Samson.

Veronica Otto's black stilettos clicked a crescendo into the office. She stopped near the fruit bowl and clapped her hands together twice. 'Meeting, everyone. Now.'

Chairs squeaked as the team got up and made their way towards Veronica. I shrank behind my computer monitor. I didn't get included in meetings, unless it was to bring someone coffee.

'Don't they teach the meaning of "everyone" at school these days?' Veronica snapped in my direction. 'Or do you not understand English?'

The group turned to stare at me. My cheeks were hot when I joined them.

When she had everyone's attention again, Veronica spoke. 'Samson passed away yesterday.'

A few gasps rippled through the room. I studied Veronica's face. Her makeup was flawless as usual, but this time I noticed the whites of her eyes were slightly red.

'I don't need to tell you what a remarkable man my husband was. He was passionate about encouraging the talents of young people, no matter what their circumstances. He could've left Concord Creek behind years ago, but he never forgot where he came from. The world has lost a shining light.' She paused, her breath quivered, and my eyes darted around for the nearest box of tissues. But Veronica didn't cry, not in front of us.

'I understand this is a difficult time for everyone,' Veronica continued. 'But the ball is still on tomorrow night, and I do hope you'll all be there. It would mean a lot to him if everyone was there to represent his great work.'

Veronica's steely grey eyes singled me out. I looked away, staring down at the powdery scuff marks on my shoes.

'You're all dismissed,' she said. 'I have work to do and so do you.'

'How did he die?' whispered a voice to my right. I shot a look up at Veronica, wondering if she'd heard. But her heels had already clicked past us, towards Samson's office.

#

The answer was revealed when I checked the *Concord Creek Times'* website that night.

'Depression,' Mum said, pronouncing each syllable slowly, as if she'd never heard the word before. 'What does this mean?'

'He killed himself,' I translated. After Dad left, I became the one who had to explain everything to Mum.

'But he is rich,' Mum said. 'How can someone with so much money get this depression?' Three decades with Dad—most of them in Australia—hadn't diluted her Malaysian accent. Nearly every time she spoke, I had flashbacks of kids at school chanting 'ching chong' at me while pulling their eyes into slits. I was so embarrassed, but Mum always seemed oblivious to it.

Sometimes I would see my classmates messing up the girls' toilets when I walked in, sneering in my direction as if they knew my mum was the school cleaner.

I rolled my eyes. 'It's an illness, Mum. It's got nothing to do with his bank balance. Now can we get on with this?'

'Okay.' She moved to the other side of the room. 'Walk here. Straight line.'

I half-stumbled, half-shuffled towards Mum, wearing a pair of her high heels. I only ever wore flats, and it felt like the heels would slide off my feet at any moment, even though Mum and I were the same shoe size.

'No good, lah. You look like a drunk,' she said, shaking her head. 'I tell you, you must practise walking in heels. So you can be ladylike for the ball.'

The annual Create Tomorrow Ball was Concord Creek's biggest charity event, according to the press release I'd read last week. I'd been interning at the foundation for two weeks when Samson had strutted over to me with a huge grin pasted on his face. I'd tried to figure out what I'd done wrong. But he just pulled a sparkly rectangular card from one of his pockets and placed it on my keyboard. It was a ticket to the Create Tomorrow Ball, and my name was scrawled in the top right corner. I'd thanked him and tried to look excited.

'Why can't rich people raise money in jeans and sneakers?' I asked, half to Mum but mostly to myself.

Mum ignored my question. 'I am so happy you are finally wearing this gown I bought for you,' she said. 'It was very disappointing that you did not go to your Year 12 Ball after I spent all that money on you.'

I gritted my teeth. 'Well, I didn't ask you to spend the money. I told you over and over I wasn't going.' I hadn't seen the point. It's not like I had friends or a date to show off. 'Anyway, I'm wearing it now. Happy?'

'Yes, it will be good to see you not dressed like a boy for once.'

I bit my tongue and dug my fingernails into my palm as hard as I could.

'What jewellery will you wear?' Mum asked.

'I don't know.'

'I can give you a gold necklace to borrow.'

'Okay, thanks.'

'What style will you wear your hair?'

'I don't know, I'll probably just brush it and leave it the way it is. It's not like anyone's there to see me.'

'This is a bad attitude. You must look good when you ask these people for a job tomorrow. You should not work for free for ten weeks for nothing.'

'They'll probably be too drunk to notice how I look.' I clomped across the tiles into the quiet safety of my bedroom. Closing the door behind me, I kicked off the heels and sank onto the mattress, rubbing my feet.

'Take me away from here, Deanna,' I pleaded uselessly to the twelve-centimetre figurine sitting on my desk. A plastic approximation of Deanna Troi—the counsellor from *Star Trek: The Next Generation*—stared back at me. I leaned over and picked her up. The toy's hair was made of plastic like the rest of her, but I imagined my fingers touching soft, dark chocolate curls that my limp black hair could only dream about. Deanna had been in my brother Cedric's room for years until he moved to the city and gave her to me when I was six and he was eighteen. Cedric thought Deanna was hot. I just wanted her to be my friend. I wanted to explore new worlds with a family I belonged to. I wanted her to tell me what people were feeling and thinking so I'd know how to react in social situations. I was too old for that fantasy now, but Deanna remained in her spot on my desk.

I looked up at the Bon Jovi poster above my pillow and gave Deanna a little squeeze. 'How about some music?' I asked her.

Seconds later, *Bad Medicine* was filling my room. I cranked the volume up until I knew for sure no one but Deanna could hear me.

'I'm never good enough for Mum. Or anyone,' I told her, placing her back on the desk. 'It should've been me who died. Not Samson.'

Chapter Two

I turned eighteen the day after Samson died, but if it wasn't for the ball, I would've planned to stay in my room. Mum says birthday parties are for Westerners, and I just think they're annoying events you have to pretend to be happy for. Besides, it's not like anyone would actually turn up if I ever had a party.

Dad, on the other hand, had grown up in England and was more of a birthday person. He arrived at our doorstep while I was practising smiling in front of the bathroom mirror, trying to look natural instead of forced, and not really succeeding.

'Happy birthday, love,' he said, when I opened the door. He handed me a red *ang pow* packet and examined my dress. 'Wow, almost didn't recognise you!'

'Thanks.'

I could feel Mum's glare behind me a second before she spoke. 'Are you staying long?' she demanded.

'Well, I was gonna give Jade a ride to the ball,' Dad said.

Mum narrowed her eyes at the *ang pow* in my hands. 'You come all this way just to drive her and go home?'

'Of course. Save you the cab money.'

I inhaled sharply. Mum had never been a confident driver—probably because Dad had taught her and he wasn't exactly a patient instructor. She could drive to and from work, but not much else.

'Fine,' Mum muttered, crossing her arms.

'Right. Come on then, Jade. You got everything?'

I nodded and followed Dad out to the car.

#

Dad's partner Wayne was in the front passenger seat, so I sat in the back. I could see Mum peeking, not very subtly, through the front curtains of the house.

Wayne took no notice. 'Looking good, Jade,' he said, making an OK sign with his hand. I nodded thanks. I didn't know much about Wayne. He and Dad had been together for almost a year. They mostly kept to themselves and Wayne never came into the house if he and Dad dropped by.

We drove mostly in silence, with Elvis Presley songs playing on the stereo. Dad had never played Elvis at home, so I figured it was Wayne's choice. At least that was one thing I knew about him now.

'You got enough money, love?' Dad asked, as we slowed to a stop.

'I don't think I need any.' My ticket had already been paid for, and the meal was included.

He pulled some more notes out of his wallet and handed them to me. 'Just in case, birthday girl. Otherwise, you can save it for another time.'

'Thanks.' I slipped the cash into my clutch and wriggled out of the car, trying to keep my legs together like Mum had taught me. My shoes pressed uncomfortably into the heels of my feet and clacked against the ground as I walked inside, following the signs to the ballroom.

I took a long breath. The room was filling up fast. Lively scraps of conversation drifted into my ears. Everyone else seemed at home in this environment. I could feel myself sweating under the dress and hoped I'd worn enough deodorant.

I found my name card at our Company table and took my seat.

'White or red?' Bethany, the accountant, gestured at two bottles of wine.

I shook my head. 'I'm underage.' I technically wasn't as of today, but I didn't want any alcohol and no one knew it was my birthday.

'I won't tell,' Bethany said, filling my glass with white wine. 'You can't come to our biggest event of the year and not drink! Those are the rules.' She winked. 'Maybe we'll spike your water later.'

I hoped she was joking. I kept my mouth fixed in a polite smile for as long as I could hold it in place.

'Jade! Come and sit with me,' Veronica called from across the table. Surprised, I got up and shuffled over to the empty seat where Samson should've been.

I didn't know Veronica well. I knew her the same way everyone knew her. She was a local girl who'd had a short-lived singing career before marrying Samson.

'You know, Samson was fond of you,' Veronica said. 'He called you a quiet achiever.'

I wasn't sure if I was supposed to respond to that, so I just smiled awkwardly.

'You've done a wonderful job with our blog over the last ten weeks.'

'Thanks.' I can never tell when someone's genuinely praising me or being condescending. I glanced back around the table. Bethany was having an animated conversation with at least two other people across my empty seat. Everyone else was discussing everything from sports to weather to their home renovation projects, like they were the most exciting topics in the world. Why did small talk come so easily to these people?

'Not many people know this, but Samson was an introvert,' Veronica was saying. 'He mentioned you in his diary.'

'What? Me?' My head spun around again but no one seemed to be eavesdropping on our conversation.

'He said he had a feeling you were the only person in the office who saw through him. That you'd understand.'

Understand what? Him? Why he died? We stared at each other and the silence ticked between us.

I could hear the band they'd hired doing a final sound-check and pointed in the direction of the main stage. 'Samson wanted me to do some social media updates,' I began, hoping to be excused.

'Yes, of course. I understand this is the last week of your internship, Jade.'

I stopped. I'd been a disappointment to Mum since failing to get into uni this year. Maybe Veronica would offer me a job. If I could show Mum I was worth something …

But all Veronica said was, 'I wish you all the best for the future.'

#

The Create Tomorrow Foundation helped sick and disadvantaged kids through various arts programs. I liked putting up photos of kids covered in paint, or playing their first song on the piano, or learning how to make movies. I was less enthusiastic about taking pictures of adults who were obviously using this fundraiser as an excuse to get drunk on a weeknight. It was daunting to ask our staff—let alone various local celebrities—for a photo, so I stood at the main entrance and took a few wide shots. When I'd uploaded the best one to the foundation's social media accounts, I wandered over to the stage where the four-piece band was playing.

I was drawn to the lead singer right away. With his eyes closed and his lips pressed to the microphone as he strummed his guitar, he seemed to be in another world. He and the other band members were all in matching suits but different ties.

The singer opened his eyes and caught me staring at him. He brushed his tousled blond hair away from his face and winked. I looked away, my cheeks burning.

A few people were already swaying in front of the stage. I could see the singer and lead guitarist trying not to laugh as they played *Dancing with Myself*. One woman, whose face I vaguely recognised from the social pages of the newspaper, tugged at my arm.

'Dance, daaarling,' she drawled. I shook my head and pulled away.

'We'll be back soon, folks,' the singer said as the song ended. 'Have a drink and enjoy the night. Maybe we'll get the Mayor on the dance floor in the next set.' He put his guitar in its rack, jumped down from the stage, and came over to me, his hand outstretched.

'Hunter. Rory Hunter,' he said. 'But you can just call me Rory.' He had a deep, mellow tone to his voice, and his handshake was snug—firm but not too tight. I guessed he was in his mid to late twenties, but there was a sparkle in his chocolate-brown eyes and mischievous smile that made him seem younger. I was surprised at how calm I felt in his presence. Meeting people usually made me feel sick.

Rory nodded his head towards the three men he'd shared a stage with. The rest of the band were now standing around their dinner table, taking turns sipping from a wine glass. Between fits of laughter, I heard them commenting on its 'nose' and 'body' in exaggerated English accents that would've made Dad cringe.

'Those three jokers are my band,' Rory said, shaking his head. 'So, what's your name?'

'Jade.'

'Just Jade?'

'Jade Milton.'

'You don't look like a Milton.' He bit his lip. 'Wait, I shouldn't say that, should I? Is that racist?'

I shrugged. 'Milton is my dad's surname. He's white, Mum's not.'

Rory nodded. 'And what brings you here, Miss Jade Milton?'

'I'm doing work experience at the Create Tomorrow Foundation.'

'You worked for Samson Otto?'

'I guess so. Did you know him?'

'Not really. We played at his cousin's wedding a few years ago.' Rory paused. 'And you? Did you know him well? Is that how you got the work experience?'

'No, but my old English teacher, Ms Greenfield, knew him for twenty years. She was the one who told me to apply for an internship.' I decided not to add that she'd recommended it after finding out how badly I'd flunked my exams last year. Then she'd written me a reference. My resume was basically a blank sheet of paper, so I knew Ms Greenfield's letter was the reason Samson had even called me in.

'Well, I'm sorry for your loss anyway.'

I nodded thanks, even though I hadn't really lost anything.

'What's your band called?' I asked. I already knew since it was printed on our programs, but I didn't feel like talking about Samson.

'The Lyrebirds,' Rory replied. 'Wanna know why?'

'Why?'

'Lyrebirds have this awesome ability to mimic the sounds around them. So, I thought it'd be a cool name for a cover band.'

As we were talking, the drummer and bass player went outside and the lead guitarist sauntered over to us. 'Who's your girlfriend?' he asked, giving Rory a friendly punch on the shoulder.

Rory rolled his eyes and rubbed the back of the guitarist's crew cut. 'Jade, this is Alex Sorensen, the best guitarist in town and my brother from another mother. Alex, Jade.'

Alex couldn't be more than a couple of years older than me. He greeted me with a solid fist bump, like we already knew each other. Later, I saw him rubbing his hands with an aloe vera hand sanitiser and wondered if my knuckles had been sweaty or something.

'How's your night been?' Alex asked me.

'Okay, I guess. I'm kinda meant to be taking pictures …'

'How about a picture of us then?' Rory suggested. He found a sober-looking lady on the dance floor and got her to snap a photo from my camera phone. I looked at it on my screen and gave her a thumbs-up. Alex excused himself and went over to the bassist and drummer when they came back inside.

'How old are you anyway?' Rory asked, when we were more or less alone again.

'I turned eighteen today.'

'Are you serious? Happy birthday!' He gently squeezed my arm. 'I take it you're not drinking since you're working?'

'Actually, I don't drink.'

'Really? Me neither. I used to love it. I was travelling a lot for gigs back then, sometimes to the middle of nowhere, so I'd get hammered every night and swear it was the last time, then do it all over again. But it loses its appeal after a while. I mean, I'm twenty-eight, so I'm meant to responsible, right?' He grinned.

Apart from Mum, I'd never met a grown-up who didn't drink. So I hung out near Rory for the rest of the night. I barely remember eating dinner. I nodded my head in time to all the songs the band played and took at least fifty photos of them on my phone, before Mum rang me to say it was getting late and she'd ordered a taxi to come pick me up.

I felt a pang of disappointment. My feet hurt, but I didn't want the night to end.

'When am I seeing you again?' Rory asked, when I told him I had to go.

'Do you want to see me again?' I said, surprised.

'Of course. We're playing at the Bluebonnet Bar on Saturday night from about eight-thirty. It'd be nice to see a friendly face.'

I bit my lip. 'I don't have ID.'

Rory laughed. 'They won't check for it if you tell them you're with me. But in case they do …' He slipped a card out of his pocket and handed it to me. 'Just give me a call.'

#

That night, my thoughts drifted to Rory. His soulful eyes. His warm smile. I wanted to reach out and run my fingers through his sandy hair. Were those messy waves as thick and luscious as they looked? How would it feel to be nestled against his body?

I shook my head at the ceiling and rolled over to face Deanna. Her spot on my desk was illuminated by a sliver of moonlight peeping through my window. 'I know, I know. It's a silly crush. But you know I haven't had one since Nathan.'

I'd lost my virginity to Nathan Conway. A year later, the clumsy, drunken thrusts still slipped into my head at least once a day.

But Rory would be different. I imagined his strong, gentle hands on my body. Nathan had been a boy. Rory was a man.

I sighed. And I was just a stupid little mama's girl. As if Rory would ever even find me attractive.

But he did tell me to go to his gig this weekend. Maybe we could be friends. That's all I really needed. A friend. Someone I could share jokes with. Someone who could drag me out of this house. Someone who understood that I didn't sit in the corner by myself because I was a snob, but because I didn't know how to join in. Someone who cared about me enough to make me a better person. Just someone.

Chapter Three

On my last day at the Create Tomorrow Foundation, the others invited me to sit with them at lunchtime for once.

'You've done good work, kid,' Hank, the general manager, said to me. 'Email us if you need a referee.'

'Thanks.'

Everyone ignored me again after that. But for the only time in ten weeks, I was close enough to hear what they were gossiping about.

'Heard Zayden might have to repeat a year,' Hank said between mouthfuls of pasta. Zayden was Samson and Veronica's eleven-year-old son.

'Didn't he get kicked out of his fancy private school in the city?' Bethany asked.

'Yep, he's enrolled at Concord Creek Primary now. How far they fall.'

There was hollow laughter, followed by an uncomfortable silence before someone dared to ask the question I'd been wondering myself.

'Do you know how he did it? Samson, I mean.'

'Took a cocktail of drugs, then hanged himself in the bedroom.'

'I heard that too, but it hasn't been confirmed anywhere.'

'Media doesn't report on suicides. They're afraid of copycats. Samson's only been in the news coz he's a local celebrity.'

I stared at my tuna avocado sandwich in silence. People cared about Samson. It mattered when he died. If I killed myself, no one would ever know.

'I still can't believe it,' Bethany said. 'He seemed so happy in the week or so before he died.'

The others murmured in agreement. I wanted to tell them it was probably because he knew what he was going to do—he wasn't wrestling with the decision anymore. But speaking up would've meant everyone staring at me and making me their next topic of gossip. So, I took a big bite of my sandwich and said nothing.

#

I didn't have any more jobs to do in the office after lunch, so I went online. Even though I hadn't spoken to the boy who took my virginity in almost a year, I felt like I knew everything he'd been up to since then.

Nathan Conway's latest update read: 'F U AMANDA.'

Heaps of his friends had already commented on it, the replies ranging from: 'OMG what happened?' to 'Forget that bitch, you deserve better.' A quick check showed me that Nathan had changed his relationship status back to single, and he and Amanda Rayner were no longer friends on any social networks.

Amanda graduated with me at the end of last year. We were both two years younger than Nathan, but unlike me, she was pretty and popular. I wasn't surprised when I found out they were together. She was more his type—I was the anomaly.

My phone beeped, alerting me to a new text message. All it said was: *Hey.*

Nathan was a lot of things, but a prolific writer wasn't one of them.

Hey. Saw your post. You ok? I replied.

Yep. Screw her. I wanna c u.

I tried to figure out how to respond, but by the time my head hit the pillow that night, I still hadn't thought of anything to say.

#

He didn't message me again until the next day when I was getting ready to go to the Bluebonnet Bar.

What r u doing tonight? Lets catch up like old times.

I dropped my phone on the bed and turned to Deanna. 'It's Nathan,' I told her.

Deanna stared back at me.

'I know what you're thinking. He probably just wants to get drunk and hook up. But he's the only guy who's ever wanted me.'

I picked Deanna up and squeezed her.

'I promise I won't go back to him. Besides, I have plans tonight.' I cupped her to my stomach. 'I've got so many butterflies right now. I mean, I'm always nervous about socialising and all that. But I'm actually excited as well. I really want to see Rory again. I can't explain it, but there's something about him.'

I put Deanna back on the desk and picked my phone up. *Can't tonight. Take care.*

He didn't reply.

Chapter Four

'I'm going out!' I called to Mum as I headed for the front door.

Mum charged me down from the kitchen. 'Going where?'

'I'm meeting a friend.'

'What friend?'

'Just a friend.'

'From school?'

'I didn't have friends in school, Mum.' I rolled my eyes. 'His name's Rory. His band was playing at the ball this week, and they're playing at the Bluebonnet Bar tonight.'

Mum squinted at me. 'I do not think you should be going out drinking with strange men.'

'I'm not. I'm going out to listen to music.' We stared at each other for a moment, before I added, 'I'm not a little kid anymore. If Dad were here, he'd tell you the same and let me go.'

Mum grimaced. 'Fine. Do not stay out too late.'

#

The Bluebonnet Bar was a ten-minute walk from my house. I'd passed it on the way to and from school but had never been inside.

'Haven't seen you round here before,' a lone bouncer said as I walked towards the entrance. 'You with the band?'

I nodded.

'Yeah? Who do you know in the band?'

'Rory Hunter.'

'He knows them all, doesn't he? Alright, go on in.'

I paused for a moment, wondering what that meant, but the bouncer's eyes were scanning the car park and he wasn't looking at me anymore. As soon as I walked inside, I noticed the grimy wooden floors and the smell of stale beer. I looked up and saw two men who seemed to be leering in my general direction.

'You here all alone, little girl?' one man called, lifting up the beer bottle he'd been cradling in his lap. 'Come sit with us. We'll buy you a drink.'

I shook my head. Had I made a mistake? Should I have stayed in my room like I did every other Saturday night? What if Rory didn't really want me there? What if he was just being polite? Was I making a complete idiot of myself?

'Aww, c'mon, don't be a stuck-up bitch!'

I clenched my fingers around the edges of my shirt. The scattered voices and clinks of glasses were closing in on me. Balls ricocheting around a pool table rang like bullets in my ears. My chest tightened. I scanned around for a bathroom I could hide in.

Just as my eyes found the female toilet symbol, two hands closed around my shoulders from behind. I jumped.

'Jade.' The familiar voice seeped into my skin. I sighed with relief and turned to see Rory Hunter staring back at me.

'You okay?'

I nodded.

'I'm glad you came,' Rory said, giving me a quick hug. He looked different out of his suit. Tonight he was wearing a faded red bandana tied in a strip around his head—like Axl Rose from Guns N' Roses, or Bruce Springsteen circa 1984—and his short-sleeved shirt revealed several colourful tattoos on his arms. I wanted to study them some more, but I didn't want to be rude or get caught staring again, like I had on the night we met.

Rory led me to another room with another bar, but this one was empty—apart from the band. Alex spotted me and waved, grinning.

'I need to go and finish setting up. We got here a bit late. My fault,' Rory said. 'Will you be all right out here?'

I nodded. There were some seats scattered around the room, and I chose one near the stage to sit in. Rory disappeared through a black curtain that marked off the backstage area and emerged a few moments later next to Alex.

By the time the band kicked off their gig with *Need You Tonight*, my heart had settled back into its chest, where it stayed, even when a few tipsy people from the front bar spilled into the room.

Alex came over to fist-bump me when the band went on a break. 'Hey! Jade, isn't it?' He had a perky but gentle voice.

I nodded.

'We're just heading outside for some fresh air. It's so hot in here. You should come hang with us.'

I followed the band outside, minus Rory, who was in a deep discussion with the sound guy when we left the room.

#

Out in the courtyard, I was assaulted by the smell of cigarette smoke. I did my best not to cough.

When we found a table, Alex introduced me to the rest of The Lyrebirds. I already knew from my online stalking that the drummer was called Dom Antonelli and the bassist was Tyler Redden, but this was my first chance to talk to them.

I knew from his online profiles that Dom was the oldest in the band—in his thirties and divorced with an eight-year-old daughter. He'd played in another band with Rory before The Lyrebirds were formed. Thick muscles bulged from his navy tank top, and he had black and grey tattoos extending down the lengths of his arms.

Tyler was almost the opposite in appearance—tall and skinny, with no visible ink or piercings on his body. He was wearing sunglasses even though it was dark outside, and a T-shirt that read: I may be vegan but I can still kick your rump.

Dom lit a cigarette. I cleared my throat and tried to take shallow breaths through my mouth so I wouldn't have to smell it.

'So, the weirdest thing happened today with Zayden Otto,' Dom said.

My ears perked up. It was the second time in two days that I was listening to people talk about Samson and Veronica's son. Small world.

'It's been six months since he started taking lessons, but I can tell he hasn't practised once,' Dom continued. 'Tells me he'll grow up to make more money than I ever will so what's the point. Anyway, I'm doing some paperwork today and he comes into the office, crying. I figure it's coz his old man just died, but then his mum walks in and says he's quitting, and Zayden starts screaming that he wants to keep playing.'

'So, what happened?' Alex asked.

'Nothing. They left. I now have some free time on Tuesday afternoons.'

I pretended to scratch my nose in an attempt to block the smoke from Dom's mouth.

'Do you know how his dad offed himself?' Tyler asked.

'I heard he OD'd,' Dom said. 'But someone at the school today said his missus found him dangling from a rope at their house.'

Alex glanced over at me. 'Wasn't he your boss, Jade?' he asked.

I felt everyone's eyes on me. I nodded. 'Yeah.' They were still looking at me, like I was supposed to say more, so I stammered, 'I mean, sort of. I mean, I was an intern at his foundation for ten weeks. But I didn't know him that well.'

My face felt hot. I thought about Zayden. Had his dad left him a note to explain?

Rory surfaced from inside the pub and made his way to our table. He flicked the back of Dom's head and grinned. 'Stop blowing your cancer at everyone, Domenic.'

Dom rolled his eyes and stuck his middle finger in the air. Alex moved over to open up a space between himself and me. Rory pulled up a chair, winked at me and sat down.

'Man, I don't know how this place still exists,' Rory said. 'The manager had a chat to me just now, and I was half-expecting him to say he was closing up early and telling us to go home.'

The rest of the band nodded in agreement. I thought about the creepy men I'd met when I walked in and was grateful there weren't more of them.

'Hard to believe there used to be lines to get in about ten years ago,' Dom said.

Alex nodded. 'My old man used to work here back then.'

'Well, original bands are used to no one being at their gigs,' Tyler said. 'But it's cover bands now, too.'

'Tell me about it,' Dom said. 'None of you came to my EP launch!' Everyone laughed, so I did too.

After a few minutes, Rory checked his watch and stood up. 'Time to go back to work, kids,' he said, which seemed like a weird thing to say, given Dom was older than him. As we headed back inside, I felt a squeeze on my shoulder. 'We'll play some Bon Jovi for you before the night's over,' Rory said. He disappeared from hearing range before I had a chance to ask how he knew Bon Jovi was what I listened to when I wanted to escape Mum.

When the band kicked into *You Give Love a Bad Name* halfway through the final set, I almost jumped up to dance before remembering I wasn't alone in my bedroom with Deanna anymore. I tried to catch each of the band members' eyes to let them know I was enjoying it, even if I couldn't let go of my body.

At the end of the gig, Rory jumped off the stage and went straight to the front bar. I found him hunched over the counter, drinking from a pitcher of water. His bandana was draped over his shoulders and his sandy blond hair glistened with sweat. He straightened when he saw me.

'How'd we go with *Bad Name*? Rating out of ten?' he said.

I thought for a moment, then replied, 'Eight. You got the words wrong, but it was good otherwise.'

He rolled his eyes and grinned before offering me some water. I took a sip, then remembered my question.

'How did you know I'm a Bon Jovi fan?'

Rory laughed. 'Mate, it's all over your profile and just about everything on the internet with your name attached to it!'

'You've been stalking me online?' I was secretly flattered.

'It's not really stalking, is it? It's not like I'm hiding under your bed.'

'You wouldn't fit under my bed.'

'You know what I mean, Miss Milton.'

I nodded. I'd been looking Rory up, too. He ran a web design business during the day and had a couple of kids and a dog. But more than anything, he had a life I wanted to be a part

of. He seemed happy and fulfilled, and I wished for that in my
life too.

Chapter Five

'I do solo gigs every Sunday at the Sherlock Arms,' Rory told me. 'You should come along. It's right near the beach so there's always girls wandering in and out in nothing but bikinis.'

I raised my eyebrows.

He chuckled. 'But more importantly, I'm there every week with no one to talk to.'

It was a half-hour bus ride to get to the Sherlock Arms from my house, but I decided to go see him that weekend. For the first time in my life—because I'd never had anywhere to go before—it sucked that I couldn't drive.

I tried not to think about my driving phobia on the way to the Sherlock Arms.

I was walking up to the entrance when something slipped from under my foot and I fell forward onto the asphalt, grazing my knees and palms.

I sat up and brushed soil off my body before looking to see what I'd tripped on. There was a grey rock, about half the size of my hand, on the footpath. I picked it up. It was slightly dusty. But there was something beautiful about it. I gave it a little squeeze, like I did with Deanna sometimes. Its jagged edges dug into my skin, stinging the grazes on my palm.

My heart started to race. I was still in pain, but I felt alive.

I got to my feet, slipped the rock into my jeans pocket and continued up the path.

#

I found Rory standing in a corner of the beer garden, wearing a green bandana, untangling audio leads. His acoustic guitar was sitting in an open case.

He looked up at me and grinned. 'You made it!'

I nodded shyly.

There was a table in front of Rory so I sat down. He picked up his guitar and began to play *Wanted Dead or Alive*. This time, he got all the lyrics right, even though I would've thought *You Give Love a Bad Name*—which didn't have as many words—would be easier to remember.

'*Wanted* tells a story,' Rory explained when I pointed this out. 'With *Bad Name*, you could put any of the lyrics anywhere in the song and it wouldn't make a difference.'

When it was time for his break, Rory grabbed his cup of coffee and a digital SLR camera and joined me at the table. He let me scroll through his photos of the band over the past few weeks, explaining the stories behind each one. He told me Alex was like a brother to him, that Tyler wore sunglasses all the time because of photophobia and that Dom had taken up smoking when he was sixteen to annoy his father.

'He always rolls his eyes when I give him crap about smoking coz he knows I used to smoke,' Rory said. 'Everyone told me it'd wreck my voice, but I didn't care. Not till my kids were born. Wasn't easy to give it up, but I did.' He took a sip of his coffee. 'Who knows, maybe Dom would have a reason to try if he saw his daughter more. But she lives interstate with her mum.'

'That must be tough for him,' I said.

26

'Yeah. Well, we don't really talk about it. But I'm glad I'm not in that situation with my kids.'

I looked back down at the camera and saw that we'd reached what were clearly Rory's family shots. I hesitated.

'Is it okay for me to look at these?' I asked. We'd only known each other for a few days.

'Course it is,' he said, and continued his commentary. 'That's my daughter, Ella, and my son, Ethan. They're four. Born twenty-three minutes apart. There they are finger-painting. What you don't see is the huge mess I had to clean up afterwards. But they love it and I try not to stifle their creativity.

'There they are on the trampoline, right before they had a fight about which of them was Buzz Lightyear.

'And there they are playing with the dog. I don't know how they got so dirty though. The dog looks pretty clean in that pic.'

Mum had never liked me playing outside. She didn't want me to get dirty, like Ethan and Ella, or fall over, like I had on my way here. And now I hardly ever went outdoors. But Ella and Ethan looked happy and I smiled with them.

'Do they do everything together?' I asked.

'Most things,' Rory said. 'But I reckon that'll change as they get older. They play this game where they copy each other when we're out, but at home, they've got really different personalities. I do my best to treat them like individuals, and not just "the twins", if you know what I mean. And I let them choose their own outfits, within reason. Ethan's fond of picking four shirts and no pants, so I have to put my foot down sometimes.' He smiled. 'When they start school, I'm gonna see if they can be put in different classes, but it might depend on how many kids are in their year.'

I noticed that in the fifty or so pictures we scrolled through, he didn't mention a wife or partner.

While I was trying to find the nerve to ask about Ethan and Ella's mum, Rory spotted a couple arriving. 'Be right back,' he said to me, and went out to greet them, leaving me alone to play with my phone and look after his hour-old coffee.

I started to feel anxious and hot. Rory was my whole reason for being here. Without him there, everyone would see that I was lonely, pathetic, out of place. There seemed to be so many people around, all looking like they belonged, and I was sure they would notice how stupid I looked. My heart was racing, taunting me. I fidgeted with my shirt, looking for something to focus on.

Finally, the three of them came in and joined me. I had to remember to breathe.

'Jade, meet my big sister, Faye,' Rory said. 'And her husband, Greg.'

Faye had the same shaped eyes as Rory, but hers were blue instead of brown, and she had her chestnut hair in a long-layered bob. Greg smiled at me through deep-set hazel eyes and a peppered beard.

I'd already looked up Faye and Greg Cunningham during my online stalking of Rory, but I pretended I didn't know anything about them. We shook hands, then Rory and Greg went to the bar. Faye studied me.

'You're the one who took those photos at the Create Tomorrow Ball,' she said.

I nodded. She began to talk about how nice the photos were and how lovely the band looked suited up. When Rory and Greg returned, Rory placed a glass of water in front of me and smiled, before turning to his sister.

'You good, sis? How's my nephew?'

'Oh, we're fine. Lyle is having a bit of trouble at school, but we'll get through it,' Faye said. 'And you? Are the twins feeling better?'

'Well, the flu's gone,' Rory said. 'Now they just have an attitude problem.' He rolled his eyes. 'Man, when Ella narrows her eyes at me and does that little pout, she's the spitting image of her mum.'

'That's why I keep saying you have to sing to them,' Faye said. 'Drown out their mum's influence with music.'

What's the deal with Ethan and Ella's mum? The question itched on the edge of my tongue, but I wasn't part of this family or this discussion, so I numbed myself with the icy cold water.

#

After the gig, Rory gave me a ride home. We drove through streets I hardly knew, even though I'd lived in this town my whole life. Concord Creek wasn't that big. Dad had moved the family here for work when Cedric was six, and I was born at Concord Creek Hospital.

Rory's left arm was facing me in the front passenger seat, and I tried to imagine the stories behind his tattoos. He glanced over at me and caught my eye.

'Do you like my tatts? Or are you staring coz you hate them?'

I blushed. 'No, they're cool. Do they mean anything to you?'

'Some of them. The footprints on my forearm are Ethan's and Ella's, from just after they were born.' He pointed to the electric guitar that took up most of his left bicep. 'This was my first baby, which got wrecked in a car accident. Not my fault, I promise.' He grinned and tapped his opposite arm, the one I couldn't see from my seat. 'On this side, I've got a memorial tattoo to my grandpa, and some random stars and stuff I got when I was bored one day.'

'Cool.' I strained my head for more conversation topics, before remembering the photos he'd shown me earlier. 'What's your dog's name?' I asked.

'Bones,' he replied, clicking his tongue at a car in front of him. 'Named him after Doctor McCoy from *Star Trek*.'

I felt my mouth slide into a grin. 'I didn't know you liked *Star Trek*.' There'd been no indication of this in my thorough online stalking.

Rory smiled. 'There's a lot you don't know about me. But I hope we get to know each other a lot better.'

Me too, I thought, but the words got stuck in my throat. I tried to think of more to say. I wanted to know everything about Rory and his family.

'You live at home, right?' Rory asked. 'Are your parents still together?'

I shook my head. 'Dad's gay. He moved in with a guy he met at work about ten months ago. I've got a brother, Cedric, but he's twelve years older than me and lives in the city. So, it's just Mum and me at home.'

'I'm sorry. About your dad.'

'It's okay. I always felt like Mum and Dad were wrong for each other. And I was right.'

'Even so … it must've been hard for you.'

I shrugged, not knowing what to say. Rory reached over and touched my arm. Despite the heaviness of the moment, I found myself enjoying the warmth that passed between us and was quietly sorry when he moved his hand back to the gear stick.

'It's really cool that you're half-Asian,' Rory said, piercing my thoughts.

I blinked. 'Is it?'

'This is Concord Creek. There aren't too many people that aren't … you know, all white. Hell, Dom's probably the most exotic person I know and I don't think he even speaks Italian.'

'Oh, I'm so exotic,' I replied, a hint of sarcasm leaking into my voice.

'Sorry, I'm stuffing this up, aren't I?' he said.

'Stuffing what up?'

'Nothing. Let's start again.' He turned to me with a grin. 'Hey, I'm Rory Edmund Hunter. I think you're cool. Let's be friends.'

'Deal,' I said, smiling back. I didn't have friends. At least I hadn't had any before. But I did now, and it felt good. I looked up at Rory. 'Edmund, huh?'

Rory rolled his eyes and laughed. 'My mum was a big Narnia fan. But unlike that Edmund, I won't sell you out to a witch for candy.'

#

As soon as I got through the door, Mum pushed me down the hall and into the master bedroom. 'I have been waiting for you,' she told me. After spending the afternoon listening to Rory's soothing honey voice, Mum sounded high-pitched and harsh.

'Why?' I asked, immediately on edge.

'I see you go out a lot this week. Why suddenly you want to go out?'

'What's wrong with going out? People do it all the time.'

'Not everyone fails their exams like you. You should have been studying harder, not playing.'

'What playing? I never had anyone to play with, thanks to you!'

'I let you keep your music so loud because you said it helped you. Now I see you were just being distracted from your duties.'

31

'I tried my best! I'm just not perfect like Cedric, okay?' I pressed my fingertips into the pocket where the rock was. 'Besides, it's done now. School's over. I don't have anything to study for so why can't I go out like a normal person?'

'You have seen this man so much,' Mum said. 'A girl like you must behave yourself.'

'What's that supposed to mean?'

'You should remember to be a good girl. How come you think you can trust this *ang moh*?'

'He's my friend,' I said.

'Why does this man want to be your friend? You don't find it suspicious?'

'Why, coz no one could ever possibly want to be my friend? Thanks a lot, Mum.' I ran away to my bedroom as fast as I could and closed the door behind me, my chest heaving.

'Why is she always on my back?' I choked. 'I'm never good enough for her.'

Deanna couldn't say anything to make me feel better. I needed to get control over my life. I needed to stop the pain in my head and heart.

I clawed the dusty, grey rock from my pocket and kicked off my jeans. Before I knew what was happening, I smacked the rock into my thighs, over and over and over, until my arm collapsed in exhaustion. A strange rush of exhilaration washed over me—calming me the way listening to Rory did.

I fingered the warm, swollen flesh I'd created.

'I don't know what just happened, Deanna,' I whispered. 'But it felt good.'

Chapter Six

'What's your favourite word?' Rory asked me the following Sunday when he was setting up for his gig.

'I don't know.'

'That's three words.' He grinned.

'I've never really thought about it,' I said. 'What's yours?'

'Sojourn.'

'Sojourn?'

'It means a short stay or trip.'

'Like you driving me home from this gig?'

'I was thinking more like a stopover in Kuala Lumpur or a long weekend in Bali or something. But I guess this could be our Sunday Sojourn.'

'Sunday Sojourn. I like that.'

Rory was playing *Here Comes the Sun* when a pair of smooth, tanned legs in short denim shorts materialised in front of me.

'Oh, wow … Jade?'

I looked up.

'Amanda. Hey.' I hadn't seen Nathan's ex since our last day of school and I couldn't remember the last time we'd spoken to each other. So I was surprised when she pulled up the chair next to me.

'It's cool if I sit here, right? I'll be gone soon. My boyfriend's about to finish his shift. So, how've you been?'

Amanda had a new boyfriend already and I couldn't even get my first? Not that it should come as a shock. Everyone in school had wanted to date Amanda Rayner.

'Good.' I gestured towards Rory. 'Just watching my friend play.'

Amanda gave Rory the once-over, then turned back to me. 'Oooh, is he your boyfriend?' she asked, way too loudly.

I shook my head. My face burned, but when I peeked up at Rory he didn't look like he'd heard anything.

'I think he should be. You look totally in love!'

I glanced towards Rory again. He was still singing, playing, seemingly oblivious. I pretended to be really interested in the table, hoping Amanda would go away so I wouldn't have to make conversation.

Amanda giggled. 'Don't get all embarrassed. I'm just teasing. But you know, anyone would be better than Nathan.'

I swallowed nervously, afraid to meet her eyes.

'Look, I know he's been messaging you and I don't want you to make the same mistakes I did.'

'How do you know he messaged me?'

'Coz he's been talking to every girl in town since we broke up. Including all my friends. And coz it's what he does.' Amanda rolled her eyes. 'Like, he literally hooks up with a dozen random girls on a footy trip, plays dumb about it when I find out and then calls me a skank for just talking to a guy.'

'I'm sorry,' I said.

'Don't be. I'm way happier now!' She looked over my shoulder and waved brightly. I turned around to see one of the bartenders. 'Gotta go, see ya!' Amanda's chair scraped sharply on the ground as she hopped up and kissed her new boyfriend. They left together, their arms touching each other's waists.

I turned back to Rory. Well, I was sure Amanda was right about one thing. Rory would be better than Nathan.

#

'Thanks for coming out,' Rory said, when he was pulling out of the car park. I was starting to learn the way home now, even though it was pointless if I couldn't drive. 'No one goes to gigs besides you. I meet people all the time and I tell them where I'm playing and they say they'll come check me out, but they never do.'

I nodded and kept on browsing radio stations because I didn't know what to say.

'You're really quiet,' he observed. 'You always just nod or shrug or give one-word answers.'

'I know. I'm sorry.'

From the corner of my eye, I saw him smile. 'It's okay. I'm just not used to it, being a musician and a dad. Not to mention dealing with clients who don't seem to remember that they hired me to design their websites.'

I nodded again, and he started to laugh.

'So, what's your story?' he asked.

'What do you mean?'

'Well, you've finished school. What do you want to do with your life?'

'I don't know. I'm probably too stupid to do anything.'

'Don't talk about yourself like that,' Rory said. 'Besides, I get a vibe from you and I think you're really smart.'

'I failed all my exams last year,' I told him. 'That's why I didn't get into uni. But if I had, I probably would've had to move to the city and I don't know how I'd cope with that.'

'I think you might've pleasantly surprised yourself. But school's not the be-all and end-all.'

35

'It is when you live with my mum.'

Rory paused, before turning to me again. 'Tell me more about yourself.'

'Is this a job interview?' I asked.

He grinned. 'Nah, I think it's illegal to ask my next question in an interview.'

'What's your next question?'

'How come you don't have a boyfriend? Or do you?' He paused again. 'Is this too personal?'

'It's okay. There's no boyfriend.'

'Yeah, so what's the story? You're gorgeous. You're not a bitch or anything. I'm surprised you're single.'

I shrugged. 'I'm a bit of a loner, I guess.'

Rory nodded. 'There's too much drama to deal with in relationships,' he said, almost to himself.

'What's your story?' I dared to ask.

Rory was silent for a long minute. I started to wonder if I'd forgotten to ask the question out loud.

'Maria's the mother of my kids,' Rory said when he finally spoke. 'But over time, we've realised we're better off as just friends rather than lovers or husband and wife, or anything like that. But we still live in the same house—we just sleep in different rooms. We raise Ella and Ethan together. We fight like a normal couple. I'm not seeing other women at the moment coz I'm just so busy.'

I nodded again, wondering if I'd still be in his life when he was ready.

'People with kids break up. I mean, you already know that,' he said. 'But if more couples took the time to breathe afterwards, they might be able to come to an arrangement where the kids don't have to lose one of their parents.'

'Yeah, it makes a lot of sense.'

We slowed to a stop behind a bus that was letting some passengers off. 'Do you sing?' he asked suddenly.

'Not really, why?'

'Just wondering. We're auditioning female singers for the band. We always used to have a girl for about half the songs until just before the Create Tomorrow Ball when I had to sack her.'

'How come?'

'She wasn't getting along with everyone. You know, the usual.'

I nodded as if I knew what 'the usual' meant.

'We had a keyboard player for a while too,' Rory said. 'We played a lot more eighties synth pop and glam metal in our set back then. But Kara got a job in the city and there aren't many good keyboard players in Concord Creek, so now we make do without.'

'I love the eighties. I know I wasn't born then, but I do.' There was just something so brazen and over-the-top about that decade that I envied.

'You're a woman after my own heart,' Rory said, smiling at me. We were silent for the rest of our Sunday Sojourn, but it was a good silence, the comfortable kind, and somehow, I felt stronger with him by my side.

#

I raced into my bedroom to update Deanna, but my phone rang before I could talk to her.

It was Nathan.

'Hello?' I said, closing my bedroom door behind me.

'That dirty slut's not answering any of my calls,' Nathan told me.

'You mean Amanda?'

'Yeah.'

'Well, she doesn't have to talk to you if she doesn't want to,' I said. 'And maybe she's heard you're going around calling her a dirty slut.' I held my breath. I'd never really stood up to Nathan before. I'd never criticised him. I'd always been too scared of turning away the only guy who'd ever thought I was worth talking to. But being with Rory had given me an injection of courage.

'When did you start taking her side?' Nathan growled. 'You don't even like her.'

'Who says I don't like her? I hardly even know her.'

There was a silence at the other end of the phone. I looked at Deanna, wondering if I was supposed to say anything, or if I should hang up. Finally, Nathan said, 'We should get together, Jade. Alone this time. I never made it up to you.'

If he'd said those words a year ago, I might've gotten on the next bus to his house on the off chance that we could fix things between us. But I didn't have those feelings for Nathan anymore.

'You're dating someone,' he concluded when I didn't reply.

'No, I'm not.' But I wanted to be. For the first time since Nathan, I actually wanted a guy.

'Tell me about him.'

'I said I'm not dating anyone.'

'But there is someone, isn't there?'

'What makes you say that?' I asked.

'Coz you're not yourself,' Nathan replied. 'And you're not thirsty for me anymore.'

I could feel my hands shaking around my phone. 'And that could only be coz of a guy?' I said, struggling to keep the squeak out of my voice. The rock I'd picked up outside the Sherlock

Arms was sitting on my desk, next to Deanna. I picked it up and squeezed it with my free hand.

'Is it a girl?' Nathan asked. 'Coz that'd be pretty hot.'

I sighed. 'There's no girl. There's a guy, but we're just friends. I don't want things to get weird between him and me.'

'So just screw him. It's fun. You don't have to date him.'

'But—'

'But nothing. You always think too much. I don't wanna hear any more about this guy unless it's to tell me that I'm bigger than him.'

When I hung up the phone, my fist clenched around the rock, so tight that my hand started to tremble from the force. I thought about the bruises I'd given myself a few weeks ago. I knew if I hit myself now, I'd feel that rush again.

I thought about Rory and put the rock down.

'I wish you could meet him,' I told Deanna. 'Rory, I mean. For the first time in a long time, I remember how it feels to be … content. Maybe even happy.'

Chapter Seven

When I arrived at our Sunday Sojourn a few weeks later, I found Rory talking to Alex, who was slumped over a table, his ear resting on his folded arms. Rory spotted me and poked Alex with his finger. Alex scrambled upright with a tired grin. 'Hey, have a seat,' he said, rubbing his eyes, while Rory went back to setting up for his gig.

Alex took a long slurp from a can of Red Bull as I sat down. 'I'm exhausted, dude. Think I'm getting too old for these late nights.'

He wasn't old at all, but I often found it tiring to be around lots of people, and I was two years younger than him. So, I could relate, even if that wasn't what he meant.

'Did you have a gig last night?' I asked.

'Yeah. Have you ever been to Summit?'

I shook my head.

'Good, don't. It's a real dodgy club we used to gig at all the time. I even saw some guy literally taking a piss on the floor next to the bar once.'

'Gross.' My eyes widened in disgust.

'We had a last-minute fill-in for the band that's been playing there for the past year or so. There were a bunch of people there we used to know, so we were catching up till about four.' Alex paused to gulp down more of his drink. 'Then Rory said, "let's do something fun" so we went back to Tyler's house and played poker till around ten this morning. Didn't get home till after ten-thirty. I only live across the road from Rory, but I almost collapsed right there in the street. And then I fell asleep for what felt like a minute, before Rory was knocking on my door. He said I had to drive him to his gig today coz he still had alcohol in his system.'

'He said he didn't drink,' I said, trying to sound light-hearted.

'He hasn't in a while, actually,' Alex said. 'But everyone kept shouting him last night. And Tyler's got a pretty impressive home bar. I reckon he could name every vegan-friendly alcoholic drink on the planet off the top of his head.'

I nodded. Maybe it was just a one-off thing then.

Alex took a small bottle of hand sanitiser from his pocket and began to smear it over his palms. He glanced over at me. 'You think I'm weird for this, don't you?'

I shook my head.

'Really? Everyone else does.'

'I think it smells nice,' I said.

Alex smiled and offered me the open bottle. I held out my hand and he squeezed a dollop of the gel into my palm.

Rory was singing *Green Limousine* as two girls in matching bikinis danced out of time in front of him. Alex grinned. 'Rory knows how to get people going,' he said. 'It's a gift.'

I nodded. By the end of the first set, both of the bikini girls had Rory's business card and were offering to buy him drinks. He turned them down, before grabbing his coffee and joining Alex and me at the table.

Faye and Greg turned up during the first break. Faye immediately started fussing over Alex, who retold the story of last night to her. As Faye turned her attention back to her brother, Greg and Rory exchanged amused glances with each other.

'You think you're an island!' Faye said, prodding Rory's chest with her forefinger. 'You think your actions don't impact on others, but they do. Look at poor Alex! Look at him!'

Rory laughed, gave Faye a peck on the cheek and waved her off. Greg offered Alex a ride home, but Alex said he was feeling more awake now. 'I'll stay on in case Rory needs me to take over the driving on the way home,' he said. I suddenly wished I had my licence so I wouldn't be so useless. Sixteen-year-olds managed it without fear. Why couldn't I?

I wasn't sure if Rory and Alex were going to be able to take me home after the gig. But when we'd finished loading his gear out, Rory pushed a toy and some tattered magazines aside to make room for me in the back next to the twins' child seats.

'You owe me one for getting me out of bed,' Alex told Rory.

'We've been owing each other one for years,' Rory replied. 'Who's keeping score?'

'Hey, I've never ruined your beauty sleep, Hunter.'

'I'll pay for next week's supply of hand sanitiser and we'll call it even.'

'Low blow, dude,' Alex said, but they were both grinning.

I smiled along and sighed, wishing friendships came as easily and naturally to me. Alex glanced back at me. 'Do you even know where you're going?' he asked Rory.

'Yeah, I take Jade home every week. I've got the route memorised. It's our Sunday Sojourn.'

'That's pretty awesome,' Alex said.

'I'm pretty awesome,' Rory said, winking in the rear-view mirror. 'Aren't I, Jade?'

I nodded. Before I knew it, we'd pulled up at my driveway. I couldn't figure out how to slide open the back door, so Rory had to get out of the van and open it for me. Giggling, I waved and watched them drive away, already missing their laughter and company. I walked into my house where Mum was waiting for me.

#

'This must stop,' Mum said.

'What?'

'You will not see this man anymore. He can put things in your drink and rape you. I read about it.'

I glared at her. How dare she? 'Rory's nothing like that. You don't even know him!'

'I know what men try to do with girls. You are not safe at bars. You will stay home from now on until you find a job.'

I clenched my fists to stop myself from hitting something— the wall, anything. Tears welled in my eyes. She couldn't do this. She couldn't take my only friends away from me.

'I hate you,' I whispered.

'You cannot speak to your mother like that!'

'I hate you!' I repeated, and bolted into my room, slamming the door behind me. I flung myself onto the bed, burying my face in my pillow.

My rock called to me.

I heard Deanna begging me not to reach for it.

'I know it's wrong,' I said. 'But why is it wrong? It works and I'm not hurting anyone.'

I grabbed the rock and rolled back onto my bed.

'I deserve all the pain I can get. If I'd stood up for myself when it mattered, I'd be okay.'

I crashed the rock into my knee, grimacing with each blow, until I drowned my feelings in bruises.

#

I wouldn't come out of my room when Mum called me for dinner. I couldn't. Rory was my only friend. If I never saw him again, what reason was there to ever leave the house?

Mum knocked on the door again.

I ignored her.

'Why do you not understand what I do for you?' she asked.

My hand squeezed the rock.

'You are my only daughter. I must protect you. You have shown you are too stupid to protect yourself.'

The rock hit my skin, sending vibrations through my body.

Mum's footsteps faded away.

Half an hour later, I heard a loud bang on the front door, followed by the sound of it opening and closing, and some voices.

'What happened?' Dad's voice drifted through the walls. I placed my ear against the gap in the door, listening as hard as I could.

'I told her she cannot see that man anymore,' Mum replied.

'Why's that?'

'He will take advantage of her.'

'All he's done is drive her home so she doesn't have to spend the money on the bus. She's old enough to look after herself. Cedric moved to the city at her age.'

'That was for his studies. Jade is not studying or working. It is my job to look after her.'

'She's got to learn to grow up sometime, love,' Dad said. 'She can't stay in her room all day. It's not healthy, is it? No wonder she never smiles.'

'Why she cannot be happy here with me?'

There was a long pause. Finally, Dad said, 'If you lock her in the house, she'll end up just like you. Too scared to do anything for herself. Not knowing how to pay a bill or fill up the petrol tank or drive on roads with more than two cars on them. Is that what you want?'

Mum didn't reply.

I just lay on the bed, my rock now tucked safely under the pillow. Whenever I flexed my leg, the skin stretched over my bruises, giving me fresh little pulls of pain. But there was something comforting about it.

A few minutes later, there was a knock on my door. 'Jade,' Dad said.

'Yeah?'

'I talked to your mum. You can still go to your mate's shows if you fancy.'

'Thank you.'

'Come out for dinner.'

'I'm not hungry.' It wasn't a lie. I had no appetite. I thought about Mum. I didn't want to end up like her. But she was all I could see when I looked in the mirror. We had most of the same features. We both struggled to do basic things. We both had no friends.

At least until Rory came into my life.

Chapter Eight

The next Saturday, The Lyrebirds were playing at the grand opening of Bonsoir, a new sleepwear and bedding store in Concord Creek. I wasn't sure why they'd hired a band instead of just having a sale to get people through the door, but I wasn't complaining. It gave me another opportunity to see my friends.

When I arrived at Bonsoir, a small crowd was already gathering. The Lyrebirds had set up their gear on a cramped stage just outside the front door. There were balloons and streamers tied to a railing that extended along three sides of the stage. The band were wearing matching satin pyjamas. I made my way towards Rory and Alex who were standing on the ground beside the stage. Rory was tying a sky-blue bandana around his head when Alex waved and Rory turned to greet me with a broad smile.

'Hey, babe,' Rory said, hugging me towards him. The PJs were soft and slippery against my skin. As he was letting me go, he slipped a piece of paper into my hand.

'Gift voucher. The owner wants us to give away ten of these. Go get yourself some sexy lingerie or something,' Rory said with a wink.

I blushed as he strolled away, his eyes on the people at the front of the building.

'What do you think of this set?' Alex asked, showing me a piece of paper as Rory disappeared into the crowd. 'I wrote it in the car.' I scanned the set list and smiled. It was stacked with songs that were loosely based on the theme of sleeping, ranging from *Enter Sandman* to *Dreams* to *Wake Me Up Before You Go-Go*.

'Some of these songs we haven't done in years. So, I don't know if this is what we'll actually play,' Alex said, grinning. 'Rory's trying to get a feel for the crowd now. But it's hard to figure out what kinda person hangs around waiting for a bedding shop to open. Or what'll attract someone who happens to be walking past a bedding shop. This is such a weird gig.'

'Typical lead guitarist. He gets paid, he's the boss's favourite and he's still complaining,' Tyler joked, drifting towards us and slapping Alex on the back. Dom followed, nodding hello at me.

A second later, I heard Rory's voice. 'We're on in two minutes, kids. Let's get to work.'

Rory squeezed my shoulder before jumping up behind his microphone. The band filed onto the stage behind him. Last in line was Dom, who tapped my shoulder.

'Hunter said you're a huge Bon Jovi fan,' Dom said, nodding towards Rory, who was already strapping on his acoustic guitar.

'Yeah, they're my favourite band.'

'Check this out.' Dom unbuttoned the bottom of his pyjama top and lifted it up to reveal the words 'Wanted Dead or Alive' tattooed in black script across his stomach.

I didn't know what to say.

'I've got this original side project with some of the guys I teach with,' Dom continued, as he buttoned his shirt back up. 'Bon Jovi's one of our influences. We released our first EP this year. I'll give you a copy. I don't have it with me right now though.'

I nodded.

'So, what do you do during the week?' Dom asked.

I stared at the ground and shrugged. 'Not much.'

'Why don't we catch up for a coffee or something? I teach drums at Concord Creek Music School and there's a sweet little cafe just round the corner from there. It's a bit hipster, but I like it.'

'Um …' I blinked. Was he asking me out? Why would he do that? Maybe he just wanted something from me? But what could I possibly give him?

'How's Tuesday afternoon sound?' Dom was saying.

Rory had known Dom for years. And I felt safe with Rory, so surely Dom was okay too. 'Sounds good,' I replied.

'Great!' Dom said. 'I'll message you.'

'Domenic!' Rory growled. 'Hurry up!'

Dom gave him a cheeky salute and patted me on the arm as he sprinted to his place behind the drum kit. I slipped around to the back of the stage to make sure I wasn't in anyone's path when the doors opened.

#

After the gig, I looked from the voucher in my hand to the front of the store and back again. Rory obviously expected me to check out Bonsoir. And it would make sense to since I was already here. But there were so many people. I never went out shopping if I could help it. It was too exhausting. If I needed something, I ordered it online and waited.

'No, you can do this,' I muttered to myself. 'No one's taking notes on your shopping.' I took a deep breath and marched into the store.

It looked bigger than it did on the outside. I drifted towards the women's section, wandering aimlessly through aisles of satin negligees, embroidered nightgowns, fluffy robes, cotton two-piece sets and onesies. When I rounded a corner, I bumped into the edge of a shopping basket.

'Watch where ya going!' a woman snapped, powering past me down the aisle.

'Sorry,' I panted, trying to ignore the sound of my heart crunching in my ears.

This would be so much easier if I were sitting on a computer. I looked for the exit and found myself in the children's section. Two sets of parents were arguing about who should get the last *Frozen* pyjamas, while their kids watched on.

Suddenly, I felt the room spin. A wave of sweat washed over me. I tried to loosen the collar around my shirt. My clothes were suffocating me. I couldn't breathe. I needed to run but I couldn't move. I was going to die right here in this damn shop, to the sound of parents who couldn't even act like adults for the sake of their kids.

I collapsed on the floor, landing on my butt. Pain shot up my backbone, but I didn't care. I lifted my knees to my head and buried my face in them.

'Mummy, what's wrong with that lady?' I heard a child's voice ask.

This feeling would pass, I tried to tell myself. It had to. It had to. I couldn't go out like this, on the floor of a bedding shop.

'Jade?'

I slowly lifted my head. Rory was staring down at me, concern etched on his face.

'What's wrong?'

I shook my head. I couldn't speak.

He put down the shopping basket in his hand and sat on the floor beside me. 'Panic attack?' he asked quietly.

My lip quivered. 'People. Everywhere,' I heard myself squeak.

'You can get through this,' he said. 'Just breathe. Focus on me. In. Out. In. Out.'

I nodded and tried to copy his breaths.

'Can you count backwards from a hundred?' he asked.

I mumbled the numbers to him. He gave me a little nod and smile with each number I counted down. My heart was slowly starting to relax and the tightening around my throat and chest began to ease.

Rory sat with me for a few minutes, waiting for my breathing to return to normal. When I was ready to get up, he stood and offered a hand to help me. I hugged him tightly, wishing I didn't ever have to let him go.

'My sister has anxiety,' he said. 'It's okay. It happens.'

'Are you buying something?' I asked when I released him, desperately trying to concentrate on anything other than what'd just happened.

'Yeah, I'm gonna look for something for the kids,' he said. 'Wanna join me?'

I wanted to leave and find somewhere with no people, but I also wanted to stay with Rory. I nodded, clutching onto his arm like it was a fireman's pole.

'What did you think of the gig?' he asked, as he picked up his shopping basket.

'In what way?'

'I felt like we were just annoying people by playing,' he said. 'I mean, it's a pay cheque, but I don't think we did anyone any favours.'

'I enjoyed it,' I assured him.

Rory smiled back at me. 'The owner of this place is an interesting guy,' he said. 'He told me he wanted live music today coz in his words, "It's not just a store, it's an experience". They probably should've just played some lullabies in the shop or something.

'Anyway, I knew him in school, but not well. He was a grade above me. Drove trucks for a few years before getting into an accident that almost killed him. When he was in hospital, he had a dream about opening a store just like this. At least, that's the story he told me.'

I nodded.

'No reaction?'

'I didn't know what to say.'

Rory grinned, squeezing my arm against his. He picked some *Toy Story* pyjamas off the rack and examined them. 'Hmm, these'll fit Ethan and Ella, but I don't really like buying them identical clothes. Random people in the street stop us and go on about how cute they look when they're wearing matching outfits.'

'Would they be wearing pyjamas outside?' I asked.

Rory laughed. 'If I take these home, they probably won't want to wear anything else for a few weeks.'

'Can you get them each something different?'

'If they were here, absolutely. They'd probably pick something out themselves. But since it's just me, it could be tricky. Like I was on my own a couple of months ago and found these superhero shirts with capes on them, so I got Batman for Ethan and Supergirl for Ella. And when I get home, they're happy for about five minutes, then Ella says, "But I wanna be Batman" and Ethan's like, "How come you don't think I'm Superman?" ... I told them to swap shirts, but they just started crying coz they both wanted to be both.'

I looked around the kids' section. 'Maybe you could get them some sheets?' I suggested.

'That's not a bad idea.'

We wandered deeper into the children's section until he found a pair of *Toy Story* bed sheets and popped them into his basket.

'What're you gonna get?' he asked.

I shrugged.

'I can leave. You don't have to buy lingerie in front of me. You can just surprise me with it later.'

I felt my face turn bright red. 'Um …' I stammered.

Rory chuckled. 'Relax, I'm kidding. You don't even have to use that voucher today. It's valid for a year.'

I nodded. I could give it to Mum, or see if there was an online store I could use it on …

'But I hope someday you'll be completely at ease around me,' Rory added, fixing his deep brown eyes on mine.

'I am,' I whispered. 'Well, compared to everyone else.' He'd been so calm when I was panicking on the floor. 'You saved me before.'

He gently caressed my hair and flashed me a warm smile before heading towards the counter to pay for the sheets. I folded the voucher into my pocket and followed him out.

Chapter Nine

I met Dom outside Concord Creek Music School on Tuesday and we walked down the road to Cool Beans Cafe. Several tables were occupied when we got there even though it was the middle of the afternoon. I felt claustrophobic.

Not again, I thought, wishing Rory were here.

My fingers scrunched the fabric around my stomach as I tried to catch my breath, hoping Dom wouldn't notice.

Breathe, I told myself. Dom's been friends with Rory for years. You're safe.

'Jade?' Dom was waving a menu in my face.

I blinked.

'What do you want?' he asked.

'Um …' I glanced at the menu and pointed to the hot chocolate while Dom asked for an espresso and a macadamia cookie.

'Did you drive here?' Dom asked as we waited for our orders.

'Bus. I don't drive.'

'Why not?'

Because I have a panic attack every time I try to even sit in the driver's seat of a parked car. Because I'm scared of everything like my mum. Because I'm me. I shrugged and pretended to be fascinated by a speck on the floor. The reasons weren't important, not now, not to Dom.

'Mind if we sit outside for a bit? I need a smoke.'

'Okay.' We moved to a table in the alfresco area. Smoking was banned on the cafe premises, so Dom had to walk out to the street. I watched him light a cigarette, and a visible wave of calm washed over him as he exhaled. As he was putting out his cigarette, our drinks were brought out to the table.

'Nasty habit,' Dom said cheerfully as he sat down across from me. 'But we all need our vices.'

I nodded and sipped my hot chocolate.

Dom handed me a CD. 'Here you go. Our debut EP. We've only sold about a dozen copies, but oh well. It was fun making it.' Dom's voice was deep and gravelly, but there was a warmth to it that I was starting to like.

While I was looking at the grey cover art on the CD, he told me about his students. His stories were so detailed that I wondered if he was breaking some kind of confidentiality agreement. But letting him talk saved me having to think of things to say, and he seemed to genuinely care about the people he taught. Eventually, he ran out of steam—or students. I looked at him. Was he watching me? My throat tightened but I pretended not to notice.

'So, what's the deal with you and Hunter?' Dom asked.

'What do you mean?'

'Are you sleeping together or anything?'

I almost choked. Why would he think that? Could everyone see that I liked Rory? Were they all laughing at me behind my back? 'No,' I stammered, my face on fire.

'You always come to our gigs on your own,' Dom said.

'I don't have anyone to go with.'

'Really? Pretty girl like you?' He inched towards me, an open smile on his face. My cheeks burned harder under his gaze. I felt his fingers brush my thumb. In reflex, I jerked my hand away.

'Sorry,' he mumbled.

'It's fine, I just … People don't touch me. I mean, I'm not used to physical contact. Like without warning, I mean.'

'No kidding,' he said. 'I didn't mean to make you uncomfortable.'

I pretended to take a long sip of my hot chocolate as I wondered for the millionth time why conversations were so hard for me.

Dom leaned back and finished his coffee. 'You know what I like about you?' he said when he'd put the cup down. 'You're not some band slut. You just dig music.'

'Band slut?'

Dom sighed. 'Talk to Hunter. He's the one the girls go after.'

I blinked, trying to process what Dom was saying. What had Rory been up to? I'd noticed that Rory probably got more admiring glances than anyone else in the band, but he was the lead singer, so it was to be expected, right? I'd never seen anything happen.

Before I could respond, a boy in a Concord Creek Primary School uniform ran towards us, calling out to Dom. I jumped in my chair.

'Domenic! Domenic, I need to talk to you!'

'Zayden! What're you doing here?' Dom asked, standing up.

Zayden Otto eyed me suspiciously before turning back to Dom. 'I went to the music school. They said you were here.'

'This is my friend, Jade,' Dom said. 'Why'd you wanna see me?'

'Teach me drums, duh.'

'You're keen for more lessons?'

'Yeah!'

'Great, where's that willing student been for the past year?'

I gave Dom a stern look to remind him that Zayden's father had just died. But Zayden didn't seem to notice Dom's sarcasm.

'I can't teach you anymore if your mum won't pay for it,' Dom said. 'It's the rules.'

'But I've got money.' Zayden swung his backpack onto the floor and rummaged through it, before pulling out a wallet and emptying a thick wad of notes onto the table.

Dom's eyes widened. 'Well, that's enough to cover the next few weeks …'

'I'll get more.'

Dom checked his watch. 'Your old lesson time's still available if you want it.'

'No shit. That's why I came to find you, Domenic.'

Dom rolled his eyes. 'Do you mind if we cut this short?' he asked me.

'That's fine,' I said. I didn't know if I should be offended or amused.

'Thanks, mate. I'll see ya soon.'

#

When Dom and Zayden had left the cafe, I rang Rory. 'What can you tell me about Dom?' I asked.

'What about him?'

'Well, I just had coffee with him and …'

'You went out with Dom? Are you dating him now?' Rory asked, a little too quickly.

'No. It was just coffee.'

'Since when do you drink coffee? I tried to give you some at Sherlock's and you looked like you'd just eaten soap.'

'I had a hot chocolate. Dom wanted to give me his EP. He probably won't even text me again.'

'I'm sure he will coz you're awesome,' Rory said quietly.

I told Rory about Zayden barging into the cafe. 'It's weird coz Dom said Zayden didn't even want to play drums until Veronica cancelled his lessons.'

'Who knows what's going on there? Maybe it's a case of you don't know what you've got till it's gone. Maybe drumming was his dad's idea and it's Zayden's way of feeling closer to him,' Rory said. 'Point is, everyone's fighting their own battles— some the world knows about and some that no one knows about.'

I thought about my bruising and nodded even though Rory couldn't see me.

'Dom said I should ask you about band sluts,' I said, changing the subject.

Rory laughed. 'Is he still going on about that? Tell him I can't help who turns up to a gig and it's his own fault for choosing an instrument that gets him hidden at the back of the stage.'

I felt like I'd missed an important piece of the puzzle somewhere, but I didn't know what to say so I let it go.

#

That Thursday night, Rory and Alex had an acoustic gig at the Sherlock Arms, filling in for the Spencer O'Neill Duo. There was a dress code at Sherlock's after 7pm, so the bikini girls that were usually there on Sunday afternoons were gone.

When I walked in, Rory put down the guitar he was tuning and planted a long kiss on my cheek.

'Are you happy to see me or do you prefer drummers now?' he murmured into my ear.

I blushed. 'I'm always happy to see you.'

Rory and Alex were three songs into the first set when a girl with shoulder-length copper curls appeared next to me. When she met my eyes and smiled, I saw that she was about my age, even though she was at least a head taller.

I'd turned my attention back to Rory and Alex when I heard the girl harmonising under her breath. She kept doing it for the next two songs, until Rory invited her up on stage.

As soon as she sang *Piece of My Heart*, I was in love and a little jealous of her. And Rory was clearly in awe.

During the set break, Rory introduced her to me as Chloe LaSalle—the newest member of The Lyrebirds. 'Chloe's been playing with Spencer O'Neill for the past year-and-a-half, but we just poached her,' Rory said.

'Welcome aboard,' I said, before turning red. It's not like it was my band to welcome her to.

She didn't make fun of me. 'Thanks! I can't wait to gig with these guys. I used to stand outside Summit and watch them through the window when I was in high school.'

'Stalker,' Alex teased.

Chloe poked her tongue out at him, then turned back to me. 'I usually do this gig tonight with Spence. He's been a great mentor to me so it's kinda weird being here without him. But I wanted to sing more rock so when Hunter asked me to join the band, I couldn't say no.' She was so bubbly, and as the four of us stood at the bar, I felt my jealousy melt away.

I was surprised at how many people were actually out drinking in the middle of the week. Rory flirted with a bartender to get a free vodka and cranberry and offered it to me. I had a taste and licked my lips and frowned, trying to figure out if I liked it.

'So, you really don't drink at all?' Rory asked.

I shook my head. Alcohol always reminded me of Nathan, and not in a good way.

Before Rory could reply, Chloe gathered our attention. 'Could I get your advice? I've been seeing this guy who works at my parents' restaurant. He was going to come to the gig tonight, but he had to change shifts,' Chloe said. 'We get along great, but I don't think he wants anything serious and I don't know how I feel about him yet. Should I end it? Should we just be friends with benefits for a while?'

'Sounds fun, if it's what you want,' Alex said.

'I don't think friends with benefits ever works out,' Rory said. I took another sip of the drink. It wasn't that bad. Maybe I could make some better memories with Rory and my new friends.

'Why do you say that?' Chloe asked.

'Someone always develops feelings.' Rory looked over at me, grinned and gave me a nudge on the shoulder. 'Jade and I used to go at it all the time, but I wanted something more and she didn't.' He said it in a way that made it obvious he was joking, and all four of us laughed. But when the moment had passed and the conversation turned to a funny video that Tyler had posted during the week, I stole a look at Rory. He met my gaze and we both just looked at each other, not saying a word as the chatter of the pub continued around us. I was sure he could hear the thump of my heart and the fluttering in my stomach.

Chapter Ten

My brother Cedric came to stay with us a few weeks later. He wasn't happy about it, but Mum had been pestering him about coming to visit before he abandoned us, as she put it. He wasn't abandoning us. He was moving to New Zealand with his partner. He hadn't lived in Concord Creek since finishing high school, but I guess moving to another country was too much for her.

In our family room, there was a framed photo of Cedric getting his Pharmacy degree. It stared down at me, mockingly.

'Cedric is such a smart boy,' Mum said proudly, when she saw me studying the picture.

'Thanks for rubbing it in,' I muttered.

Mum raised her eyebrows at me. 'It is not too late for you to get into uni as well,' she said. 'You just have to be interested in doing the work.'

I went to my room, snatched the rock from my desk and smashed a fresh bruise into my leg. It helped a little. 'I did my best in school,' I told Deanna. 'Even when it hurt to get out of bed. Why can't she see that? I just wasn't good enough. I can't be her perfect daughter.'

#

Cedric spent most of his time in Concord Creek catching up with old friends instead of spending time with his family. I could hardly blame him, when the only thing at home was Mum asking him question after question.

It turns out I was often the topic of conversation.

Cedric knocked on my door in the middle of the first week. I let him in. He nodded his approval at Deanna. 'You've taken good care of her,' he said. 'I'd still do her.'

'Don't talk about her like that,' I said.

He raised his eyebrows, opened his mouth like he was going to say something, then closed it and shrugged.

Cedric was the reason I loved *Star Trek*. I watched anything he watched that wasn't too gruesome. I wanted to be cool and smart like my brother. The twelve-year age gap between us meant it was one of the few things we shared growing up.

'So, Mum tells me you've been spending a lot of time with a guy called Rory,' Cedric said, taking a seat at the edge of my bed.

I raised an eyebrow and nodded. 'What else has she been telling you?'

'Well, she's asking me stuff like, "Why is Jade always with this man?" and "What is he doing with her?". I just told her it's good for you to go out and have friends. You've never really done normal things like that before.'

I rolled my eyes at Deanna.

'You've gotta understand something when you live with Mum though,' Cedric continued. 'You don't need to tell her everything about your life. But you have to make her feel like she's part of it. Chat to her about ordinary things and explain them in layman's terms. Otherwise, she'll never trust you or any of your friends and she'll drive you insane with her questions.'

'Is that why you left?'

He didn't reply. 'Is Rory your boyfriend?' he asked, picking Deanna up and adjusting her spindly arms.

I shook my head. 'We're just friends and he kinda treats me like a sister. But …'

'But?' Cedric said, when I stopped.

I stared at Deanna as Cedric placed her back on the desk, recalling all the times I'd spent silently wishing for some real friends to play with. Deanna was the closest thing I had to a best friend. And like me, she was mixed-race. I always thought that if I could somehow travel to the twenty-fourth century and meet her, I wouldn't feel so alone.

'Well, I met his drummer for coffee and Rory was like, "Are you dating him? Do you prefer drummers now?" And we had this moment about a month ago where we were just staring at each other …' I trailed off, wondering if Cedric would think I was stupid and reading too much into things.

Cedric bit his lip for moment before speaking. 'Okay, let me give you a little lesson about guys,' he said. 'They all want to sleep with the girls they hang out with. You know when you have a group of guys and there's always that one girl in the group? The one they all treat like a little sister, the one they've all known forever? Each guy in that group wants to sleep with her, whether it's on a conscious or subconscious level, whether they have girlfriends or not. Not saying they all have a crush on her, but they all want to sleep with her.'

I flushed red and looked down. Cedric had never spoken to me like this before. Well, of course he hadn't. I'd been a little kid when he left Concord Creek and now I was trying to be an adult.

'Are you sure about that?' I asked. I mean, our own father wasn't interested in women. Although I didn't think Rory was gay.

'I'm a guy, aren't I?' Cedric said. 'Look, maybe it was subconscious for Rory until you told him about the competition and he got jealous. Maybe he knew it all along and just didn't show it.'

'So, what do I do now?' I asked.

'That's up to you. But if you really want it from this guy, I bet you anything you can get it.'

Chapter Eleven

The Lyrebirds began a Friday night residency at the Bluebonnet Bar that week. Rory's sister Faye rang me from a band rehearsal to let me know. 'Rory wanted me to tell you,' she said. 'It's good news. There are hardly any places for bands to play these days. Venues are closing down or not putting live music on anymore. And Rory would never admit it, but he could use the money.'

I was looking forward to seeing the band again. I hadn't seen Rory since the night we shared that moment at the Sherlock Arms, almost a month ago. The Lyrebirds had been fully booked out with private gigs for three weekends in a row. I didn't realise just how much I'd grown used to seeing Rory every week until I couldn't. I'd watched a lot of TV, listened to music and talked to Deanna but the loneliness made me cry myself to sleep more than once.

There seemed to be a few more people around on Friday night than I was used to on Saturdays. I tried to be happy for the band while sucking in slow, deep breaths to calm my nerves.

But while there were almost too many people for me, there weren't nearly enough for Rory. 'The manager told me it's packed on Fridays,' Rory said when he came over to greet me. 'He's obviously got low standards. If this is the most people they get, doing this gig every week's gonna be tough.' He sighed and disappeared to help the band finish setting up.

I sat down and looked around. I immediately recognised Maria – the mother of Rory's kids – from my online stalking, even though I'd spent most of my time looking Rory up rather than her. She looked shorter in person than I'd imagined her to be—although she was probably still taller than me. I didn't have the nerve to get too close to her. She was dancing with two friends near the stage.

Faye and Greg soon arrived, but Faye was in a bad mood. She wouldn't say why.

'Have you met Maria?' Greg asked me during the band's break.

I shook my head and looked in her direction again. She and her friends were chatting to Rory. Her hand was sliding up and down his arm. I looked away, my stomach dropping. I reminded myself that Rory had said he was still friends with her. I had no right or reason to be jealous.

Greg and Faye drifted off to talk to Alex, Tyler and Dom, while Chloe led me outside through a side door in the band room. 'God, I need some air with Princess Maria in the building,' she said.

'Why?' I asked.

'She's just rude to me for no reason. Hunter said she was like that with some of the other girls he's been in bands with. But she needs to get over herself. Alex told us how they met. She's basically a band slut that got knocked up.'

There was that phrase again. Band slut. And again being used by someone to talk about Rory. I glanced at the door. Did he really care about me? Or was he just being nice to me so I could be another notch on his bedpost? Just how many women had he been with?

I turned back to Chloe. 'Have you and Rory ever …'

Chloe's eyes widened. 'No way. Love him to bits but he's like my weird uncle or something. I prefer guys closer to my age.'

Chloe was only a year older than me and closer to Rory's age than I was. I felt my cheeks blush. In the dark, Chloe didn't seem to notice. We fell into silence.

'It's nice to see you again,' I stammered. 'I mean, it's been a while.' The last time I'd seen Chloe was the night we met, but she'd added me as a friend online. We discovered we both loved Bon Jovi, so we'd been sending each other old concert videos.

I'd also exchanged text messages with Rory almost every day, which made the time away from him a little more bearable. And Alex had sent everyone a selfie with the one-litre bottle of hand sanitiser Rory bought him, while pointing out that he couldn't exactly carry it around in his pocket.

Chloe smiled. 'Yeah, it's nice to see you again too. Wish you'd been around last week to help knock some sense into Hunter.'

'Why, what happened?'

'Oh my God, he was so off his face. Ended up going home with two women from the party we were playing at.'

Did they have sex? I almost asked, before biting my lip. What do you think, Jade? Don't be so naive.

#

I tried to be indifferent towards Rory when we went back inside, shrugging when he asked how I'd been and brushing him away when he put his arm around me.

'What's wrong?' he asked.

'Nothing.'

'It's obviously not nothing.'

He waited for me to say something but I didn't reply. I wanted to. I wanted him to know everything about me. But I didn't want to have to say the words. If I did, I'd never be able to take them back. Saying things out loud made me vulnerable. It was one thing to trust someone not to embarrass you in public. It was another to trust them with the essence of who you were, deep down, under all the walls and layers you'd built up over eighteen years.

'I'll sit here and wait all night. Then the manager will get angry at us coz we're not playing. The band will get fired. They won't get paid. They'll lose their homes and have to wander the underbelly of Concord Creek begging for loose change …'

'Alright, alright,' I snapped, but Rory was grinning at me. I sighed. 'I know we haven't known each other for very long. But you mean a lot to me … and it kills me that I mean nothing to you.'

Rory looked stunned. 'You're not nothing to me. Don't ever think you're nothing to me. You're more to me than you know.' He gave me a quick kiss on the side of my mouth, lightly brushing my lips before the band returned to the stage.

I couldn't remember a single song they played after that.

Chapter Twelve

Maybe it was what I'd said about not meaning anything to him, but Rory and I started talking on the phone every weeknight. He'd ring me when he was in his shed 'tinkering with tunes' after his kids had gone to sleep. I'd listen to his impersonations of annoying clients he was making websites for and his stories about what the twins had been up to that day. Sometimes he'd put me on speaker and let me listen to a song he was working on, even though it was hard to hear it clearly over the phone. Our calls didn't usually last longer than twenty minutes, but I always felt better after hearing his voice.

'Heard from my ex today,' Rory told me a couple of weeks later. 'Layla. The last woman I dated before Maria.'

'Oh?'

'Yeah, when she friended me a few months ago, I asked her if she had any photos from when we went to Italy together. She told me she'd deleted them all. I was kinda disappointed, but then I forgot about it.

'Well, this morning, I'd just dropped Ethan and Ella off at kindy when Layla called and said, "My mum found a flash drive with those photos you wanted." I thought, "great". And then she goes, "Remember those naked pictures we took of each other in Venice?"' He paused, as if waiting for me to say something. 'Nothing?' he prompted when I didn't respond.

'I don't know what I'm supposed to say to that.'

'Neither did I,' Rory said chuckling. 'Her mum never liked me either, so I'm not even sure if I can get those photos back.' He paused again. 'So, just out of interest, are there any naked pictures of you in existence?'

My stomach fluttered, suddenly remembering how Nathan had sweet-talked me for weeks, making me feel pretty. I swallowed hard. 'Yes,' I murmured.

'That's hot,' Rory said. 'Is there any way I can get my hands on them?'

Was this how sexting began? What was I supposed to say? I looked down at my body that was bruised and lumpy in all the wrong places. The first and last person to find me attractive was Nathan, and almost two years ago he'd coaxed some nudes out of me. But Rory didn't really think of me the way I sometimes thought of him. Did he?

'Have I offended you?' Rory asked.

'You didn't offend me.' I drew in a long breath. 'I can trust you, right?'

'Wait, are you gonna show me?'

'I think so.'

'That's awesome. Of course you can trust me. I'll keep it in the vault under lock and key.'

When we got off the phone, I looked at Deanna. I'd deleted the photos I sent Nathan, which was probably a good thing since I was barely sixteen when I took them and I didn't want Rory to get into trouble. But I remembered how to do it. I'd usually lie on the bed, so my stomach was flat, and I'd always made sure my face couldn't be seen, in case Nathan's footy mates got their hands on them.

'Your boobs sit nicely,' Nathan had said to me when he'd seen my photos for the first time. What would Rory say? Would he like me? What if I turned him off completely? What if he said nothing at all?

I stripped off my clothes and lay back on my bed with my phone until I had two photos I was happy with.

Well, here goes. I swallowed the lump in my throat, took a deep breath and emailed Rory the photos.

My phone buzzed. It was a text message from Rory.

Are you sure you want me to see them? I can delete the email if you've changed your mind.

I realised I'd been shaking as I hit send, but seeing him offer me a way out settled me down.

Will things get weird between us after this? I texted.

Hopefully weird is awesome :), he replied.

It's ok, you can look. I'd trust you with my life.

And I knew it was true.

Photos are amazing, he texted back a few minutes later. *Thanks for making my night.*

#

The next night at the Bluebonnet was a strange one in a couple of ways. Dom convinced Faye to do shots of tequila with him, but only Faye seemed to be affected by the alcohol. It made for some interesting—though unintelligible—conversation, as well as some off-key backstage singing. Tyler asked if they made sunglasses for your ears. Chloe said it was like seeing your mother get drunk. Alex just watched with a smile on his lips and a glop of hand sanitiser in his palm.

And of course, it was the first time I'd seen Rory since he saw my nude photos.

He spotted me in the band room and came over to give me a hug. 'Please send more photos,' he said in my ear. 'You can't tell me you've only got two?'

'It's a long story,' I said.

'I like stories,' Rory said softly, but he didn't press the issue. When the band returned to the stage, he seemed to wink in my direction as Alex played the opening lick of *Friday I'm In Love*.

'That wasn't weird tonight, was it?' he asked me at the end of the gig.

I shook my head.

We were alone backstage. The rest of The Lyrebirds were packing up their gear and Greg had taken Faye home early.

'Has anyone ever told you how beautiful you are?' Rory said.

I shook my head again. Nathan had called me cute and hot at various times, but never beautiful.

Softly, slowly, carefully, Rory's fingers stroked my hair, my cheek, my chin, my neck. My heart was pounding, but I didn't have the urge to move away like I did when other people touched me.

He glanced over my head at the stage, then back at me. 'Goodnight, beautiful,' he said, placing a quiet kiss on my lips.

#

I paced around my room, trying to make sense of what had just happened. He'd kissed me. He'd seen my photos and actually wanted more.

Before putting my pyjamas on, I studied myself in the bedroom mirror. Sucking my stomach in, I frowned at my bruises and stretch marks. Did Rory see something I couldn't?

My eyes fell on a bottle of concealer on my bedside table. I gave it a shake before carefully painting over my bruised skin. When the makeup had set, I lay back and closed my eyes until I got a shot I was reasonably happy with. About an hour-and-a-half later, I had two more pictures I could send to Rory.

Chapter Thirteen

I couldn't explain it with any logic, but Rory made everything seem brighter. When the birds outside my window woke me up on Saturday morning, I didn't mind. I even put on my sunglasses and went for a walk. At the front of my old school, there were some pretty yellow flowers I'd never really noticed before. I bent over to breathe in their scent. The grass on the school oval where I first met Nathan looked and smelled freshly mown. A butterfly fluttered past as I circled back towards home. I'd never realised how pretty Concord Creek really was.

Mum was flicking through the newspaper when I got home. She looked up suspiciously as I entered the family room. 'Why you go out so early?'

'I just took a walk.'

'Walk to where?'

'Nowhere.'

Mum glared back at me. 'You out with that *ang moh* again, huh?'

I bit down angry tears and went to my room.

My first thought was to smash myself with my rock. But Rory was the reason I felt hopeful for the first time in a long time and I wanted to hold on to that feeling. I sent him a text and waited.

Good morning … Mum's driving me nuts! :(

A few moments later, my phone beeped. *Good morning beautiful girl. Mums tend to do that. Think it's in the job description. Don't let it get you down.*

I hugged my phone to my chest and smiled. *I'll try not to*, I replied.

#

When Faye and Greg turned up to the Sherlock Arms on Sunday, I was worried I wouldn't get any time alone with Rory to talk about the pictures. But while the Cunninghams were eating at their table, Rory beckoned me over to the edge of the verandah.

'Nice view, isn't it?' he said, sipping a flat white.

I nodded. I saw Rory take a picture of the perfect blue sky on his phone and upload it with the caption: 'Stunning day at the office.'

'I've had people tell me I should move to the city for more work, but I think we're pretty blessed right here,' he said, putting his phone in his pocket. 'Wanna go for a walk?'

'Sure.'

Rory drained the last of his coffee and led me down the path towards the beach. My feet sank into the loose sand, making each step an effort. I felt fat and unfit. Rory looked over at me.

'C'mon, it'll be easier to walk near the water,' he said.

I followed him, one slow step at a time, until we reached the edge of the water. Here, the sand was more tightly packed and definitely easier to walk on. My leg muscles began to relax. I listened to the splash of waves, the crunching of our shoes on the wet sand.

'Bones is gonna be all over my feet when I get home. He loves coming to the beach,' Rory said. 'Do you have pets?'

I shook my head. 'My parents don't like animals, so we never had any.'

'That's a shame. I think pets are great for kids. And adults too, for that matter. Not that there's anything wrong with you.' He gently squeezed my hand.

There are lots of things wrong with me, I thought. But Rory made me feel like I could get better.

'So, you mean to tell me your stockpile of photos is four?' he asked.

Did other girls take nudes of themselves all day? I wondered. 'I took them for you,' I said. 'I had others, but I deleted them. It's a long, messed-up story.'

Rory caressed my hair and motioned for me to follow him back up the soft, white sand towards the shade of some trees. I was exhausted by the time we got there. He checked his watch and sat down. I planted myself next to him.

'Are you gonna tell me the story?' Rory asked. 'Was he a boyfriend? Lover?'

'Sort of.'

'Yeah, well, when you're seeing someone, you send each other photos. What's wrong with that?'

I stared at the ground, studying the pattern of shadows formed by the leaves and branches above us. 'I only sent them to him coz I wanted him to like me. He was a jock and I was a loser, but ...'

'You're not a loser,' Rory said firmly. He squeezed my hand again. 'So, is this guy still around?'

'Well, I still know him. We're friends on everything online.'

'Do you still see him?'

'No. We've talked a few times but I haven't met up with him.'

Rory draped his arm around my shoulders. 'They're good photos. I mean, it's hard to take photos of yourself. Most people probably take four hundred and keep two. Except me, of course. Mine would all be awesome.' He rolled his eyes and we laughed.

He glanced at his watch again. 'We'd better get back to it,' he said, standing and offering a hand to pull me up. We took the path along the top of the beach back towards the Sherlock Arms. I wanted to tell him about Nathan but the words wouldn't leave my tongue. Rory kept looking over at me while he talked about his kids, as if he was waiting for me to speak. But he didn't push it. I appreciated it and was slightly disappointed at the same time.

As I tried to fall asleep that night, I decided to reveal my secret to Rory when I woke up the next day.

Chapter Fourteen

'His name is Nathan,' I blurted out when Rory answered the phone on Monday afternoon.

'Huh?'

He was listening now. And I was about to tell him my biggest secret. I immediately felt the air tightening around my throat.

'Breathe, Jade,' Rory said, taking a couple of deep, audible breaths to demonstrate.

'The guy. The jock. I've never told anyone the full story before,' I said.

'Is it that long a story? Or do you just not feel like telling anyone?'

'I've known him since I was fifteen, so I guess it's kinda long. But I tend to keep stuff to myself as well.'

'Well, maybe it's time to start sharing.'

'I'm not even really sure where to start.'

'How about the beginning?' Rory suggested.

And where is that? I wondered. When I met Nathan? When we had sex?

'Can I see you? In person?' I asked.

There was a pause at the other end. 'Are you at home?' Rory asked.

I nodded, remembered he couldn't see me and squeaked out a yes.

He paused again. 'I'll be there in an hour or so.'

#

I was waiting out the front of my house when Rory's van pulled up in the driveway. He smiled when I climbed inside.

'Maria's away for work till Thursday. Ethan and Ella are at Alex's place,' Rory said. 'They love him. He's their cool uncle.'

We began to drive in aimless silence as Rory waited for me to speak.

'I was fifteen and he was seventeen when we met,' I began.

#

I'd stayed back late at school to finish an assignment in the library. Nathan was doing laps of the school oval when I cut across it to get home, trying not to stare at him. He was shirtless, a light glaze of sweat on his lean but muscular frame. He called to me.

'Kick-to-kick?'

I stopped, tugging the straps on my backpack. 'What?'

Nathan brandished the football in his hands. 'The footy. Wanna have a kick with me?'

'I don't know how.'

Nathan laughed. 'I'll show you.'

#

'Jade?'

Rory's voice jolted me back to the present. I realised I'd been silent for some time. The van had also stopped moving. I looked around and almost laughed. He'd pulled up at Pelican Oval, where Nathan's footy team—the Concord Creek

Pelicans—trained and played their home games. But today it was empty.

I unbuckled my seatbelt and tried to gather my thoughts. 'He seemed so much more mature than me.

'After a while, he started to crack onto me. We'd do video calls and … show each other … what we looked like. He was the first boy to see me naked.' I swallowed the lump in my throat, avoiding Rory's soulful brown gaze.

'High school was so cliquey. People like him just didn't talk to people like me. But he did. He made me feel special. He taught me about footy. I started going to his games.'

'So, what happened between you two?' Rory asked.

'He invited me over. It was the day after Easton Rock beat Concord Creek by fifteen goals in the prelim final.'

'I remember. It was on the front page of the *Times*.'

I nodded. 'I thought he'd be out somewhere with all his teammates, but he said he just wanted me. So, I told Mum I had a study group to go to and went to see him.'

#

Nathan was strangling the neck of a beer bottle when he opened the door. He greeted me with a hug and a sloppy kiss. I followed him into the living room where one of his teammates was lying on the couch. I knew everyone called him Pauly, but I'd never met him properly. I smiled shyly at him, wondering what was going on.

'Have a drink,' Nathan said.

'I'm not old enough to drink.'

Nathan and Pauly looked at each other and laughed. 'C'mon, Jade. You know how you're always so stressed about everything?' Nathan said. 'Alcohol helps. Trust me.' He thrust his beer forward.

I took a sip and screwed up my face. 'This is gross.'

'That just means you haven't found the right drink yet. Do you like sweet stuff?'

I nodded.

'Thought you might. That's why I bought you some Cruisers.' Nathan led me to the kitchen and opened the fridge, revealing a shelf of coloured bottles. He opened the first one on the left and handed it to me. I took a sip and nodded.

An hour-and-a-half and two bottles later, I was giddy and giggling while Nathan and I made out on the floor. Pauly went to the bathroom. After a minute or so, Nathan took my hand and pulled me into the bathroom too.

'I get first dibs,' Nathan said, putting down the toilet seat lid and placing me on top of it. He yanked my jeans and underwear away from me and spread my legs.

I stared at his penis. I'd seen it on my computer screen but never in person. In my peripheral vision, Pauly was already jacking off.

Before I could say anything, Nathan was inside me. I cried out in pain. I felt like I was being stabbed and sandpaper was grazing my insides.

'Shh, I'm being really gentle,' he whispered, his breath thick. 'I haven't even gone in all the way.' I closed my eyes and tried to sing a Bon Jovi song in my head.

'Is it feeling better?' Nathan asked.

'A little,' I lied.

After a few more thrusts, Nathan pulled himself out and gestured to Pauly. 'I think he wants it even more than me,' Nathan said, laughing. 'Go on.'

Numb, I stumbled towards Pauly. His body glued me to the wall. He pierced me hard, again and again. When I looked down, I was bleeding all over the tiles.

'Shit! Why didn'tcha tell me?' Pauly exclaimed as we stared at the red puddle around my feet. I didn't know if he was talking to me, or Nathan, or both.

'Sorry,' I mumbled, avoiding eye contact. My head was spinning, beating in my brain. My face, my arms, my legs, all felt like they were vibrating. The world was blurry and way too hot. I closed my eyes, but it didn't help. I stumbled to the sink and threw up everything I'd drunk.

I heard swearing behind me. The tears stung my eyes and burned my cheeks as I washed my mouth out, vowing not to get drunk ever again.

'Clean yourself up in the tub,' Nathan ordered. 'We'll get rid of the blood on the floor.'

'Did you know she was a virgin?' I heard Pauly whisper, but I couldn't make out Nathan's reply.

There was blood dripping down my thigh. I hurried into the bathtub to rinse myself off, then stuffed tissues between my legs. I vaguely remember getting dressed, being bundled home in a taxi with some breath mints and bleeding on and off for three days.

Nathan rang me the day after. 'I'm really sorry about yesterday,' he said. 'We were so drunk.'

'Yeah,' I mumbled.

'I shouldn't have had Pauly there. It should've just been the two of us.'

I didn't answer.

'I forgot you'd never had a drink before. I should've told you to pace yourself.'

Finally, Nathan asked me if I was okay. It didn't take much to convince him that I was.

#

'I'm glad you shared that with me,' Rory said. 'I hope you're okay. It's a pretty intense situation.'

'I'm okay as long as you're here.'

'I'm always here to talk if you want. About anything. You've become a really good friend. I don't want you to think you have to go through things like that on your own.'

Rory unbuckled his seatbelt and pulled my shaking body into his arms, letting me cry all over his shirt. But this time they were tears of relief.

'Who else knows about this besides me?' he asked.

'No one.'

I felt his body shift as he kissed the top of my head. 'Why'd you make me the first?'

'I've never had anyone I could talk to.'

'You don't think your mum—'

'No,' I snapped. 'Sorry,' I added a moment later.

'It's okay. Why not?'

I sat back up in my seat, running my hands nervously over my jeans that hid the bruised flesh underneath. 'We were in the living room one day, watching the news. And then a report comes on about a girl who was gang raped at a party. And my parents blamed her for getting drunk in the first place. So, I knew I could never tell them what'd happened to me.'

Rory reached over to hug me again. 'Have you had any other experiences with sex, or is that it?'

'That's it. People don't like me in that way.'

'I can assure you that's not true.' He broke the hug to flash me a smile.

'I was so scared for about a month after … it.'

'Scared of what?'

'That I was pregnant. Or I'd been infected with something. I had to wear a disguise when I went to the clinic to get tested, in case anyone from school recognised me.'

'You're hardly the first person at school to have sex.'

'Sure, but it wouldn't have stopped them writing "Jade Milton is a skank" all over the toilet cubicles the next day.'

'School sucks, babe. Thank God the real world is so much bigger.' He put his arm around me and I relaxed into the warm silence.

'So, why'd you show me those photos?' he asked, after a minute.

'You wanted to see them.' My heart was racing again. Surely he could hear it.

'You wanted me to see them,' he said, with a sly grin, 'and you wanted me to like them. And I love them.'

My cheeks were warm. I flashed him a coy smile. We stared at each other, my face growing redder as his smirk widened.

'C'mon, let's get some fresh air,' he said at last. He opened the door and stepped out of the van and I followed suit. When he'd locked it, he came over to my side and took my hand.

'Is it weird being here?' Rory asked, as we started to walk around the oval. 'I didn't know this place had memories for you when I drove here. I just wanted to find somewhere quiet.'

'It's a bit weird.'

'Do you want to leave?'

I squeezed Rory's hand and shook my head. 'No. It's fine.'

We passed the goalposts. 'I played a bit of junior footy here,' Rory said. 'Came back years later to do a couple of gigs. Had dozens of people I don't even remember telling me it's a good thing I sing better than I kick.' Rory grinned. 'Did you ever play sports?'

'No, Mum didn't want me doing things that could get me hurt.'

'Getting hurt is a part of life. You can't wrap yourself in bubble wrap and you shouldn't want to.'

'Try telling her that. Actually, don't … She's already tried to ban me from seeing you.'

We climbed inside the Pelicans' dugout and sat on the interchange bench, facing the oval.

'Your mum doesn't like me much, does she? She hasn't even met me.'

I shook my head. 'But I like you.'

'I like you too, babe. I like you a lot.' He leaned towards me and brushed my hair behind my ear. Our eyes locked. My breath caught in my throat. I imagined diving into his sweet, chocolatey eyes and losing myself in him forever.

'How would your mum react if her beautiful eighteen-year-old daughter stayed out all night?' When I hesitated, he added, 'Like if you texted her to say, "I'm watching *Star Trek* with Rory."'

'I'm not sure. She wouldn't let me stay over someone's house to play board games a couple of years ago, even though it was school holidays and there were a dozen other girls there. That's probably why I've never had friends for long.'

'Some parents try to hold on forever. Maybe you should say, "If you don't want us watching *Star Trek*, we'll just get high and have sex."'

'I don't think that'll work.'

He smiled. 'Yeah, probably not. Do you want me to take you home now?'

'Not really.'

'Why don't you come over? I need a break from this actor's website I'm working on anyway and I've got all the original series episodes. We can watch one together and still get you home before it's late.'

I nodded. He took my hand and walked me back to his van. My heart thudded with each step. I was finally going to Rory's house.

Chapter Fifteen

Bones, the fuzzy little dog I'd seen in Rory's photos, pattered up to meet us as we entered the house. 'Hey buddy,' Rory said, scooping the dog up and inviting me to pet him.

I ruffled my fingers through his fur. 'What sort of dog is he?' I asked.

'He's a cavoodle,' Rory said. 'Kinda looks like a teddy bear, doesn't he? Ethan and Ella sure think so.' He grinned and filled up the dog bowl. 'That should keep him occupied for a while,' he said, as he washed his hands. 'Would you like anything to drink?'

He opened the fridge and I selected some apple juice that he poured into a glass for me. My hands were trembling. I took a long sip of my juice and stared at Rory.

'You seem nervous,' he said. 'Just relax. We're good friends, hanging out.'

I nodded.

'C'mon. Let's do something I know you'll like.'

I followed him into the living room. A smattering of well-worn stuffed toys and some coloured textas lay on the rug in the centre of the room. There was a flat screen TV against one wall and an L-shaped couch on the opposite wall.

Rory put on one of my favourite episodes of *Star Trek: The Original Series*, the one when Kirk and Spock travel back in time and Kirk falls in love with a social worker named Edith—only to discover that Edith has to die because the history they all knew would completely change if she didn't.

I kept glancing at Rory. Should I touch him like I wanted to? I slid towards him on the couch and stroked his hand. He didn't pull it away.

'Do you believe in fate?' I asked as the closing credits appeared on the screen.

'Maybe,' he said. 'When I was younger, I thought starting a family would be a simple case of finding the right girl, settling down, having the perfect number of kids—whatever that might be. But the kids came a bit unexpectedly, and obviously Maria and I never got married or anything. So, my family doesn't look quite the way I pictured it. And she and I manage to argue over the stupidest things sometimes. Everyone's so much more relaxed when she's away. But if she hadn't come into my life, I wouldn't have Ella and Ethan. And they're two awesome reasons to wake up in the morning.' He squeezed my hand. 'How about you? Do you believe in fate?'

'I'm starting to.' I bit my lip in thought. 'I mean, I didn't really want to go to the Create Tomorrow Ball. I felt like I should coz Samson died. And if I hadn't gone, I would never have met you.'

'And I wouldn't have met you. But I'm glad I did. I love having you in my life.'

He cupped my face with his hand. My heart tremored. He smiled and kissed me, tenderly and deliberately.

Nathan's kisses had been wet and clumsy. Rory's lips were warm and soft on mine. My mouth parted for him, savouring his smooth taste.

All too soon, he pulled away. 'I should get you home,' he said, looking reluctant.

I nodded, disappointed.

He held me against his body for a few minutes and I drank in his warmth until he started to stand up. With one last kiss, we left the house and returned to his van.

'Can I make a request?' he asked as we pulled into my driveway. It was about dinnertime.

'Sure.'

'Can you personalise your next lot of photos?'

'How?'

He leaned across and pressed his lips on my forehead. 'Write my name in lipstick on your thigh.'

I froze. My thigh was covered in bruises. I'd have to paint over them and hope it looked natural with lipstick on top of it. And I'd have to buy lipstick, because I didn't normally wear it. But I nodded.

'And I'd love some hand-delivered ones,' he murmured into my ear.

'You want me to turn up naked at your house?'

He grinned. 'Well, you don't have to turn up naked. You can turn up with clothes and then become naked. But if you want to turn up naked, I'd be happy to receive you.'

#

I counted down the days until Friday night came around again and I could be with the people who made me feel safe and accepted.

When I got to the Bluebonnet, I approached the band room as usual. The black curtains separating it from the rest of the bar were drawn tight. Tense, simmering voices floated into my ears. What was going on?

'You think just coz they call you Uncle Alex, you're some kind of parenting expert? You don't know the first bloody thing about raising kids!' I'd never heard Rory yell before, but it was unmistakably his voice behind the curtain.

'It's my job to protect them if you won't.' Alex. He spoke more quietly and I had to strain to hear him, but there was a threatening tone in his voice I'd never encountered before.

'The hell is that supposed to mean?'

'You know what to do, mate. Why don't you ask Ella and Ethan what they want?'

'You're supposed to be my brother!'

There was a thud, like the sound of an object being punched or kicked. I jumped, then Rory stormed out from behind the curtain, his eyes blazing. He didn't even acknowledge me. He stalked towards the front bar. I felt like I should run away, hide in the bathroom, lock myself into a cubicle until the band came on and the music started and everything was okay again. But how could anything be okay after what I'd just overheard?

Shaking, I peeled back the curtain, just a crack. Alex was sitting alone, his head in his hands. I was about to walk away and find the others when he looked up. 'Hey, Jade. Come in.'

I shuffled in and took a seat next to him. 'Where is everyone?'

'Outside. Staying away from me and Rory.'

'What's up with you two?'

'I told him I thought Ella and Ethan should live with me for a while.'

'What for?'

'I don't know how much Rory's told you. But him and Maria have a pretty crazy relationship. And kids pick up on everything. The stuff you try to hide from them and the stuff you don't even know you're doing. I had a mum who didn't want me, and she never actually said it out loud, but I could tell. Even when I was the twins' age. Anyway, she left one day when

I was twelve and Dad raised me on his own after that. Most days I wish she'd just left as soon as I was born.' Alex was wringing his hands as he talked and the sound of his skin whispering together made me even more anxious.

'Sometimes I look at Maria and it's like I've seen her before in my mum,' he said. 'Like when the kids want to show her something they're all excited about and she doesn't even pretend to care. They gave her a birthday present the other day and she just put it on top of the fridge without unwrapping it. I know when you're a grown-up, it's easy to see a kid's world as being kinda trivial. But it's not to the kid. And when you ignore something that's important to them, they start to see that they don't really matter. Trust me, dude, you never forget that feeling.'

Alex stopped fidgeting, took his hand sanitiser out of his jeans pocket and squirted a little into his palm. He offered the bottle to me and a second later we were both smoothing the gel over our hands.

'I don't want Ethan and Ella to grow up feeling like I did,' Alex said. 'But Rory and Maria are my friends. Or at least they were. So, I wasn't gonna butt in …'

'What changed?'

'When I had them over on Monday, Ella asked if I could find her a new mum. I said, "you've got a mum." Ella's like, "no, she hates us." I said, "she doesn't hate you, she was probably having a bad day." And Ella said, "why is every day a bad day?". She's only four, dude. It broke my heart.'

I touched Alex's arm, hoping it was a comforting gesture. He turned to me and gave me a soft pat on the back of my shoulder. 'Thanks, dude. You know, if Rory thinks you're taking my side, he'll go off at you too.'

The Lyrebirds started the gig with *Don't Speak*, which would've been funny if it weren't so depressing. Rory and Alex refused to look at each other for the whole set. There was hardly any interaction between the rest of the band either. Chloe kept her distance from Rory and Alex, while Dom and Tyler—who were positioned at the back of the stage—alternated between staring at the ceiling and each other.

During the break, I followed The Lyrebirds—minus Rory, who stayed inside to talk to the Bluebonnet's manager—out to the courtyard.

'You really gonna leave the band?' Dom asked, lighting a cigarette.

Alex shrugged as if he simply didn't care anymore. I felt my throat getting hot.

'You've been Hunter's best friend forever. You must've fought before,' Chloe said.

'Not like this,' Alex said. 'I'm not welcome at their home anymore, which is gonna make things difficult.'

'Well, Maria's hated me from day one so I don't know the difference,' Chloe murmured.

'We can rehearse at my place,' Dom said. 'Been working on my studio and it's awesome now.'

'Since when do we rehearse?' Tyler said. 'I've counted three times in the last year, and two of those was coz we had a new band member.'

'Touché. I'm just saying, no one actually needs to go to Hunter's house again.'

I wanted to talk to Rory but he was nowhere to be seen. I wish I'd gotten a glass of water from the bar, to wet my throat or just for something to do. But I was so nervous I'd be peeing all night if I had so much as a sip of anything.

Tyler reached over and lightly punched Alex in the bicep. 'I'll miss you, bro. You're the second best muso in this band. After me, obviously.'

'Yeah, but you've only got four strings to play with,' Alex said, finally smiling.

'Yeah, but my instrument goes deeper than yours.'

Chloe and Dom chuckled awkwardly. I tried to smile, but I felt the walls of my safe place beginning to crack.

Chapter Sixteen

On the way to the Sherlock Arms on Sunday, I remembered the blazing fury in Rory's eyes on Friday night and began to panic that he wouldn't want to see me. He hadn't even spoken to me on Friday. I pinched my bruised skin, trying to get some second-hand relief, but by the time I got to my stop, my arms and legs were aching from trembling so hard. I stumbled off the bus, dizzy and short of breath. The driver looked at me like I was on drugs.

Rory put down the acoustic guitar he was tuning as soon as he saw me. 'You right, babe?' he asked, hugging me.

I nodded into his chest.

Faye and Greg were sitting at a table to the right of where Rory was setting up—this time with their son, Lyle, who was fifteen. Other than a brief smile when his parents introduced him to me, he just played with his phone and picked at a bowl of wedges.

Rory finished his first set with *Better Man*, then came over to sit in the space between Lyle and me. Rory smiled and ruffled his nephew's hair. But when Faye asked about Alex, I felt the mood at the table turn cold.

'That idiot's trying to break up my family,' Rory muttered.

Greg raised his eyebrows but stayed as silent as Lyle.

'How bad must things be for Alex to threaten you?' Faye said.

Rory shook his head. 'He just projects his own mummy issues onto everyone. Maria would never hurt the kids.'

'She doesn't need to. All she has to do is not show that she loves them.'

Rory glowered, just like he had at the Bluebonnet two nights ago.

Faye reached across me and touched her younger brother's hand. 'You and Alex are so close. You know he loves Ella and Ethan. And he's a wonderful guitarist. Are you really going to let this end a friendship and a band?'

'I'm not doing anything,' Rory said in a deadly tone that signalled the end of the conversation.

#

On the drive home in Rory's van, I was too scared to say anything at first. Eventually, he was the one who broke the silence.

'Bad news. I had to delete your photos,' he said. 'One of my mates needed to use my laptop.'

'If you still have the emails, you can download them again,' I pointed out.

'That's true. But I've been trying to control myself. You must've known that sending me those pics would put you in a position of power over me.'

'You wanted me to send you more. The personalised lipstick ones. But I haven't yet. It's … on my to-do list.'

'Can you put me on your to-do list?'

The question hung in the air. My heart jumped and my mind scrambled for a response.

'I mean, I could be on the bottom of your list,' Rory continued, 'but hopefully I'd work my way up. But you'd have to tell me when I get to the top of the list. Otherwise I'll never know and I'll never get to be naked with you.' He said it like it was a joke, complete with his trademark grin. But when I turned to meet his eyes, we both realised he was serious. And I realised I'd never wanted anything or anyone more.

'I want you. On my list,' I managed to stammer. 'But I don't know if I can. Ever since … what happened with Nathan and Pauly … you're the closest anyone's gotten to touching me like that.'

Rory bit his lip in concentration. We were in my driveway already.

'You're really uncomfortable about this,' Rory said. 'You're squirming in the seat.'

I looked down at the body that had betrayed me.

'Did you tell them to stop?' he asked.

I closed my eyes and shook my head. 'I never said anything. I didn't know what to do.'

'Did you feel guilty or ashamed?'

I nodded.

'Why?'

'I went there. I drank too much. I put myself in that position.'

'It doesn't matter who was drunk. It sounds like they set you up. Nathan knew his mate was in the bathroom. They took advantage of you.'

'But I wanted it. I wanted him to love me.'

'Not like that, I'm guessing.'

I stared at the faded jeans covering my knees.

Rory reached over and squeezed my thigh, where unbeknown to him, there was a pool of bruises. But there was something warm and comforting about his touch. I gave him a watery smile.

'How do you feel about it now?' he asked.

'I don't know.'

'Maybe you should talk to someone and work out how you feel, so you can begin to put it past you.'

I thought about Deanna on my desk and the rock under my pillow. I figured Rory meant talking to a professional, but I wasn't ready to let anyone new into my life. 'I'd rather talk to you.'

Rory licked his lip, looking pensive. 'Do you think about sex much? Does it bother you that you're not having it?'

I shrugged. 'Maybe. Sometimes.'

'Would it help if you were with someone you trust?'

I turned to meet his eyes. Was he asking what I thought he was asking? 'I think it might.'

He took my hand in his. 'Do you want to have sex? With me?'

'Yes,' I heard myself whisper. 'Just not right now.'

'When? In ten minutes? An hour? I need to prepare,' Rory said cheekily.

'I'm on my period,' I blurted out.

Rory blinked in surprise, then burst into laughter. I blushed.

'Sorry for being so awkward,' I mumbled.

'Don't be,' he said, kissing the back of my hand. 'You're fine just the way you are.'

#

I thought about the night I'd tried to tell my parents about Nathan and Pauly. The evening news was on TV. Dad was still two weeks away from officially coming out and moving in with Wayne.

95

I'd been trying to put my words together when the story came on about a woman named Emily, who'd just done a talk at my school.

Years earlier, she'd gone to a party with her sister, but they'd been separated in the crowd. Emily was drinking with some older boys and passed out. When she woke up, there were three guys looking down at her. One was inside her, one was taking photos, another was recording the whole thing. They'd gagged her with a T-shirt so she couldn't scream while they all took turns with her. They threatened to send the pictures to everyone she knew if she reported it. But she went to the police anyway. She told her story, over and over. And now she was travelling around the country, speaking out about sexual assault.

I thought she was brave to stand up for herself and other women and girls. My parents didn't feel the same way.

'It's sad what happened to her,' Dad said. 'But surely if you're gonna get blind drunk with so many boys around, you need to accept some personal responsibility.'

'They raped her,' I whimpered.

'A girl must learn to have control,' Mum said. 'Not drink so much. Not look like a prostitute.'

I burned in silent shame.

But now Rory knew my secret. And he didn't judge me for it. He didn't tell me it was my fault. And that meant more to me than I could express in words.

#

I didn't know what was going to happen with Alex and the band, but as long as I had Rory, I'd be okay. Having him in my life made me want to live, and knowing he saw something in me made me want to be a better person. Instead of hitting the snooze button until lunchtime, I started getting up when my alarm went off at 8 am. On Monday, I tried to write my resume. On Tuesday, I applied for some jobs. And on Wednesday, I started looking at uni and TAFE courses, trying to figure out what I really wanted to do with my life.

'Why you up so early? You going out again? Where are you going?' Mum asked, bursting into my bedroom without knocking.

'Why?'

'I just ask. Cannot even ask, ah?'

'I can go wherever I want. If you had any friends, you'd go out too, instead of bothering me.' I knew it was the wrong thing to say as soon as it left my mouth, but it was too late.

'Don't be rude.'

If it were anyone else I would've said sorry. But it was Mum. And she made me tired and angry.

'What you doing now?' she demanded.

'Nothing.'

'Show me. You talking to that man who turned you against me?'

I flicked off my computer screen before she had a chance to read the perfectly innocent course outline on it. 'Unlike you, my friends actually care about me.'

'You are so ungrateful. I raised you. All by myself after that *ah kwa* walked out on you.'

I turned away, blinking back tears until Mum left the room. She hadn't raised me all by herself at all. It'd only been a year since Dad left so it's not like I was a little kid then, even if she treated me like one. She was being ridiculous and I hated myself for crying over it. When she was gone, I shut the door and reached for my rock.

#

Almost on cue, the phone rang. I put my rock away and picked up my mobile. 'Hey.'

'Half of the band that normally plays at Summit tonight is sick,' Rory said. 'So, we're filling in for them. You coming?'

I remembered what Alex had told me about how dodgy the club was. 'Isn't that where you go to get peed on at the bar?'

'We used to play there all the time and we're fine.'

Fine as in they'd never been hurt? Or fine as in the friendship was back on track? Remembering how angry Rory had been last weekend, I didn't dare bring up Alex yet.

'There aren't any buses in that direction and I don't think I've got enough money for a cab.'

Rory sighed. 'Okay, babe. It's gonna be a shit gig without you.'

'You're pretty close to the top of the list,' I told him.

'I take that back. You've just made my day. Summit's gonna be a breeze.'

I smiled, even though he couldn't see me. When we hung up, I curled up on my bed and squeezed my pillow, my heart thumping. I would see Rory again on Friday. Were we going to have sex then? I got butterflies in my stomach and an ache between my legs every time I thought about it.

But taking pictures was one thing. Having sex was another. Would he even be able to touch my naked body without it recoiling? Would I bleed again? What was I supposed to do with my hands? What if he saw my bruises?

And how would it even happen? He lived with Maria and the kids. I lived with my mother. He knew I couldn't drive.

At least my period had finally ended. I found a black dress and stockings to wear on Friday instead of my usual T-shirt and jeans—trying not to get my hopes up, but wanting to be ready, just in case.

Chapter Seventeen

I was nervous about the gig for a whole bunch of reasons, but it was a relief to see that Rory and Alex were at least on speaking terms again. Rory even grinned when Alex did his duckwalk during *Thunderstruck*.

During the set break, Rory joined the rest of us outside. I can't remember what we talked about. All I remember is the heat from Rory's leg against mine and my fingers intertwining with his under the table.

'I think we'd better get back to work,' he said after about half an hour. How could he sound so casual? As the others got up and went inside, Rory's hand found the small of my back.

'Is it wrong what we're doing?' he asked, and the first hint of insecurity flickered across his eyes.

I stared back at him, suddenly self-conscious. It was a huge step we were taking, if we took it. But I knew there'd never be anyone else it felt right with. He was my best friend. 'I think it's okay. As long as it's what we both want.'

Backstage, I overheard Rory tell Alex they were taking me back to his place tonight.

After the gig, I climbed in the back seat of Rory's van and Alex drove us home. We chatted for a little while on the front lawn until it got too cold to stay outside. Alex grabbed his gear and said goodbye, crossing the street to his house.

Alone, Rory and I went inside.

#

'Let me show you around properly,' Rory said after locking the door behind us and taking off his shoes. 'It's just me and the dog right now. I kicked her out. The kids are with Faye and Greg for the weekend. It's been like a ghost town here today.'

I tried to mask my surprise. What happened to him and Maria being friends and raising the kids together? Alex had hinted at their 'crazy relationship' but Rory never seemed unhappy with the arrangement.

As I debated whether or not say anything, Bones trotted over to greet us, his tail wagging. Rory ruffled his fur and put him in the laundry. We did a brief tour of the house. When I peeked into the master bedroom, I noticed there was no mattress on the bed.

'She took the mattress with her,' Rory explained, looking slightly embarrassed. 'I'll get a new one. But I've been sleeping on the couch for the last two years anyway.'

We returned to the living room. Rory untied his black bandana and dropped it on the floor before switching off the lights.

'Mood lighting,' he said, his grin illuminated by the streetlight streaming through the window. 'Take a seat. Make yourself at home.' He lay down on one side of the L-shaped couch. I sat down on the other side, near his head, loosely raking my fingers through his hair.

'You don't use as much product as Nathan did,' I observed.

He smiled up at me, looking more relaxed than I'd ever felt. 'Come here,' he murmured. I looked confused. He chuckled. 'Alright, I'll come to you.'

He sat up, gently pulled my hair back from my face, and kissed me. His soft lips drew a trail down the curve of my neck and my breath hitched.

Rory unbuttoned his shirt and lay back down on the couch. 'Lie on top of me,' he said.

'I don't know what to do,' I admitted.

'It's okay. Just be with me. We won't do anything you don't want to do.'

I slipped off my shoes and gingerly lay myself over him. His fingers lightly wandered a path down my body, sliding under my dress. As I listened to the calming rhythm of his heartbeat, my breathing began to slow, matching the rise and fall of his chest.

'You're pretty comfortable with me, aren't you?' he said.

'Mm-hmm,' I mumbled, breathing in his scent. I'd never felt more comfortable with any person in my life. Rory could sing away the storms in my heart and kiss away the fears. He was the reason I woke up in the morning, the thing that made me want to live to see another day, another week. Was this how it felt to be in love?

'Can I take my pants off?' he asked.

I nodded and peeled myself off his body, biting my lip in anticipation as he removed his trousers and briefs. And there he was, the person I loved more than anything, with eyes only for me.

'Should I take my clothes off too?' I asked.

'Only if you're ready.'

I nodded and slid off my stockings and underwear. With the lights off, my bruises couldn't be seen. I started to pull my dress over my head, but my elbow got stuck in one of the straps. I'd never undressed in front of anyone before. I tugged my arm back and forth, trying to free myself.

I heard Rory's soft chuckle and a heartbeat later he was standing in front of me, helping me get my dress off. A quick unhook of my bra and we were both as naked as each other.

He took my hand and showed me how to touch him. 'Are you sure you want to do this?' he asked.

I nodded.

'Stay here,' he said, disappearing into the bedroom. He returned with a condom and guided me back to the couch. This time, I was on my back and he was over me, on me, as he explored every inch of me.

He ripped the condom out of its packet and rolled it expertly onto himself. Then he spread my legs carefully and slid himself inside me. I winced. It wasn't the searing pain I'd felt in Nathan's bathroom, but my body was telling me I wasn't used to this.

'Are you okay?' Rory whispered.

'Yes,' I breathed.

He began to move slowly in me. I tried to match my breathing to his rhythm. He thrust into me and I winced again.

'Sorry,' he said.

'I'm okay.'

'Do you want to stop?'

I shook my head. 'Please don't stop. I want you.'

We started to kiss, gradually finding the right pace for us. It was a strange feeling, having him in me, but he seemed to be enjoying himself, while still caring about whether or not I was in pain, and that made me like it too. When I felt Rory's body shudder against mine, I realised we were both a little out of breath.

He planted a gentle kiss on my mouth. 'That was awesome,' he said. 'See what you've been missing out on?'

I poked him in the ribs and we collapsed into a fit of giggles.

He slipped off his condom and went to throw it away.

I could now see Rory's dog staring at me from the middle of the room, panting and wagging his tail. When had Bones escaped from the laundry? How long had he been watching us? I waved at him, then felt like an idiot as he cocked his head to one side.

Rory returned and flicked the lights back on, grabbing a red texta that was lying on the floor. 'One more thing on our to-do list,' he said. 'Since you never got to take those pictures. It's not lipstick, but it's easy to wash this off. I've had it on my face heaps of times.'

He knelt between my legs and stopped.

'What happened here?' he asked.

I looked down at my thighs. With the lights back on, there was no hiding my bruises.

'I'm just really clumsy,' I said. 'I keep bumping into things at home.'

He studied my face. Could he see I was lying? Could he hear my heart thumping?

But he just leaned forward and kissed me. 'Try to be careful, okay?'

I nodded. He scribbled his name on an unbruised spot on my thigh and pulled me towards him in a tight embrace. 'You really are beautiful,' he said.

'So are you,' I replied. 'Or handsome or whatever guys like to be called.'

'Thanks, babe.' He was massaging my hair, the warmth of his fingers sending electricity through my scalp and down my body. 'I hope I'm still on your list and that wasn't our last time together.'

'Me too. You'll always be on my list.'

Chapter Eighteen

When I woke up on Saturday, I could feel all the places Rory had been. It made me smile. We'd cuddled on his couch for about half an hour and then he'd called me a taxi, mindful that I wasn't supposed to have sleepovers.

My mood didn't last though. Mum barged into my room as I was getting out of bed. 'You are home,' she said flatly.

I rolled my eyes at her.

She scowled at me. 'I see you are quiet and you sometimes look worried.'

It's taken you eighteen years to notice this? I wondered.

'I cannot sleep last night. You came home so late.'

'We went back to Rory's place to talk.' It wasn't technically a lie.

'Who is we? Who had this idea?'

'Rory's guitarist drove us.'

'Rory has children, do they not get disturbed when you go there so late?'

'His sister was babysitting them.'

'Why they need a babysitter? Where is his wife?'

I sighed. Rory's personal life was none of Mum's business, but I couldn't think of anything else to say. 'They split up. She moved out of the house.'

'Why does his wife not want him?'

'How should I know? And I'm not going to ask. That's really rude.' Maybe I should've thought of a lie. The problem with telling Mum that Rory and Maria weren't together anymore is that it opened the door in Mum's mind for what Rory and I actually did.

Mum squinted at me. 'You must be careful with these *ang moh*. They are not your family.'

'Mum, stop doing this. They're my friends. They're not big drinkers, they don't do drugs and they always make sure I get home safely.'

'I know you are big enough, but do not do anything foolish you will regret.'

I blinked as she walked out of the room. Did she just try to give me the sex talk? It was so vague that she could've been talking about skydiving for all I knew.

'Well, I've got no regrets,' I whispered to Deanna. 'I'm glad he and I did it. I'm glad it was with someone I love and trust.' I went to my desk to pick her up. 'You know, for the first time in my life, I've got friends and not just people I know. It'd be nice if my own mother could be happier for me.' I gave Deanna a little squeeze for comfort. 'But at least I've got you and Rory.'

#

I used the rest of Saturday to figure out what sort of woman Rory had liked enough to make babies with. I already knew her name was Maria Ashton and she was a makeup artist. I watched her video on using makeup to cover tattoos for tips on how I could hide my bruises better.

I found Maria on the Concord Creek Mums' message board by searching for her name, along with Rory's, Ethan's and Ella's. Her posts began about four years ago, not long after she gave birth to the twins, and stopped just before their second birthday. I started to browse through the threads and scrolled down to her introductory post.

Hi, I'm Maria. I'm a young mum of fraternal twins (a boy and girl). I was freaking out when I found out we were having two! But it runs in the family … My mum has twin siblings and I was a twin myself but my sister was stillborn. So glad to have found this forum. Everyone seems so supportive here. I went to a couple of prenatal classes before Ella and Ethan were born and got some dirty looks for being so young. I'm 19, not 12! But they were mostly in their late 20s or 30s or older. Is it my fault they waited until they were old????? Anyway, I never went back. Me and my amazing man Rory got through it on our own and we're still going strong.

It was the kind of story Bon Jovi could write songs about, I thought. I clicked on a thread entitled: 'How did you meet your partner?' and read on.

I went out to Summit one night. His band was playing. He sang With Or Without You and I fell in love. After he finished the gig I went over to him to see where we were going next. He said he'd had a feeling about me. Went back to his place and had the best night of my life. Started seeing each other a bit then made it official four months later. I moved in with him and fell pregnant with the twins soon after that.

It hadn't taken long for me to fall for Rory either. That was something I had in common with Maria. But even if he'd asked me to go home with him that first week, I don't think I could've have done it. I started to feel anxious. What if Rory wanted someone more spontaneous than I could ever be?

Shoving away the thought, I found a thread Maria had started when the twins were about eighteen months old.

My hand flickered instinctively to my stomach, even though I knew there was nothing there. What would Rory do if he knocked me up? Would he take me in and protect me from Mum? What would Maria do? How would Ethan and Ella take it?

I flopped onto my bed and bruised myself until the frantic thoughts racing through my head began to clear.

#

I finally saw Rory again at our Sunday Sojourn. I wanted to talk about what we'd done, what Mum had said and all the thoughts and emotions flooding through me that I couldn't even name. But I waited for him to speak.

'Maria's been living with her mum since she moved out,' Rory said. 'Her mum's told her, "You're not staying here with two kids as well." Which is fine, coz I want Ethan and Ella living with me. I'm picking them up from their grandma's place after this gig.'

And what about us? I wanted to ask. But where I'd been relaxed in his arms at his house two nights ago, I was suddenly tense with nerves again. What if he regretted what we'd done? What if this was just a one-night stand? How could we be together if he was the only one at home looking after the twins?

Faye had told me she and Greg were coming to the Sherlock Arms for this gig, but they never showed up. Instead, a dozen loud women arrived midway through Rory's first set. They sat inches away from me, ignoring my presence, but I could hear the names 'Rory' and 'Maria' float up above their noise. Someone was wearing a perfume that tickled my throat. I tried to listen to what they were saying.

'Did you see what Maria posted last week?'

'That stuff about having a great night with a real man?'

'Yeah, Rory never added her, so I sent him a screenshot. She deactivated her profile right after I told him.'

My heart sank. Did Rory just sleep with me because he was angry at Maria? Hadn't he said they were both free to date other people?

When Rory finished his set, he introduced me to the women as his friend Jade. I felt their sneers on me for the rest of the afternoon, even after Rory went back to work.

The woman he'd introduced as Stacey slid towards me. 'So, how long have you known Rory?' she asked.

'A few months,' I replied.

'Oh, I've known Rory for years,' she said. 'There's so many photos of us lying on the road outside Summit.'

She slithered back to her friends and the whole group went back to ignoring me. I felt the air closing in on me. I gripped the edges of my seat, trying not to look like my chest was strangling my lungs, but no one noticed or cared anyway. I must've looked like I'd been running a marathon. My hands quivered when I tried to rub the sweat off my forehead.

Before Rory finished his last set, I bolted into the bathroom. I sucked in some deep breaths and splashed water on my face. My knuckles were white as I held onto the edge of the sink, trying to get myself back to normal. I heard Rory finish his gig outside.

When I finally left the bathroom, Rory was waiting for me outside the door. 'Do you want me to drive you home today?' he asked.

I nodded. Didn't he always do that? It was supposed to be our Sunday Sojourn.

'That group is my worst bloody nightmare,' he told me. 'They're friends from way back, but huge gossipmongers. You must've heard them talking.'

I nodded again.

'I need you to wait for me down the road. I'll load out of here as fast as I can and then come and get you.'

'You don't want a hand packing up?' I asked.

He shook his head. 'Those girls won't stop interrogating us if they see you helping me. I'll be quick.'

Why does it matter if Maria's with someone else now and Rory's single? I wondered, but Rory had walked back out to where he was playing.

I went outside and waited for him. Was he ashamed of me? We drove home in silence, my head spinning with unasked questions.

Chapter Nineteen

I had no one else to talk to. Except maybe … Cedric. He and I weren't close, but he did know about Rory.

Cedric was in the process of settling into his new home in Wellington and hadn't been online much. I sent him a text message and asked if I could get some guy advice.

My phone rang eight minutes later. I jumped. I'd been expecting him to just message me back.

'What's up, sis?'

'Rory and I had sex.'

'Oh gee, thanks for letting me know,' Cedric said dryly.

'But I think he just did it coz he's lonely and pissed at his ex. She's been bitching about him online and going on about some other guy. They split up a while ago, but she only moved out of the house in the past week or so. And he and I haven't spoken about what happened at all, so I don't know what he's thinking.'

Cedric paused. 'I'm sure it wasn't just down to being pissed at his ex,' he said. 'This thing between you sounds like it was a long time coming. His ex bitching about him may have been the final push towards him doing it, but it probably would've happened anyhow, albeit a little later. But he's a guy, Jade. He's not gonna bring it up. We don't do that. That's something you have to bring up.'

'How do I do that without making it awkward?'

'Well, you can't really. It's gonna be a bit awkward no matter what you do. But don't let him think you're feeling awkward about it, coz then you won't get a hundred percent honest conversation out of him.'

#

I waited for Rory's weeknight call on Monday, but it never came. I texted him. He didn't reply. I began to panic.

When I still hadn't heard from him on Tuesday, I sent a text message to Faye asking if Rory was okay.

He's fine. Just stressed. Alex is still thinking about leaving the band. Rory's looking at possible replacements.

My stomach fell. It wasn't easy for me to find people I felt comfortable with, who accepted me the way I am. I didn't want the band line-up to change.

A few minutes later, Faye sent me another text. *I told Rory you messaged me. He's grateful and will call you soon.*

But he never did.

Chapter Twenty

I considered not going to the Bluebonnet on Friday. But I had to see Rory and confront him, if nothing else. I didn't know what I was expecting, but it'd been a week since he took me back to his house and he was acting like it never happened. Having sex—and more to the point, a positive sexual experience with no blood and strangers in bathrooms—was a big deal for me. I thought he knew that.

Rory and Alex were civil to each other without being overly friendly. As they were sound-checking and tuning up, Tyler decided he wanted to change his strings. I was the only other person in the room, so he asked me to shine a torch over his bass guitar while he operated on it. I wondered if it'd be easier to see what he was doing if he took his sunglasses off, but I didn't say anything.

Tyler told me his cousin Brad was on the list to be The Lyrebirds' new lead guitarist if Alex really decided to quit. 'But between you and me, I don't think he will,' Tyler said in his low drawl. 'We all complain about the band and the crappy bars sometimes, but there's enough musos in this town that can't get a gig and none of us want to be them.' Tyler glanced over his shoulder at Rory, who was idly strumming chords on the main stage, oblivious to our conversation. 'Don't tell Hunter that though. I don't mind seeing him sweat.'

'Why're you telling me this?' I asked.

Tyler shrugged. 'You're so quiet, I figure you wouldn't say anything to him. Dom said you guys aren't sleeping together.'

I felt my face and neck prickle with heat. 'What we do or don't do is nobody's business,' I stammered. Was everyone gossiping about us?

Tyler looked sheepish. 'Sorry, mate. It's just … I'd worry about you if you were banging Hunter.'

'Why?'

'Coz … How can I put this? He's rocked a million women's faces.'

I raised my eyebrows at the garbled Bon Jovi reference, but Dom chose that moment to enter the band room and Tyler went over to talk to him. I slinked into the corner, Tyler's words ringing in my ears as I agonised over their meaning.

#

Faye and Greg soon arrived and the three of us sat down. I felt bad for not dancing when hardly anyone ever came to check out the band, but my body kept me pinned to my seat. When Chloe was singing *I Love Rock 'n' Roll*, three women pranced into the room from the front bar.

'Is that …' Greg began.

'Oh God, yes. Layla,' Faye finished.

My stomach curled. Rory's ex-girlfriend? The one with the nude photos of him from Venice?

'You guys stay here,' the apparent leader of the group was saying. 'I'll go over there and get his attention.'

She flicked her fingers through her hair and strutted towards the stage in time with the song. Rory noticed her with surprise. When the song finished, he announced, 'Layla's in the house, ladies and gents.'

Her girlfriends cheered next to us. Faye pursed her lips. My throat felt constricted. There was no one listening but Layla, her friends, Faye, Greg, and me—Rory's last notch. Is that all I was to him? Was he rubbing it in my face?

Rory picked up his acoustic guitar and started playing the opening lick of the Eric Clapton song bearing Layla's name. As he sang about getting lonely with no one by your side, I gripped the hem of my dress and longed for my rock.

#

It was a chilly night, so the band stayed inside instead of going out to the courtyard during the set breaks. Layla was all over Rory, massaging his shoulders and whispering into his ear. I didn't want to watch, but I couldn't look away. When she went to the bathroom, Rory came over to Faye, Greg and me.

'My past is so annoying,' he said. But he didn't look annoyed when Layla came back and ushered him into a corner to herself again, feeding him sips of her cocktail.

Alex, Dom and Tyler went straight to the bar, while Chloe joined us.

'Who is that girl?' Chloe asked. Layla's arms were now encircled around Rory's waist.

'Rory used to date her years ago,' Faye said.

'Does he want to fuck her?' Chloe said, echoing the words I was afraid to speak.

'I think he's just thinking, "I might as well. She's here. Why wouldn't I fuck her?"' Faye rolled her eyes in disgust.

I felt like throwing up. After sucking in a series of sharp breaths, I took a sip of water. It sent an icy chill down the length of my body.

By the end of the night, Layla had announced that she was taking Rory home. Rory was too drunk to drive his van and had no choice but to leave it in the car park because Alex had driven his own car to the gig.

'Don't be ridiculous,' Faye scolded. 'Come home with us.'

'It's fine,' Rory said, swatting her away with a stupid grin on his face.

'You're such a jerk,' Faye said. 'You kicked Maria out because you think she was screwing someone else and now you're about to do the same thing.'

The colour drained from my face. He used me. He'd really used me.

'No, I'm not,' Rory said. 'I'm going home.'

'Home is where you damn well should be. With the woman you love and your kids.'

Rory went to hug his sister goodbye, but she pushed him away. When he tried to embrace me, I did the same. He didn't seem to notice. Layla pulled him into her car and he was gone.

'Idiot,' Faye said.

'He's a grown man.' Greg, who'd been silent until now, finally spoke. 'You can't control him anymore.'

'So, has Maria moved back in?' I asked, trying to sound casual despite the growing lump in my throat.

'Yes, she was only gone for a few days,' Faye said. 'Their relationship's always been on and off like that.'

I felt like I'd been winded. No wonder Rory had been so distant. He'd only been buttering me up so he could sleep with me to get back at Maria.

I muttered goodbye to Faye and Greg and turned towards home.

#

The tears started streaming down my face as soon as I took my first steps out of the car park. I ran down the street until I was

115

safely out of sight of Faye and Greg and started bawling. I didn't care how ugly I looked. I didn't care if my makeup was smudging.

When I'd tired myself out and my tears had slowed to a trickle, I began to walk home, the heaviness of my heart weighing me down with each step.

#

Back in the safety of my bedroom, I found the rock and slammed it wildly against my ribs. If Mum were to lift my shirt tomorrow, she'd be confronted by angry blotches of purple skin that I wouldn't be able to explain. I'd always been careful about my bruises, making sure I could pretend I'd gotten them by bumping into a chair or something. But I didn't care anymore. I just needed the pain to go away. I hit and hit and hit, finding my own tortured rhythm until I dropped the rock in exhaustion.

My body slipped into the quiet euphoria I felt every time I bruised myself. But I knew it was only temporary.

Chapter Twenty-One

I almost didn't get out of bed for our Sunday Sojourn, but I really had to confront Rory about Layla and Maria.

He looked up as soon as I entered the beer garden of the Sherlock Arms and flashed me an innocent smile. My throat closed up. I looked around. It was just him and me this week— no Faye or Greg, and no nightmare friends and exes from Rory's past.

I opened my mouth to speak.

'Man, that girl I went home with on Friday …' Rory mused, cutting me off before I could start. 'We were at her place and within about a minute I wanted to leave. Don't tell Faye I said that.'

I frowned. Did that mean he hadn't slept with Layla after all? Not that it made up for not telling me about Maria. I still needed to talk to him about that.

He started his gig singing *Wicked Game*. Nervous sickness flooded through my body as I tried to script the right words in my mind. What should I say? I still wanted him to be my friend, if nothing else. He'd been the only light in my life in a long time. What would I do if I lost him completely? But he'd been really hurtful this past week and he needed to know that.

'You've been quiet,' Rory remarked after the gig as we were carrying the last of his gear out to the van.

'I've kinda been wondering about something, but I don't know if it's worth saying …' I began.

Rory turned to me. 'Of course it is. Everything is worth saying.'

'I don't want you to get upset.'

He raised his eyebrows. 'I don't want to get upset either, but if you need to talk to me about something, then you need to talk to me about it.'

I tried to swallow some deep breaths to calm my nerves. It didn't work. My hands found one of the bruises under my shirt and I pinched the skin.

He waited a moment for me to speak, then gestured at me to get in the car. 'Maybe you'll talk to me when we're driving.'

I climbed into the van and buckled up my seatbelt, wondering why it was so hard for words to travel from my brain to my mouth without getting lost. My eyes squeezed shut as Rory drove away from the Sherlock Arms.

'Did you use me to get back at her?' I finally blurted out. I didn't need to say Maria's name.

'Okay, so very well put. Understandable question. And no, I didn't,' Rory replied carefully. 'I have no reason to get back at her. I'm not a spiteful person like that. I think it happened coz you're beautiful and we connect. Well, I think we do anyway.'

I tried to formulate a reply, but none came.

'You can't not respond after I say that.'

I fought back angry tears. 'It's been playing on my mind for over a week. You took me home, made love to me, then acted like nothing happened!'

I punched the side of the door and realised we were almost home. He pulled into my street, stopped the car and turned to me.

'It's complicated,' he said at last. 'Whatever I do at the moment, I want to be sure that it's the best thing for Ethan and Ella. Maria's their mother and she's got nowhere to go so I let her come back to the house. But it's proving awkward. She said she wants to try to make our relationship work, but I know she's seeing someone else. I've played every venue within a stone's throw of this town. The managers ring me the second she walks in with this guy. I just want her to come clean to me about it so the whole family can move on, but I don't think she will.'

And where does that leave you and me? I wondered.

'It wasn't about getting back at her,' Rory continued, reaching over and cupping his hand over mine. 'If it was, I'd be gloating to her about it. And I'm not. It's something that's between you and me.'

He leaned towards me and planted a chaste kiss on my lips. 'I'm sorry I've been distant. It's not because of you. I've just got so much going on at home and I have to put my family first. Just give me some time.'

#

Rory and I texted a little during the week, mostly about things like *Star Trek*. I missed him. When I wasn't thinking about him, I spent most of my time in bed, struggling to get up. The next time I saw Rory was at the Bluebonnet Bar on Friday. He bounded over to me and literally swept me off the ground with a tight hug.

'How are you, beautiful?' he asked, pecking the side of my mouth.

I shrugged.

'It's okay, I won't make you talk.' He squeezed me around my waist—the only person who could do that without me

119

squirming, I realised—and went back to sound-checking for the gig.

Maybe I could cut him some slack. He was going through a complicated, stressful situation. But I was still really confused about where I stood with him. And as the gig wore on, it became clear to me that he was drinking more and more these days. For the second week in a row, he had to leave his van in the car park and come back for it the next day. But no one else in the band seemed concerned about his drinking, so maybe it was just me. Or maybe I was the only one who really cared about him.

#

By the time our Sunday Sojourn rolled around again, I'd figured out that I liked Rory better on Sundays. He had to drive home so he couldn't get drunk and he usually just had coffee and a glass of water. Without the alcohol, he morphed back into the sweet, sometimes cheeky guy I'd fallen in love with.

Faye and Greg were at the Sherlock Arms when I arrived, but they barely acknowledged me. They seemed to be arguing under their breaths.

'I can't take it anymore,' I thought I heard Faye say.

Greg muttered a mostly inaudible response, but I overheard 'need to make an effort.'

I felt like an intruder, even though we were outside in the beer garden and I was in a public place. Before the end of the gig, Faye announced that she was leaving and walked out, leaving Greg to apologise and scurry after his wife.

'What was that about?' I asked.

'Hard to say with Faye but it's always something dramatic,' Rory replied.

I didn't prod any further, but I wondered if I'd ever be close enough to Faye to understand what was going on. I realised I wanted to. It was clear to me now that I loved Rory, but I wanted to love his family too.

When we'd finished loading his gear into the van at the end of the gig, he turned to me. 'Do you want to take a walk?' he asked. 'I'd like to show you something.'

'Okay.'

He took my hand and we strolled down to the beach. The deep orange sun was beginning to set over the glistening water. An oversized ball bounced past us as our feet met the sand and a girl who would've been about the twins' age chased after it, her mother close behind.

'I never want you to be afraid to tell me how you're feeling,' Rory said. 'You know you can talk to me about anything.'

'I don't really talk to people.'

'I get that. But I think you and I have been through enough together that you should try to talk to me from time to time.' He smiled and we continued to walk down the length of the beach, engaging in small talk. Or rather, he made small talk and I nodded, trying to think of things to say, as usual. Rory told me about how much he disliked social media, but had no choice but to use it for both his jobs. His eyes lit up when he told me about the playdough village Ethan and Ella had built together this week after fighting over colours for half an hour. I'd been so angry and hurt at Rory's aloofness after our night together, but as he talked I felt my irritation melt away.

We stopped at a seemingly random bus stand that had been placed at the top of the beach. It was nowhere near the closest bus stop. The stand had been decorated with painted flowers and each flower had a little coloured handprint instead of the petals.

'Ella and Ethan's kindergarten class painted this,' Rory explained. 'Well, they did the handprints and a group of Year 6 kids did the stems and leaves.'

'It's pretty,' I said.

He pointed to a red right handprint at the bottom left corner of the stand. 'That's Ethan's,' he said. Sliding his finger across to the left yellow handprint next to it, he added, 'And that's Ella's.'

I noticed the pinkies on each hand touched slightly, forming a line of orange where they connected. I smiled.

'Have you taken them here to see this?' I asked.

'Yeah, we were here yesterday. I was so proud. We took heaps of pictures. I just hope it doesn't get vandalised. It probably will, but maybe not as quickly as if they'd stuck it on the road and used it as an actual bus stand.'

I nodded in agreement.

He smiled, kissing the back of my hand. 'You should meet Ethan and Ella and find out if you like kids.'

My heart danced eagerly before I remembered the situation with Maria. 'Would that be weird for them?' I asked.

Rory sighed. 'It's tough. They don't really understand what's going on. But they kinda do. Whenever Maria and I speak to each other, they start talking really loudly, trying to drown us out. Not coz we're screaming or anything—we try not to do that in front of the kids. But I guess they pick up on the tone of the conversation. And there's no easy way to explain that Mum and Dad won't live together anymore.' He shook his head grimly. 'She's an idiot. She knows it's over. It can't go on like this. But she did tell me this morning that she'd pack while I was doing this gig and be ready to go when I got home. I think she's gonna live with her dad since it didn't work out with her mum before.'

My mind scurried for a response but none came, so I just smiled awkwardly.

He grinned. 'It's okay, you don't have to say anything when you can't think of anything to say.'

'You know me pretty well,' I said, shyly returning his smile.

He swept my hair behind my ear and kissed me. 'I know we haven't been having our phone chats lately. But you should feel free to call me more,' he said. 'Even if it's just to say hello. If I'm busy, I'll just call you back.'

I nodded. I didn't know how to talk enough on the fly to fill an awkward silence, but I did feel good about Rory again and that was the most important thing.

Chapter Twenty-Two

I spent Monday researching 'Best Jobs for Shy People' and Tuesday looking at uni and TAFE courses without getting any clearer about what I wanted to do for my future. Part of me missed high school, even though I'd hated it. It was easier to say you were studying than to admit you did nothing all day.

But if I were still in school, I wouldn't have met Rory or gone to his gigs. And I couldn't imagine going through each day without him. How had I ever survived this long without knowing I had his voice at the other end of the phone and his warm embrace at the end of the week?

On Wednesday, I was reminded that I would never have met Rory without Samson and Veronica.

'Hello?' I said when my phone rang that morning. People didn't usually call me, and certainly not from numbers I didn't recognise.

'Jade. It's Veronica Otto. I'd like to catch up with you for a coffee.'

Veronica? What for? I wondered, panicking. 'Um, when?'

'Next week. Tuesday afternoon. Four o'clock.'

Obviously Veronica had assumed I wasn't working then. And she'd be right. My cheeks burned silently.

'Let's see. I think I can make it then,' I said slowly, hoping Veronica would think I did actually have a life with other commitments. 'Whereabouts are you thinking?'

'I need to get back to work so I'll text you the address. I look forward to seeing you again.'

She hung up. Why did she want to see me? Why was she looking forward to it? Was I in trouble? Had I done something wrong during my internship that she'd only just found out about?

My phone beeped. I read the address, my stomach fluttering. It was Cool Beans Cafe, where I'd caught up with Dom. And where Veronica's son had stormed in, demanding his drum lessons back.

There was a sharp knock on the door. Mum came into the room. 'I heard you talking to someone,' she said.

I sighed. 'Yeah, it was Veronica Otto.'

'She is the wife of the man who killed himself?'

I nodded.

'Why she want to talk to you?'

'I don't know, she wants to catch up for coffee next week.'

'Maybe you can ask for a job.'

I knew I wasn't going to do that.

'He has a son, I read in the newspaper. Why he kill himself?'

My face tightened. 'How should I know? It's none of my business. Or yours.'

#

When Mum left the room, I rang Rory. I told him about Veronica's call and our planned meeting at Cool Beans Cafe.

'I'll be face-to-face with her next week. What am I gonna do? What is *she* gonna do?'

'I can't tell you why Veronica wants to see you,' Rory said

calmly. 'But you're stressing about something that hasn't even happened yet. Just go meet her. You'll be in a public place, and most people around town know who she is. What can she possibly do?'

'She can still make me uncomfortable without punching me or anything.'

'Point taken. Tell you what, if you feel threatened at any point, go to the bathroom and call me and I'll think of an emergency to get you out of there.'

'Okay.'

'But I'm sure it won't be that bad. At least it'll give you some breathing space from your mum.'

I smiled. He really did know me. 'Anything else?'

'Yes, order their pumpkin soy milkshake. I thought it'd be disgusting, but it's surprisingly good.'

'Okay.' I paused. Now that I had him on the line, how could I make the conversation last longer? 'What've you been up to?' I asked.

'Had a parent-teacher meeting this morning,' he said. 'The kids are socialising well with everyone. Ethan has a slight speech impediment we're monitoring, but it's not that uncommon at their age. Right now, they're both playing in the backyard.'

I imagined them outside, Rory watching on, and tried to picture myself in the scene. I hadn't expected to have kids in my life at my age. Or maybe any age. But to my surprise, the thought of it didn't scare me.

'Do you really want me to meet them?' I asked him.

'Yeah, I do. Maybe not right at this minute, but sometime soon.'

Chapter Twenty-Three

'What if they hate me?' I blurted out when Rory answered the phone the next day. I'd been online, researching "Meeting your partner's kids" since I got up. Even though Rory wasn't technically my partner yet, I was still nervous about getting it wrong.

'Huh?' Rory said.

'Ethan and Ella. I want to meet them, but …'

'They won't hate you. We'll take things slow. I'll introduce you as my friend, so there's no pressure.'

'Okay,' I whispered.

'Whatever happens between us, we'll always be friends, okay?' Rory said. 'And when they get to know you, they'll see how awesome you are.'

'I hope so.'

'Don't stress about this, babe. I don't expect or want you to be Maria. Just be yourself.'

#

Just be yourself. The words echoed in my head for the rest of the day. Who was I? I was the girl who had anxiety attacks. The girl who talked to a plastic figurine and hit herself with a rock in private.

And the girl who loved her best friend more than anything. Rory's friendship was the best thing about me. Fate had brought us together. And now he was what kept me going when I wanted to knock myself out. The thought of seeing him again and hearing his voice and feeling his arms around me gave me something to look forward to when I had nothing at home.

As I headed out of the house on Friday, my mood began to lift. Rory knew I was imperfect and he accepted that. He wanted me to be myself. And I wanted to be the best possible version of myself for him, and for his family.

#

The Lyrebirds were playing *Chasing Cars* on Friday night when one guy broke away from his mates and descended on me.

I tried not to make eye contact with him. He parked himself on the seat next to me, spreading his legs apart until his knees touched mine. I jerked my leg away.

Undeterred, he said, '*Ni hao ma?*'

I didn't speak Mandarin and it seemed presumptuous of him to assume I did. I said nothing. Beads of sweat prickled on my skin. My mind scrambled for a strategy to get away from this guy without making him angry.

He stared at me with an expectant grin on his face, waiting for my reply. I blinked and shook my head, my chest tightening. 'I wanna take you home with me,' he growled in my ear.

'I don't do that with guys I've just met,' I stuttered.

'That's cool. Maybe I can change your mind.'

I shook my head and tried to concentrate on the band.

He pushed his face into my line of sight and narrowed his eyes. 'Can't you take a compliment?'

My hands wrung the hem of my dress. A group of women from the front bar swayed into the room. The band kicked into 'Respect', with Chloe taking lead vocals and the women squealed in a piercing pitch that hurt my ears. The group of men who had been with my 'admirer' watched us with wide grins plastered on their faces.

'Think you're too good for me, huh?' the man sneered into my ear. 'You're not hot enough to be a snob. I'd toss you straight back on the boat you came from when I was done.'

His hands touched my stomach and I leapt to my feet. I looked at Rory, pleading with my eyes and ran into the band room, hoping the man wouldn't follow me through the curtains. I huddled into the corner, hugging my knees to my chin, tears welling in my eyes.

Rory turned to the side of stage, his eyebrows knitting together in puzzlement. He unplugged his acoustic guitar and placed it in its stand. Yelling at the rest of the band to keep going, Rory stepped into the backstage area.

'What's wrong?' he asked.

'That guy.' I told Rory what he'd said.

Rory stalked out of the room. I got up and peeked through the curtain as he strode past the man—who'd rejoined his mates—and out to the front bar. A moment later, Rory returned with a pair of security guards who threw the entire group out in a flail of swear words.

'Thanks,' I breathed, when Rory came back through the curtain.

'No one should be spoken to like that. I'll always have your back,' he said, tenderly kissing my forehead.

#

During the band's break, I noticed we seemed to have split into three groups.

Dom and Tyler sat in one corner of the band room, debating musicians and musical styles I'd never even heard of. Tyler had just started teaching at Concord Creek Music School, so he and

Dom were seeing even more of each other than they had before.

Alex and Chloe sat in another corner. I couldn't hear what they were talking about, but a couple of times I saw Chloe's hand linger on Alex's. I expected Alex to reach for his ever-present aloe vera hand sanitiser, but it stayed in his pocket until just before the band went back on stage. He always used it just before and after he touched his guitar.

And then there was Rory and me. I was trying to work out if Chloe and Alex were now a couple or just close friends, when Rory called me over. He held up a bottle in a scrunched-up brown paper bag. 'Want some?'

I shook my head. 'What is it?'

'Spiced rum.' He pulled me down into the seat beside him and took a swig. 'Maria came over to watch the kids tonight,' he said. 'It's the first time she's seen them all week. And she just walked in, told them to sit down, then got her laptop out and ignored them.'

I draped my arm over his shoulder, trying to show him that I cared and that I was there for him.

'She's got no idea how much damage she's doing to Ethan and Ella. She might as well not be there even when she is.' He sighed. 'They'll be okay. They've got me.'

I wanted to kiss him, but I didn't know how he or the rest of the band would react. We weren't in a relationship. He'd asked for time. And I wanted to give it to him.

I thought about Maria. How she could be so cold to her kids? But I didn't know her. So how could I judge her? She'd been a mother her entire adult life. Maybe she was exhausted and sick of missing out on things that other people her age had taken for granted. I didn't think I'd be able to raise a child at my age, let alone two, but Maria had had no choice.

Chapter Twenty-Four

Rory was visibly distracted at our next Sunday Sojourn. 'Maria's been sending me abusive messages all day,' Rory fumed. 'And then she just asked me to go to a concert with her in the city next weekend coz her friend can't go anymore. She doesn't get how this "not being in a relationship" thing works.'

'What concert is it?'

'Don't care.' He looked at me as if he wanted me to say something. I blinked and made a movement that was somewhere between a nod and a shrug. He rolled his eyes and grinned.

'Talking to you is like having a conversation with myself,' Rory said. 'That's why we get along so famously.'

I nodded and he laughed.

'What do you say to your therapist?' he said playfully. '"Nice couch"?'

'Do you think I need therapy?' I asked.

'Everyone could benefit from a little therapy.'

As we finished loading his gear into the van and hopped inside, Rory said, 'The house is empty at the moment. The kids are at their granddad's place.'

I met his eye, wondering what he wanted to do.

'Do you want to grab some dinner and come back to mine?'

'I'd love to.'

We pulled away from the beach and drove to Brightlights, a twenty-four-hour fast food joint down the road from the Bluebonnet Bar. 'I like to cook when the kids are with me,' he said, as we looked at the takeaway menu. 'But it's easier to buy something on the way home when it's just me. Well, you're here tonight too, but I didn't want to cook something you don't like and make you feel obliged to eat it.'

'I wouldn't mind trying your cooking someday.'

He smiled. 'I'll keep that in mind.'

We ordered a pizza and some hot chips to share. As Rory drove us to his house, I texted Mum to let her know I was eating dinner out and turned off my phone.

Bones started barking as soon as Rory unlocked the front door. He wagged his tail and yapped excitedly at our feet when we entered the house. 'Sorry, mate, this isn't for you,' Rory said. He put our food down on the kitchen table and opened a can of dog food for Bones.

'Do you want a watermelon smoothie?' Rory asked, washing his hands. 'I was making them with Ethan and Ella today.'

'Sounds good.'

He poured my smoothie and set it on the table next to my plate. We settled down to eat. I was suddenly self-conscious. I picked at a mushroom on the pizza, my hands shaking. What if I got food stuck in my teeth, or it ended up on my face, or I spilled something, or I choked or burped or did something embarrassing?

'Are you okay?'

I nodded.

'You sure? You're not eating anything.'

I blushed harder. 'I don't usually eat in front of people.'

'You're really anxious about this.'

I avoided his gaze and nodded. I heard the scrape of his chair moving towards me and felt his hand close over mine.

'You don't have to be shy with me. We've seen each other naked.'

I gave him a wan smile.

'Besides, I've had my kids put more food on these walls than in their mouths. There's nothing you can do that I won't have seen before.'

I squeezed his hand and he kissed my cheek. 'Just take your time. I won't watch you,' he added, returning to his place across the table and focusing on his own plate. Bit by bit, I managed to get some food down.

#

After dinner, we watched another *Star Trek* episode together, the one where our heroes discover they've switched places with their evil counterparts from a parallel universe.

'It'd be interesting if there was a Mirror Universe out there, wouldn't it?' Rory said, as the closing credits started to roll.

'Would the other me still be scared of eating in front of my best friend?' I murmured.

Rory turned to me. 'The other you would probably be the opposite of this you. Which would suck, coz you're an amazing person. And if there are things you don't like about yourself, you've got your whole life to work through them.'

He cupped my cheek, caressing it as he pulled me into a deep kiss.

He took my hand and led me into the bedroom. There was now a mattress on the bed, much to my relief. I held my breath as he rummaged for a condom in the drawer.

'I'm still not sure if I know how to … you know …' I trailed off, blushing.

'Don't overthink it,' he said. 'I just want it to feel good for you.'

He lowered me onto the bed, his soft lips never far from my skin. And even though he was older and more experienced than me, I felt like his equal.

#

We lay together afterwards, entangled in each other's bodies, breathing in unison. I softly traced the outline of his tattoos with my finger and he smiled drowsily at me.

I knew right then I could never love another person the way I loved Rory. He knew me better than anyone ever had. He completed me. With him, sex wasn't bloody and embarrassing and shameful like it had been with Nathan. With Rory, all I wanted was more.

#

It was almost midnight by the time Rory drove me home. On the way, I considered telling him the truth about the bruises I hid throughout my body. But I didn't want him to crash the van in shock. Maybe I could just stop hitting myself for him and then I wouldn't have to tell. He hadn't mentioned them this time, but the only light on in the room had been a dim bedside lamp.

I dodged Mum's questions about why Rory was bringing me home so late by heading straight to my bedroom and avoiding being alone with her for the rest of the weekend. I didn't want to talk to or even think about Mum. I just wanted Rory.

My body still wasn't used to sex because I could feel where Rory had been every time I touched myself down there or

134

clenched the right muscles. But I didn't care. It made me feel closer to him.

Chapter Twenty-Five

I was still slightly sore when I went to meet Veronica on Tuesday. I got there half an hour early and hid in the bathroom. I was desperate to give myself a bruise in one of the cubicles. The wave of relief would give me the strength to face Veronica. But I stopped myself. I didn't want to turn to that anymore. Not when I had Rory.

Veronica was entering Cool Beans Cafe when I emerged from the bathroom. I flashed a weak smile and she strode over to me, her grey eyes cold and blank.

'What would you like?' she asked, marching to the counter.

'Pumpkin soy milkshake, please,' I replied, remembering Rory's recommendation. Veronica ordered a cappuccino and we took a seat.

'I suppose you're wondering why I wanted to meet you,' Veronica began.

'A little,' I replied.

'My son Zayden has his drum lesson nearby. He's been stealing money from me for it.'

I didn't know what to say and was relieved when our drinks arrived—much faster than they had when I was here with Dom.

'He never practised when Samson was alive,' Veronica continued. 'Samson was constantly nagging him about it. It wasn't a good look for the founder of a children's arts charity to have a son who didn't even draw stick figures, you see.'

Would people have cared that much? I wondered. Maybe they would. Unlike the Ottos, no one paid attention to what I did or didn't do.

'Now all Zayden wants to do is play drums,' Veronica said. 'So, I let him. I pretend that abysmal noise doesn't give me a headache. I pretend I don't know he's stealing from me. It's the least I can do. It's probably my fault his father's dead.'

Why are you telling me this? I thought. I sipped my milkshake. It was rich and creamy, but I couldn't enjoy it with this conversation going on. 'It's not your fault,' I managed to say, my words sounding hollow.

'I wasn't much older than you when I met Samson,' Veronica said, as if she hadn't heard me. 'I knew he was going to be special. He was so full of ideas and dreams. If something didn't work, he'd try something else. He never, ever gave up until the day he died.'

I shifted uncomfortably in my seat. There were days I felt like 'giving up'. Before I met Rory and The Lyrebirds—and before the bruises—watching *Star Trek* and listening to Bon Jovi were all that got me through.

'We never intended to have children. It seemed like an unnecessary distraction. But then I fell pregnant with Zayden. And Samson found he loved being a father. He started the Create Tomorrow Foundation because he wanted all young people to have a voice, and he believed the arts were a universal language. Being Zayden's dad changed him. Samson started thinking about other people besides himself. Until he decided to die, that is.'

I resented Veronica's suggestion that Samson's suicide was selfish. How could she ask someone she loved to exist in misery for the rest of his life just so that she could feel better about herself? What if he thought he was a burden and that Veronica and Zayden were better off without him? Maybe he felt that ending his life was the most selfless thing to do. No, she didn't understand. She never would. I took another sip of my milkshake and bit my tongue.

'I was a good mother when Zayden was a baby. Everyone said so.' Veronica seemed to be talking to the air now. I wasn't sure if she even knew I was sitting across from her. 'But as he got older, he started pulling away from me. He wanted to be like his father, who took risks and reaped the rewards. Not his mother, who sang a few pop songs, starved herself to look pretty for a few years, then had the good fortune to marry a successful entrepreneur.'

'You're still pretty,' I said, then kicked myself. Why did I say that? But I couldn't say she was still a good mum, because I didn't know. And the other thing I still didn't know was why I was even here with Veronica.

Veronica's face made a tight smile that didn't reach her eyes. 'Have you been in a long-term relationship?' she asked.

I shook my head.

'Well, let me tell you something. It doesn't matter how in love you think you are. It doesn't matter how committed you think you are. When you've been together long enough, you drift apart. Until one day you realise that you're with the person because you're so used to them and not because you love them anymore.'

I gulped hard. I still didn't know what to say and my drink was almost half-finished. Maybe I could pretend I needed to pee, and climb out the window. I tried to recall the layout of the bathroom. I was pretty sure there'd been a small window above the bench top, but I was probably too short to get up there, let alone squeeze through the hole.

'I had no idea Samson even kept a diary,' Veronica went on. 'But I found it easily after he died. Sometimes I wonder if he wanted it to be the first thing I found. He wrote about how alone I made him feel.'

Veronica took her first, long sip of her coffee, then fixed her haunting grey stare on me.

'Then he started to write about you. How he could see, even in your interview, that you were smart, but no one knew because you didn't shout it out. That you understood people even though you never said anything. I wanted to hurt you.'

I tightened my grip on my glass, eyeing the door.

'But I calmed down,' Veronica continued. 'And I thought, with all the time he devoted to the foundation, perhaps you knew him better than I did at the end.'

'But I hardly knew him at all,' I said, and it was true.

'No, I suppose no one really did. There was the Samson Otto everyone saw on TV and in the social pages. And then there was the man who talked to no one but his diary.'

Can I go now? I wondered. I was three-quarters of the way through my drink and Veronica needed comfort or friendship or something that I wasn't able to give.

'Zayden's drum teacher, Domenic, played at the ball,' Veronica said, changing the subject. 'I heard you're friends with him and his band.'

I nodded. 'How did you know that?'

She arched her perfectly-shaped eyebrow. 'People tell me things, Jade. When my son runs screaming into a cafe waving my money around, they tell me.' She took another careful sip of her drink. 'So, are they good?'

'Huh?'

'The band. Are they good? Someone else booked them and I wasn't listening at the ball.'

'Yeah, they're awesome.'

She smiled thinly. 'Well, perhaps I'll see you at a gig sometime.'

I coughed. Good thing I'd swallowed the last mouthful of my drink. Veronica at the Bluebonnet Bar? I couldn't quite picture it.

'Don't look so surprised, Jade. I was young once. Samson and I had to change our lives when we had Zayden, but he's old enough to look after himself now.'

I smiled back, but inside my heart was falling. Going to Rory's gigs was my reprieve from the stress of being at home. I couldn't cope if Veronica—who'd given me enough anxiety during my short internship—started invading my space with the band. I could only hope she was just being polite and had no intention of actually going.

#

I called Rory as soon as I was safely back home in my bedroom.

'Did you meet Veronica?' he asked.

'Yes.'

'See? You survived.'

'Uh-huh.'

'What happened?'

'I don't know, it was just really weird.' I recounted the conversation to him. 'Why would she come to me with this? We only knew each other for ten weeks. And it's not like she came into the office every day.'

'How long were Veronica and Samson together? Close to twenty years? And at the end of his life he wrote that you were the one who'd understand him. She's probably as scared and

140

confused as you are, except that she's also got a kid to raise on her own now.'

I sighed. 'I guess you're right.'

'Hey, I'm always right,' he said.

I giggled. 'Yes, sir.'

'I'm glad you agree. So, Veronica aside, how are you?'

'I'm good. About Sunday …' I felt myself blushing.

'Did you not enjoy yourself?' he asked.

'No, I did. I mean … I really did.' My neck felt prickly and hot. 'That's the first time sex has felt good,' I whispered. 'And I'm glad it was with you.'

'I'm glad too, babe. We should make this a regular thing between us.'

I felt my cheeks lift into a smile. 'We should. But sex is still a really big deal for me,' I admitted.

'Why is it a big deal? I mean, it's a big deal for me coz I can't seem to find enough time for it.'

I laughed. 'Well, a few weeks ago, no one could touch me. I couldn't even imagine it.'

'Yeah, so you're making progress. This is good, right?'

I was about to reply when I heard cries of 'Dad, Dad!' at the other end of the phone, followed by Rory's muffled reply.

'Sorry, Jade, I've gotta go,' Rory said when I could hear him clearly again. 'Speak soon. I love you.' He hung up.

I collapsed onto the bed, the pounding of my heart echoing in my brain. He loved me? He'd never said it before. He loved me. Did it mean the same thing to him that it did to me? All I knew was that I loved him back. And thinking about him made me feel happier than I ever did when I talked to Deanna or bruised myself.

Chapter Twenty-Six

I came crashing down that Friday when I went to the Bluebonnet Bar. Rory was visibly drunk before the gig had even started. As soon as I stepped into the band room, I realised I was in the middle of a battlefield. Alex sent Rory a torrent of swear words then took Chloe's hand and marched outside.

And then Layla and her two stupid friends rocked up. They were loud and drunk too.

'I hate it when you all turn up with clothes on,' Rory murmured. 'You know how much pain you're putting me in by not being nude?' He was holding a silver hip flask. I wanted to slap it out of his hands.

'I remember all the times you were nude at my house, babes,' Layla slurred back, her arm curling around his waist.

I clenched my shaking fists.

'But we all got responsibilities now, hey?' Layla turned to her friends. 'You know, his kids are so sweet and gorgeous. And they have the most amazing blue eyes,' she said.

'Do they take after him?' one of the women asked.

Layla snorted. 'Obviously not!' she scoffed, before pinning a wet kiss on Rory's face.

I stormed out of the band room unnoticed, tears prickling my eyes. How had Layla met his kids? She was the ex before Maria!

As I passed the bar on my way out, I collided with Tyler.

'Sorry, Jade … Hey, are you okay?'

I lowered my eyes, not wanting Tyler to see me cry. 'Yeah, I'm just tired,' I lied.

Tyler studied me for a moment. 'Well, I'll see you back there, okay?'

'I don't know, I'm not feeling well,' I mumbled. That wasn't a lie. My belly was churning with rage.

'Are you going home?' Tyler asked.

'What do you mean you're going home?' Dom had returned from his cigarette break to take his place by Tyler's side.

My face felt hot.

'She said she's not feeling well,' Tyler replied.

Dom bent down, placing a hand on my forehead. I flinched under his gaze and his smoky breath. 'I reckon you're alright. We'll just play some Bon Jovi and you'll be fine!'

I smiled weakly. But as Tyler turned to the bartender, Dom put his arm around my shoulder. 'Look, if you're really feeling sick, I'll call you a cab. But if Hunter's being a jerk or something, I can kick his arse for you.'

'Don't do that,' I said quickly, and Dom's eyebrows shot up.

'That's it, isn't it?' Dom said. 'Jeez, you're probably the most loyal friend he's ever had. You're always here and there's nothing in it for you. At least when he treats the band like crap, he's paying us.'

'He pays me in … other ways,' I said. My face flushed again. What if Dom realised I was sleeping with Rory after all and thought I was a 'band slut'? 'I mean, he's a really good friend to me when he's not off his face,' I added quickly.

Dom rolled his eyes. 'Let me tell you something. My old man was the nicest guy in the world ninety percent of the time. The other ten percent, he was a really mean drunk. And the fact that he couldn't remember any of it the next day didn't change the fact that it happened. I hardly even talk to him anymore coz I never know which Dad I'm gonna get.'

I remembered what Rory had told me about Dom taking up smoking to annoy his father.

As if he'd read my mind, Dom added, 'I know I'm not perfect myself. Doesn't mean I'm not right.'

Alex and Chloe walked back inside, fingers interlaced, before I could think of anything to say to Dom.

'Hey, dude!' Alex grinned, giving me a fist bump.

Chloe gave me a quick hug. 'Sorry you had to witness all that abuse earlier,' she said to me, glancing sideways at Alex.

'He deserved it,' Alex replied, but his mood seemed to have lifted.

Tyler sauntered back towards us, sipping a cola-coloured drink in one hand. With the other, he passed me a glass of water. 'Feeling better?'

I nodded and took the water. It was ice cold with a slice of lemon in it.

'To work, then?' Alex said, scrubbing his palms with his hand sanitiser.

I peeled off from the others and found a seat as they took to the stage. Confusion and anger at Rory swirled in my head. But I was buoyed by the feeling that the band at least had my back.

#

I considered not going to see Rory on Sunday. But it was only when he was drunk that I didn't like the person he became. And I didn't want to give Mum the satisfaction of thinking she'd won in her quest to keep me home alone. So off to the Sherlock Arms I went.

Rory was frowning at his phone when I arrived. 'Hey, babe,' he said when he looked up and gave me a hug. So far, so good.

Then he had to ruin it. 'Layla hasn't texted me back. That's really unlike her. I wanted to make sure she got home okay on Friday.'

I dug my fingernails into my palm, leaving red welts in my skin. So, Rory could worry about Layla, yet he didn't even seem to notice or care that he'd hurt my feelings. Hell, he hadn't even bothered to say goodbye to me on Friday night. He'd been too wrapped up in Layla and her friends, who'd been trying to get him to party on with them at Summit after the gig.

I didn't say anything for the next three hours. A man approached us after the gig as we were packing up in silence. 'That was really good, mate,' he said to Rory.

'Cheers,' Rory replied, shaking his hand.

'You here often?' the guy asked.

'Been here every Sunday for about a year-and-a-half. They haven't gotten sick of me yet.'

'Well, I might see you around then. I'm new to the area.' The man pointed to me. 'Your missus, is she Vietnamese? My wife's from Hanoi.'

'She's not my missus. Just a friend who loves music,' Rory said. 'Her mum's from Malaysia.'

I gave the man with the Vietnamese wife a tight smile and threw a tangled audio lead into Rory's gig box. Just a friend? I thought of all the things we'd done on his couch, in his bed … Was that what you did with "just friends"?

We drove home without another word. I was about to get out of the van when we reached my driveway, but Rory grabbed my hand.

'How are you?' he asked.

I stared at him and shrugged.

'Good? Okay? Not okay? I only see you on weekends now, so I wonder how you are during the week.'

'I'm okay,' I muttered.

'I'm okay, too,' he said. 'I mean, I'm really enjoying being a dad and getting to spend a lot of time with Ethan and Ella. But it breaks me too, you know?'

I shrugged again.

'Like I'll internally start to unwind when I've put the kids to bed. But inevitably one of them'll wake up and need to be settled again. And then the other one gets up. And then they'll both be jumping around telling me they're not tired.' Rory sighed. 'They climbed onto my bed at six this morning demanding breakfast. It was eight o'clock by the time I was finished cleaning eggs off the floor.'

I still didn't know what to say so I leaned over and gave him a silent hug. 'I missed you,' I said at last.

'What do you mean?' he asked.

'I like you when you're like this. Being real and sharing your life with me. Not like how you were on Friday night.'

Rory was quiet for a long time. 'I don't actually remember anything about Friday,' he said, staring at the dashboard. 'I know you were there. I know Layla was there. I think Alex was mad about something. But it's all hazy.' He looked at me evenly. 'I'm sorry if I did something to upset you. I didn't mean it.' He swept the hair off my forehead and kissed it tenderly. 'I love you.'

I looked at his sombre eyes and sighed into his neck. 'I love you too.'

#

I didn't go straight inside after Rory left to take over from his babysitter. I needed a walk to clear my head, away from Mum.

How was it that Rory could make me feel so rotten on Friday nights and so warm on Sundays?

An hour or so later, I found myself near Cool Beans Cafe. Maybe I could enjoy a stress-free drink this time. I went inside.

Alex and Chloe were sitting across from each other at a table in the corner, gazing into each other's eyes. I blushed and was about to shuffle out when Chloe spotted me.

'Jade!' she called, waving me over.

I went over to them, smiling nervously.

'Come join us,' Chloe said.

'I don't want to interrupt,' I began.

'Nah, it's cool,' Alex said. 'We're all friends here. And the dirty stuff happens at home.'

I laughed awkwardly and pulled up an empty seat.

'So, how're things with you and Rory?' Chloe asked.

'What?'

'He just had a gig at Sherlock's, right? Alex said you always go.'

'Oh. Yeah, we're fine.' I hoped I hadn't turned too visibly red.

'Did he tell you?' Alex asked.

'Tell me what?'

'I'm leaving the band.'

My heart fell. I thought about the picture of Rory, Alex and me at the Create Tomorrow Ball on the evening we'd met, our faces frozen in perfect smiles. My life had changed that day. And Alex had been a part of it too. It was one thing for Rory to invite me to The Lyrebirds' gigs, but Alex had made me welcome on the first night. He was the one who'd invited me to hang out with the rest of the band. When Rory was being a drunk jerk, the others would at least be nice to me and I was sure that was because Alex had set the tone. What would happen to me now?

'When?' I asked.

'My last gig's the Creek Carnival on Saturday.'

I let out a long sigh, trying to find the right words. 'I'll miss you.'

'Thanks, dude.' He grinned and held out his fist and I tapped it with mine.

'You may not have to miss him for long,' Chloe said.

Alex smiled and reached over to touch Chloe's hand. 'We've got about forty songs we've been working on together and we're gonna try to get some duo gigs.'

'Keep me posted,' I said.

'Will do,' he promised.

Chloe decided we should order food. I didn't want a repeat of my anxiety when I had dinner with Rory, so I told them I wasn't hungry. I got some green tea because the menu said it was soothing. Mum texted me to ask where I was and when I was coming home, then again to tell me she was worried. I told her I was having dinner with some friends and switched off my phone. I spent the rest of the evening at the cafe with Alex and Chloe, who didn't once treat me like I was the third wheel, even though I could tell I was.

Chapter Twenty-Seven

I didn't go to the Bluebonnet Bar on Friday night. From the time I woke up that morning, all I could think about was seeing Rory drunk, or with Layla or someone else from his past.

I went back to bed and pulled the covers tight around my neck. Deanna looked back at me from her spot on the desk, but I had nothing to say, not even to her. I just felt sick and numb. By the time I would normally leave the house, my eyes were so red and puffy that it hurt to keep them open.

My mother knocked on the door. 'You are not going out?' she asked.

Even though I'd slipped a door wedge under my door to stop it from opening, I closed my eyes so it wouldn't look like I'd been crying if she managed to get into my room.

'Hey. Hey.' The knocks grew louder.

'What?!' My voice sounded thick and scratchy, like I'd just woken up with a bad flu.

'Why are you not going out? Did that *ang moh* do something bad to you?'

'No!' I shot back. 'I'm sick!'

'Open the door, I can give you medicine.'

'I don't want medicine. I want to rest in peace.'

I ignored Mum's remaining taps on the door until she shuffled away and I buried my face in the dampness of my pillow.

#

I was still in bed when Rory rang me on Saturday morning.

'Where were you last night?' he asked.

'Home.'

'Why?'

I didn't reply.

'Hello?'

If I opened my mouth, he'd hear me cry, and I didn't know if I was ready to be naked in that way. I didn't want him to be interested in other women. I didn't want him drinking. I wanted to be enough for him. And I didn't know if he'd love me once he saw how broken I was inside.

'Jade, I can tell something's bugging you. You were really quiet on Sunday. Like more than usual. Or maybe a different kind of quiet. I don't know. But I consider you one of my closest friends and I know something's going on with you. And I want you to know I miss you when you're not there.'

I started to sob.

'Jade, talk to me, please.'

'I can't.'

'Why not? Shouldn't you talk to your friends when something's bothering you?'

'I don't talk to anyone about what's bothering me.'

'I meant what I said at the beach. About not being afraid to talk to me about anything. Why do you feel like you can't talk to anyone?'

'Because … you're my best friend. And yet, sometimes sitting there with you at the Bluebonnet feels like the loneliest place in the world.'

Rory paused and I could hear him draw a long breath at the other end of the phone. Finally, he said, 'Well, you're an introvert. So, maybe every now and then you need a break from people to recharge.'

I sighed. No, that wasn't it.

'I get lonely too, sometimes,' he continued. 'Even at gigs when there's heaps of people around me.'

'It sure doesn't look like it,' I muttered.

'I'm an entertainer. It's my job to look like I love it when everyone's there. And I guess it beats playing to no one.'

Did he really want me and not someone like Layla? 'I missed you last night too,' I admitted. 'But I couldn't get out of bed and I was crying so hard it looked like my eyes were infected. Sometimes everything hurts so much that I just feel numb. Sometimes I feel like I can't breathe and sometimes I wish I could stop breathing altogether.'

'I hear you. There are days I don't want to get out of bed. Then I remember Ethan and Ella are counting on me,' he said. 'But I'm glad you were able to tell me how you're feeling. You know if there's anything I can do to help, I would.'

I sniffed. 'Okay.'

'Are you depressed?' he asked.

The question threw me off balance. 'Um, what do you mean?'

'Look, I can't give you a medical opinion. But depression's something Faye's struggled with most of her adult life and it's crippling for her. Maybe you should go see a doctor and see if that's what's going on for you.'

'I don't need a doctor. You're the only person in my life I trust. Which is somewhere between cool and terrifying.'

'Having someone you trust is a good thing,' Rory said. 'And it means a lot to me to have you in my life. Do you think you can put aside what's making you cry and try to come to the carnival today? I'm bringing the kids.'

It was going to be Alex's last gig too, I remembered. 'I'll be there,' I promised.

Chapter Twenty-Eight

The Creek Carnival was an annual funfair held at Pelican Oval. Cedric used to take me there when I was a little kid, but the novelty wore off quickly and I hadn't been there since I was six.

When I walked through the gates this time, everything looked pretty much the same as it did back then, except that the rides seemed bigger than I remembered. There also seemed to be a lot more people. Where did they all come from? How did they fit? Why did they all look so carefree? I sucked in a series of deep breaths and pushed my fingernails into the skin over my wrists. It wasn't a bruise, but it'd have to do. Trying to shut out the voices and shrieks around me, I scanned the field for signs of the band. Finally, I spotted the stage. With a sigh of relief, I made my way towards it.

Rory was restringing his acoustic guitar. He stopped to give me a quick peck on the cheek. 'Faye and Greg are on their way with Ethan and Ella.'

'Cool.' I think I managed to sound calm, even though my heart was playing a thrash metal beat in my chest.

'So, Alex told you it's his last day, huh,' he said.

'Yeah.' I glanced over at the other end of the stage where Alex was playing a fast lick I didn't recognise. 'Were you going to tell me at some point?'

Rory stared at the grass. 'I guess part of me thought I'd be able to change his mind.'

'Did he give you a reason?'

'Just that it was time for him to explore his own vision. What does that even mean? We play covers. He and Chloe play covers. Nothing would change.' Rory looked over at Alex and sighed. 'You know, I was in another band when I moved across the road from him and his dad. He was still in school, but he could shred like nothing I'd ever seen. But he doesn't have the need to show off all the time, like some people I've played with. He just feels the song and plays what the song requires.'

I didn't know what to say so I put my arm around Rory.

'Look, I get it,' he continued. 'Not everyone wants to be in the same old band playing the same old songs to the same old people for the rest of their life. And that's okay. But we started The Lyrebirds together. It was supposed to be his band as much as mine.'

Rory picked up his camera and slung it around my neck. 'Can you be our photographer today? It's been a while since I got any pictures and …'

'It's your last chance to get any with Alex?' I finished.

'Can't hide much from you, can I?' He gave my shoulder an affectionate squeeze, then looked past me and waved. I turned around. Faye and Greg were walking towards us, carrying a sleepy twin each. I didn't see their son, Lyle anywhere. Greg was also holding a picnic basket.

'They fell asleep in the car,' Greg explained.

Rory nuzzled Ethan's and Ella's hair until their eyes drifted open. A grumpy Ella swatted her dad on the nose.

Faye laughed. 'You deserved that!'

Alex scrubbed his hands with sanitiser and hopped down from the stage. 'My favourite twin tornadoes!' he exclaimed.

'Uncle Alex!' the twins squealed in unison, suddenly awake, waving their arms at him like tiny windmills. Alex pulled a funny cartoon face in reply and ruffled their hair.

I noticed the mixture of hurt and jealousy that flashed across Rory's face a moment before he smoothed it into a smile.

'Ella, Ethan,' he said, directing their attention towards me. 'This is my friend Jade.'

Ethan and Ella studied me with blank blue eyes. Obviously, they weren't identical twins, but you could tell they were siblings. I smiled awkwardly. At least they didn't cry as soon as they laid eyes on me.

Rory nudged them and told them to wave, but I had a feeling he was actually talking to me. So, I waved and was glad when Ethan and Ella did too.

#

Rory laid a picnic rug on the lawn, while Faye and Greg placed the twins on the ground. I watched Ethan and Ella trot around our feet until Ethan stumbled and crashed into Ella. Ella squealed and the two four-year-olds started wrestling each other on the grass.

I looked around in shock, wondering if I should do something to break them up.

'It's okay, they're just playing,' Rory said to me. 'Happens all the time. I don't bother splitting them up anymore.'

Ethan pushed Ella off him and stood up. 'I'm hungry,' he announced.

'I'm hungry too,' Ella said, scrambling to her feet.

'I made sandwiches,' Faye offered.

'No, I don't want sandwiches,' Ella said, crossing her arms.

'I don't want sandwiches,' Ethan echoed.

Faye sighed and looked over at Greg, who turned to Rory. 'Well, I saw a food truck around the corner,' Greg said. 'I could get them some chips?'

'You'll probably have more luck with nuggets this week, to be honest,' Rory replied, reaching for his wallet.

Greg waved him away. 'It's on me,' he said, heading towards the food truck.

Faye put her arms around the twins. 'You'll get to see Dad play today. Are you excited?'

Ethan and Ella looked at each other and back at Faye without replying.

'They'll probably start crying when they hear all the noise.' Rory laughed, pulling the twins towards him and giving them a kiss each.

Ella sat down and started rummaging through the picnic basket until she found a plush bunny to play with, while Ethan looked around, taking in the sights and sounds around him.

The rest of the band was already on stage, ready for the first of their three scheduled sets. Dom leaned into a microphone and—in a freakishly accurate impression of Rory's voice—hollered, 'Let's get to work, kids! Hurry up!'

Rory rolled his eyes and joined them.

I took as many photos as I could, trying to capture everyone from every angle I could reach. Some of my pictures featured the whole band, some just one or two members and some were little more than a blur. I deleted those so Rory wouldn't think I was a rubbish photographer.

Ella ran around me untying my shoelaces and giggling at her handiwork. Soon, Ethan started to copy her. Every time I bent over to tie them back up, one of the twins came over to untie them again. Somehow, I didn't find it annoying. Maybe it was because I loved Rory, and he loved the kids, and that made me love them too. Maybe it was because I envied the fact that something so simple was making them happy.

When I had about fifty photos, Greg called me over. Not wanting to trip over with Rory's camera around my neck, I shuffled slowly towards the picnic rug.

'I got you some chicken strips and chips. Hope that's okay,' Greg said, handing me the warm box.

I nodded and sat down to nibble at my food. I glanced at Ethan and Ella before tying my shoelaces again, but the twins were now engrossed in their food instead of my feet.

'They're a handful sometimes. Or a footful in this case. Lyle was the same at their age but now he just plays games in his room,' Faye said. 'You're a good sport.'

With Faye and Greg's attention either on the twins or on the band, I could see they weren't really looking at me, so I managed to get my food down. But for the most part, I was thinking about Ella and Ethan. Could I handle them becoming a part of my life? And could they handle me being a part of theirs?

#

During the band's first break, Rory took Ethan and Ella exploring. The rest of the band joined Faye, Greg and me.

Dom lifted his T-shirt sleeve to reveal a nicotine patch. 'I'm trying to quit,' he announced. Everyone else was full of encouraging words, but I couldn't think of anything inspiring to say, so I gave him a thumbs-up. Then Tyler mentioned he'd seen a hot chick operating the bouncy castle, so he and Dom wandered off to find her.

Alex leaned back onto the picnic rug while Chloe rested her head on his chest.

'When's the wedding?' Faye teased.

Alex and Chloe looked at each other and grinned. 'Let's just see if we can handle doing gigs together without killing each other first,' Chloe said. Alex pulled her up and gave her a long kiss. I smiled and blushed, feeling like I should look away. Chloe and Alex went to get lunch a few minutes later and I was left alone with Faye and Greg.

'So, how are you, Jade?' Faye asked.

'Good.'

'You and Rory are getting pretty close.'

I searched Faye's eyes for a clue about what she thought of that, but I couldn't read her. So much for Samson saying I understood people. 'Yeah, I guess so,' I replied.

'That's nice,' Faye said. I still couldn't figure out if she was happy or not. Nervous sweat was starting to poke through my skin.

'Rory needs a good friend right now,' Faye added. 'Maria's fighting him for custody. She's told him today's the last day he gets with Ethan and Ella.'

My jaw dropped. 'Can she do that?' I asked. Why hadn't Rory told me any of this?

'Oh, she definitely plays nasty when she wants to. She's trying to punish him. She doesn't care that she's punishing her kids too.'

I stared at the blades of grass beneath us, racking my brains for something to say, to assure Faye that I was the right person for Rory. Did she know we'd slept together? Did she care? Did I know how to be the good friend he needed?

'Being Rory's friend is the most important thing in the world to me,' I said at last.

Faye smiled. 'I'm sure it is,' she replied.

\#

Rory returned with Ethan and Ella in tow. The twins were each slurping on juice boxes–apple for Ella and berry for Ethan. Dom and Tyler were the next to come back, arguing about who the bouncy castle girl liked more. Alex and Chloe arrived soon afterwards.

I took some more photos of the band before Ethan and Ella started tugging at my jeans. When I looked down at them, Ella pointed towards the merry-go-round. 'Butterfly,' she said.

I couldn't see any butterflies—only the horses on the merry-go-round bobbing up and down. I frowned in confusion.

'Come on,' Ethan said, and they took off, past Faye and Greg. I followed them in a panic, wondering if they were old enough to sit on a merry-go-round, if I had enough money with me and if the three of us could even fit together on one horse.

Ethan and Ella seemed to be able to communicate with each other through looks. They pulled each other to a stop at the face painting tent. Inside, two girls not much older than Ella were being turned into tigers.

Ella pointed to the girls and looked up at me.

'You want your face painted?' I asked.

Ella nodded.

'Me too?' Ethan asked.

I opened my wallet and was relieved to see I still had the money Mum had given me this week.

Greg appeared at my shoulder and I jumped.

'I came to make sure you were okay, but it looks like you're on top of things,' he said in an amused voice.

When the girls in front of us were done, Ethan and Ella hopped into the chairs in front of the two face painters, swinging their legs. I turned on Rory's camera and began snapping pictures.

Five minutes later, Ethan had been turned into a puppy and Ella was a rainbow butterfly. I took one last photo of their smiling faces before Greg and I led them back towards the stage where The Lyrebirds were playing. Rory widened his eyes and blew a kiss when he saw us.

'When are you having kids of your own then, Jade?' Faye asked, laughing.

I went red. But deep down, I was elated that the twins had apparently liked me. I wanted them in my life. They were so happy and free. I didn't want that to change. I didn't want anyone to take that away.

Chapter Twenty-Nine

For the rest of the set, I sat with Ethan and Ella on either side of me, holding the camera in front of them as I scrolled through the photos I'd taken. They squealed with delight whenever 'Dad' and 'Uncle Alex' appeared on the display. At the next break, the band joined us on the lawn and Rory cuddled the twins into his lap.

'Thanks for taking such good care of them,' he said.

'I was just telling Jade she's about ready to be a mum,' Faye said.

I shook my head quickly, then realised Rory might interpret that to mean I didn't like kids. 'I love kids, but I don't think I'm ready to be a parent yet,' I explained. Not to mention, I didn't even have my own income—Mum was still giving me an allowance whenever she got paid for her cleaning work.

'Who's ever ready?' Rory said. 'You're forced to become ready when the kids pop out.' He bent down to kiss Ethan and Ella. I snapped another photo. Rory looked up when he heard the click and winked at me.

'Hey, is that …?' Tyler began, breaking into my thoughts.

'Yeah. Heads up,' Dom said, nudging me.

I turned to see Veronica and Zayden Otto walking over to us. My stomach started to knot. Why were they here? Okay, heaps of people went to the Creek Carnival each year. Rich people were probably no different. But why were they coming towards us, here, now? What was I supposed to say? What if I ended up looking or sounding like a complete tool in front of the most important people in my life?

Dom had no problems composing himself. He stood up and stepped forward to shake Veronica's hand.

Veronica looked at Dom's hand, placed hers behind her back and gave him a curt smile and nod. Zayden rolled his eyes. Dom slowly put his hand down and cleared his throat. 'Good to see you, Zayden, Mrs Otto,' he said politely.

'Hi Domenic. Hi Jade,' Veronica said, despite my best attempts to hide behind Faye and Greg. I waved awkwardly.

Everyone looked at each other, unsure of how to break this uncomfortable silence until Rory jumped up.

'Mrs Otto, I didn't get a chance at the Create Tomorrow Ball to express my deepest condolences to you and your family.'

'Thank you. Please call me Veronica.'

'Rory.'

Veronica smiled properly for the first time. 'You're a very good singer,' she said.

'Thanks.'

'Really, you have such a seductive quality to your voice. I used to sing but I wasn't nearly as good as you. How long have you been singing?'

'Well, I was always screaming and banging on things as a kid. But professionally for about ten years in various bands.'

'I must come see you again sometime.'

'You can look us up. We're called The Lyrebirds.'

I cringed. Please, no. He could not be inviting her to the gigs. I couldn't think of anything worse than having Veronica cut into my Rory time.

Zayden glared at his mother. 'Dad's only just died!'

Veronica grabbed the back of his collar, jerking him upright. 'Home. Now!' she hissed, and with that, the Ottos were gone.

#

Twenty minutes later, the band went back on stage for Alex's last set as lead guitarist of The Lyrebirds. I took a few more pictures but put the camera away for the most part. I just wanted to savour these final moments. I didn't know when I'd see Alex again.

The band finished on *Sweet Child O' Mine*, with Chloe taking lead vocals and Alex making his guitar sing me to tears. Hoping no one had noticed, I wiped my eyes as I watched the band pack up their gear like every other gig, except that it wasn't.

I wasn't in love with Alex the way I was with Rory, but I felt a different kind of love. Alex's friendship meant a lot to me and I wish I knew how to say it without embarrassing myself.

One by one, everyone said their goodbyes. When it was my turn, Alex grinned and held out his fist for his trademark bump. 'Hey, don't be so sad, dude,' he said. 'It's a small world. You can't get rid of me.'

'I'll print out that picture of us at the ball and stick it above my bed next to my Bon Jovi poster.' I kicked myself. Why couldn't I say something intelligent? 'I mean, take care of yourself.'

'Always do, Jade. See ya round.' Alex and Chloe gave everyone a final wave, before picking up his guitars and heading out to the car park.

Rory stared after Alex and Chloe's disappearing silhouettes until Faye walked over and put her arm around him. Rory shrugged her away and turned his attention to Ella and Ethan.

163

Faye and Greg offered me a lift home. I gave Rory my tightest hug before we left, kissing him near his ear. 'Love you,' I murmured under my breath.

'Love you, babe,' he whispered back, gently brushing my cheek and smiling when he broke the hug. 'Say bye to Jade,' he told Ethan and Ella.

'Bye bye,' they chanted, flapping their hands at me. I waved back, hoping it wasn't the last I saw of them.

#

I followed Faye and Greg out to their car. The events of a long day raced through my head as we pulled out of the car park and onto the streets of Concord Creek. Did I have what it took to be Rory's lover and friend? Would Maria really take Ethan and Ella away? Was Veronica going to start going to gigs? Could I survive being more than just a kid myself?

Faye penetrated my thoughts.

'Are you in love with Rory?'

I felt my stomach leap into the back of my throat. Every inch of my body prickled with heat. 'What?' My voice sounded very far away, like it was coming from outside the car.

'You obviously have quite the crush on him,' Faye said.

This time I couldn't even force a single word off my tongue. Had she told me Rory needed 'a good friend' because she knew I was trying to be more? What was I supposed to say?

I saw my expression in the rear-view mirror as my mouth tried to remember the English language.

'I think we're out of bread,' Greg said, changing the subject. 'Better swing by the shops after we've dropped Jade home.' He then tuned the radio to an oldies station that was playing *Summertime Blues* and turned up the volume.

My face was burning red for the rest of the drive home, but at least Faye didn't ask me any more questions. How did she know? Was it so blatantly obvious on my face every time I looked at Rory? Or had he said something to her? And was that a good or bad thing?

He'd never come right out and said he wanted me to be his girlfriend. But he said he loved me. And I loved him. I wanted us to be official. I knew he had his flaws, but it felt right with him in a way it never had with Nathan.

Chapter Thirty

'Does anyone know about us?' I asked Rory at the Sherlock Arms the next day.

'I'm sure lots of people are aware of our existence,' he answered without skipping a beat.

'No, I mean … you know …'

Rory looked up from the guitar he was tuning. 'You mean, the part where we've seen each other naked and done things and liked it?'

I giggled. 'Yeah, that.'

'Well, I haven't told anyone and I won't. You're not some conquest to me. This is something special that you and I share.'

'I haven't told anyone either.'

He smiled and gave me a quick, blink-and-you'll-miss-it kiss on my lips.

I was on a high until Veronica showed up.

'My son Zayden went to his friend's house and I told myself, I must hear that lovely singer's voice again,' she explained, even though no one asked.

'Well, it's always nice to have company,' Rory said, strumming the opening chords to *Hungry Heart*.

No, it's not, I thought.

'Lovely to see you, Jade,' Veronica added, as if she'd only just noticed I was there. She sat down at my table. I wanted to tell her that I hadn't invited her to, but I knew she wouldn't care. I gave her a tight smile, which grew tighter as she stared lustfully after Rory.

When Rory finished his first set, he sat down with us. Veronica inched her chair towards him. 'Those were your children at the carnival yesterday, weren't they?'

'Yep,' he replied.

'How old are they?' she asked.

'Four.'

'Oh, I love kids,' Veronica said, clapping her hands together. 'Aren't they the most precious?'

I raised an eyebrow. Her own son didn't even like her!

'Samson and I wanted more kids, but we never got the chance.'

I wanted to remind Veronica that she'd told me they never intended to have any kids in the first place, but Veronica must've known I'd be too scared to speak up. Inside, I was screaming with rage—at her, and at myself.

'I'm really sorry,' Rory said.

'Yes, me too. I always felt Zayden should have a brother or sister.' She smiled. 'Perhaps it's not too late.'

I almost threw up in my mouth.

Rory flushed pink and cleared his throat. 'Speaking of kids, I need to call the babysitter and check on them.' He picked up his mobile phone and walked outside.

I cursed him silently. Now I was alone with Veronica. She turned her attention to me.

'He doesn't have a wife,' she said.

I blinked. It hadn't been a question, so I didn't know if I was meant to respond. And it was none of Veronica's business, anyway.

My phone vibrated in my pocket. It was a text message from Rory.

I'm sitting in the van.

'I have to, um, check something out at the beach,' I said.

Rory reached over and opened the front passenger door for me when I got to the van. I climbed in.

'Are the kids okay?' I asked.

Rory laughed. 'I didn't really have to check on them. Faye and Greg have the kids today. They would've called me if something was wrong.'

'So … you've still got custody?' I asked.

Rory nodded. 'Yeah, she and I had a long talk last night. I convinced her that they should stay in the home they've grown up in. Especially since she has no fixed address at the moment. She's been moving from her mum's to her dad's to her brother's to her best friend's and back again. And I don't think she even wants to be a mother anymore. I offered to let her have Ethan and Ella today while I was doing this gig, but she wasn't interested.'

I squeezed his hand. 'I really enjoyed meeting the kids.'

'I'm glad you met them too,' he replied. I interlocked my fingers in his and we fell into a comfortable silence.

'Do you think the manager will notice if I just don't go back in?' he asked.

'All your stuff is there,' I pointed out.

He chuckled and sighed. 'Alright, let's go back to work.'

#

It was easier to sit through the rest of the gig with Veronica after spending that time with Rory. When he'd finished work, we packed up and left her at the table sipping a glass of wine.

'What're you doing tonight?' Rory asked, as we climbed into the van.

'Nothing.'

'Do you want to drive somewhere and hang out for a bit?'

'Okay. But what about the kids?'

'They wanted to have a sleepover. I'm picking them up from Faye and Greg's place in the morning.'

'Where do you want to go?' I asked.

'I'll figure something out,' he replied mysteriously, and started the engine. As we neared my house, Rory took a different turn and ended up on the road adjacent to the high school oval.

I turned to Rory and lifted my eyebrows. 'Why're we here?'

'High school wasn't a great time for you, was it?' Rory said.

I shook my head.

'But you seem to like being with me.'

I nodded.

'Well, I thought we could make some better memories here together.'

'How so?'

'What do you want to do?'

I looked at him and shrugged.

'We can sit here and talk or listen to some music. We can go outside … I've got some chips and a rug in the boot. We can drive around in circles. It's up to you.' He pressed his lips sweetly on the back of my hand.

I bit my lip and tried to make a decision. 'How big's the rug?' I said at last.

'About two by two metres. Why?'

'I thought it might be cool to lie down and look at the stars or something. Does that sound stupid?'

'Not at all.'

Rory took a picnic rug out of the boot of his van, hoisting it over his shoulder before gesturing at me to lead the way. I strolled across the oval, Rory a step behind. We stopped about twenty metres from the goal posts, which had been crooked for as long as anyone could remember.

'This is where I met Nathan,' I said.

Rory lay the rug down and we stretched out over it. His callused fingertips brushed my hand as we tried and failed to remember the names of constellations. Eventually, we rolled onto our sides, facing each other. His fingers slid under my hair, caressing my ear and neck. I breathed in his scent and smiled.

'Do you still think about Nathan?' Rory asked quietly.

The question threw me for a moment. Nathan crossed my mind nearly every day. After all, his posts were still popping up whenever I went online. And I was always comparing Rory to him. I thought I'd loved Nathan until Rory taught me what love really felt like.

'Yes,' I said. 'But only coz I wish I'd waited for you.'

A look of surprise flashed across Rory's face before he relaxed into a grin and started singing *Like a Virgin* in a breezy falsetto. I giggled.

'I think I should leave those vocals to Chloe,' he said, chuckling.

I kissed him and nestled into the crook of his neck. 'You make me feel safe,' I mumbled into his chest. 'I wish we could stay like this forever.'

He didn't say anything, but he held me snugly against his body until we dozed off.

#

I crept into the house just after midnight with a box of sushi rolls from Brightlights. Rory had made a quick stop there before taking me home, since we hadn't ended up eating any dinner.

Mum burst into my room on Monday. 'Why were you home so late?'

'I had dinner with Rory,' I told her, daring her to object.

She squinted at me. 'I hope you do not let him out of your sight when you are with him,' she said.

'What's that supposed to mean?'

'I know what his kind is like.'

As she walked away, I clenched my fists, fighting the urge to hit myself. I stared at Deanna. She stared back at me.

'I know you know what I want to do,' I said with a sideways glance at my pillow. My rock was hiding underneath my pillow, waiting for me. 'I'm trying not to, okay? I'm trying to think about Rory. He makes me feel like … like I don't need the bruises when I've got him.'

Chapter Thirty-One

That Friday was Brad McMillan's first gig as lead guitarist of The Lyrebirds. He was lean like his cousin Tyler, but not quite as tall, and he didn't wear sunglasses at night. His mousy hair was pulled back in a long ponytail.

'Hope I remember all the songs!' Brad said to me after we'd been introduced.

Tyler smacked Brad on the bum and grinned. 'You'll be fine. We're the only ones who'll notice if you screw up.'

'Thanks, Ty,' Brad replied sarcastically.

Tyler offered Brad a bottle of beer from an esky on the floor, but Brad waved him off. 'I'm driving the boss home tonight, remember? In his van!'

'I was in the band almost a year before Hunter trusted me with the keys,' Tyler said, shaking his head. 'Bass players are always discriminated against.'

Brad grinned and turned back to me. 'So, Jade, are you studying or working?'

I felt my face turn red. 'Um, I'm … between jobs,' I mumbled.

'Oh, okay. So, you're a big fan of the band?'

I nodded.

'Well, I'll do my best not to disappoint you. Or Hunter … I don't wanna get yelled at on the way home.'

I gave Brad what I hoped was an encouraging smile.

Almost on cue, Rory burst through the curtains into the band room. Before I could say anything, he rummaged through his backpack. I heard a rustling, crackling sound and his fist pulled out a brown paper bag. I gritted my teeth as he took a long swig from it.

He put the bottle away, turned to me and said, 'Veronica's here.'

#

Much to my disappointment, Veronica sat beside me when the band started playing. She had to yell to be heard above the music and even then, I could barely hear her. I just tried to focus my attention on the band's Queen medley, hoping my concentration would make Veronica go away. She started yelling something else about the Create Tomorrow Foundation. I couldn't make out all the words and didn't bother to ask. By the end of the first set, she'd gotten up and walked out to the front. I assumed she was at the bar, but I didn't see her again.

When I checked my phone, I decided to look up her profile. Her latest status update, posted five minutes ago, read: 'Young people these days have NO respect for their elders. You would be nothing without us!'

I started to shake. Was that post about me?

'Is she gone?' Rory mouthed at me towards the end of the band's first set.

I shrugged, but I hoped so. I already had Rory's drinking and a band without Alex to worry about tonight.

#

I slipped through the curtain into the band room. Dom, Tyler and Brad were talking in one corner, while Rory sat in another, looking drained. I was about to go to him when Chloe returned from the bathroom and beckoned me outside.

I waited for her to speak, but she seemed to be struggling with her words in the way that I usually did. I racked my brains for something to say that might help. 'Hey, how's Alex?'

'He's good. Spent about nine hundred bucks restringing his guitars this week.' She grinned and shook her head. 'They're his babies. And it's okay, I've always known that marrying a muso means we'll probably never roll around in a mansion.'

'You're getting married?' I asked.

'Well, not yet. We're not even officially engaged. But we've talked about it a lot. I know, it's happening so fast, isn't it? But sometimes you click with someone and you just know they're "the one".'

I nodded. Rory. No one had ever made me feel so complete. I was meant to be with him, even if we had to work on certain things, like his drinking and my social anxiety. Maybe we'd need to compromise, but that's what relationships were about, right?

'Does Rory have an alcohol problem?' I asked before I could stop myself.

Chloe sighed. 'I don't know. Alex said it'd been ages since Rory drank at all. Something about getting too old for it and wanting to set a better example for Ethan and Ella. Then when the situation with Maria took a dive, he started again. Just a little at first. But it's worse now, right?'

I nodded.

'Alex was telling me about one of the first gigs they did together. He accidentally touched something on the bar counter and Rory found him in the bathroom twenty minutes later, still washing his hands. But Rory didn't yell at him or anything. He just said, 'We have to go back to work.' And Alex managed to stop and finish the gig, even though his fingers bled coz the skin was so raw from all the washing. He told me Rory was the first friend he ever had who didn't make him feel like a freak.'

'Why did he leave the band?' I asked.

'He said he wanted to see if he could make it on his own. But I think he's also scared that he wouldn't be able to help Rory the way Rory's helped him.'

We fell silent. Could I be what Rory needed? What should I do? All I knew was that I loved him and I'd do anything for him.

#

Rory jumped to his feet when Chloe and I went back inside. 'I thought you'd left me too,' he said dramatically. 'Time to get back to work, kids.'

'As if I'd walk out in the middle of a pay cheque,' Chloe said. 'And Jade loves you too much.'

I felt my face turn pink and smiled nervously.

As Chloe, Dom, Tyler and Brad filed back onto the stage, Rory clasped my hand.

'Are you in a rush to get home after the gig?'

'I'm never in a rush to get home.'

Rory laughed. 'Maybe you should move out.'

'Where would I go?' I'd live with him if I could, but I didn't want Ella and Ethan to hate me or think I was trying to replace their mum. Maybe Rory would suggest it sometime in the future, when the twins had gotten used to me. After all, it hadn't taken long for Maria to move in after she and Rory started seeing each other.

'You'll find something.' He brushed my cheek and lip with his thumb. I wanted him to kiss me, but I knew he probably wouldn't with the rest of the band waiting for him. His eyes

175

glanced up towards the stage. 'I better go sing for my supper,' he said. 'Don't go anywhere.'

#

I watched the last set from inside the band room. As soon as The Lyrebirds played their final song of the night, Rory's eyes found mine. He jumped off stage and wrapped me against his body. 'You've been on my mind all night,' he said in a low voice.

'You've been on mine too.'

'But the kids are at home so I can't take you to my house and you can't take me to yours.'

'What do you want to do?' I asked.

He flashed me a lopsided grin. 'Well, we could do it in the car park.'

I started to cough.

'I'm kidding, I'm kidding,' he said, looking embarrassed.

I bit my lip. 'That's too bad,' I heard myself murmur.

Rory's dark eyes widened, darting towards the stage where the band was packing up and back to me. 'Are you serious or joking?' he asked.

I gave him a coy shrug and he shrugged back, holding me in place under the intensity of his stare. I giggled nervously and blushed.

'It's up to you,' he said. 'It'll be awesome though.'

'Okay,' I managed to say.

He grinned and gestured for me to follow him outside. We stopped to retrieve a couple of condom packets from his van.

'Did you plan this?' I asked.

'No. But I wanted to be prepared for anything. I can't stop thinking about you, Jade.'

I remembered how close I'd felt to Rory on the picnic rug under the stars. We didn't need sex, but I wanted it with him.

Together, we found a quiet spot behind the Bluebonnet that was hidden by thick, leafy bushes.

'It's a bit seedy,' he admitted.

I could hear bits of voices coming from the other side of the building—drunk people being kicked out of the bar. Was this really going to happen? Here? The thought scared and excited me all at once. I started to giggle again.

'Tell me what you want,' he murmured.

I pulled him down towards me and kissed him, long and hard. He tugged me deeper behind the bushes. I could feel the leaves tickling my back and the earthy scent of the plants. I clung to Rory, breathing him in.

His hand slid down to my waist and slipped under my dress, massaging the ache between my legs. I buried my face into his chest to muffle the sound of my cries. His fingers became more urgent, I gripped his shoulders tighter and then I came hard in a sticky mess on his hand.

'Sorry,' I gasped.

'No, don't be sorry,' he whispered. 'Don't ever be ashamed of your body.'

I almost told him about my self-harm there and then. Instead, I crouched down and did my best to return the favour.

#

'Well, that was exciting. I've never done that before,' he said, as we rearranged our clothes.

'Me neither,' I replied, even though he already knew that. My legs trembled like jelly and I could still taste him on my lips. 'I love you.'

'Love you, babe.' He smiled at me, the moonlight catching the cheeky glint in his eye and his mouth found mine.

'I want to tell you something,' I said, when we broke the kiss.

'What is it?'

I took a deep breath. Only Deanna knew the truth about my self-injury. But if Rory was my future, then he should know too.

'Sometimes I hit myself,' I said. 'Like when I'm anxious or upset or overwhelmed. I give myself bruises.'

I waited for the look of shock on his face, but Rory just took my hands in his. 'That's not such an uncommon thing to do,' he said gently. 'But you're not alone when you have those feelings. I'm always here for you. All you have to do is pick up the phone.'

I hugged him as hard as I could.

As we headed back to the bar, his fingers teased the hair at the nape of my neck, sending more warm shivers down my body.

'Where the hell've you two been?' Tyler asked. Only he and Brad were still in the car park. All of Rory's and Brad's gear was packed up and sitting on the ground outside the van. Rory unlocked it and began loading it inside.

'We were hungry, so we went down to Brightlights,' he replied, his voice and face giving nothing away.

'And you didn't get us any chips?' Tyler said.

Rory shrugged. 'Sorry, I only had enough money for me and Jade. Thanks for packing up for me, guys.'

I threw an apologetic look at Brad, who'd been left waiting around to drive his boss home at the end of his first gig. He flashed me an awkward smile.

'Well, the manager wanted to lock up and go home so we had no choice. But you're welcome,' Tyler said dryly.

I blushed and said goodbye to everyone and Rory pulled me into a tight hug. 'I'll call you tomorrow, beautiful,' he said softly, giving me a peck near my ear.

I scampered home with a guilty smile on my face, still tingling with what we'd just done and free from the burden of my secret.

Chapter Thirty-Two

I woke up the next day with seven mosquito bites spread across my arms and legs, and even one on my neck.

Did you get bitten by mozzies last night? I texted Rory.

Yep. It's killing me, he replied. I waited for him to call me like he'd promised, but he didn't. I tried ringing him after dinner, but he didn't pick up his phone. Had he forgotten? Had something happened? I wanted to feel the closeness I'd felt last night, and his radio silence left me cold and confused.

I went to the Sherlock Arms on Sunday hoping to find out why he hadn't kept his promise.

Veronica was already there.

She was rubbing one hand up and down Rory's back as he tried to set up for the gig, while her other hand was curled around a glass of wine. 'I can help you. Tell me what to do,' she said.

'You're gonna spill that all over my pedals if you're not careful,' Rory replied. 'I don't need help.'

'You men. You're all the same. Thinking you can do everything on your own.'

'I've been doing this on my own for years. Just go sit down, okay?'

Get out of his way! I thought. Veronica looked for a moment like she was about to keep arguing, then shrugged and took a seat at the table closest to Rory.

Rory looked up and offered me a half-smile when he saw me. He looked like he hadn't had any sleep, and it was fifteen minutes past his usual start time when he was finally ready to begin playing. I reluctantly pulled up a seat at Veronica's table and tried to pretend she wasn't there.

He was singing *Don't Dream It's Over* when Veronica turned to me. 'How old are you again, Jade?'

'Eighteen.'

'And Rory is almost thirty, yes?'

I stared at her. What's it to you?

She gave me a thin smile and turned back to Rory.

When Rory finished his set and came to sit with us, Veronica placed her manicured claws on his hand. 'Are there always so many half-naked women here?'

Rory shifted his hand away from Veronica in a swift movement, feigning the need to check his phone. 'Yeah, usually. They go to the beach then pop in here for a couple of drinks.'

'I did a bikini shoot when I was younger,' Veronica told us. 'But there was a time and place for it. I simply don't have the body for it now, of course.'

'You look good and perfectly healthy,' Rory replied.

'Oh, that's so lovely of you to say,' Veronica gushed. 'Any good woman would be lucky to have you and your gorgeous kids in their life.'

I felt like gagging. While I was thinking about how I could make Veronica go away, someone knocked into the back of my chair.

'Sorry,' giggled a girl about my age, dressed in an Australian flag bikini. Her older male companion, sporting red board shorts and a thick rug of chest hair, winked at us and pinched the girl's buttocks before the two of them scurried away to the bar.

'You know what I find pathetic?' Veronica said, as we watched the couple feeling each other up like they were already in the bedroom.

Or behind the bushes at the Bluebonnet Bar, I thought, feeling wet and guilty and confused.

'When teenage girls are involved with grown men,' Veronica continued. 'I honestly think it's sickening.'

My face flushed. I glared at Veronica, then at Rory. He couldn't let her get away with such an obvious attack on me!

Rory cleared his throat. 'We don't know how old they are but I'm sure they're both legal,' he said mildly. 'I'd better go back to work.'

Hyperventilating, I ran into the bathroom and bolted myself in a cubicle. My chest and throat felt constricted, like thick ropes were squeezing the air out of them. I balled my hands into tight fists to try to stop them shaking. Why didn't he defend me, or us, or our relationship? Didn't he understand the gravity of what I'd told him on Friday night? Would he notice if I passed out in this cubicle and he never saw me again? Would he care? Was he looking for bushes he could poke Veronica in right now?

I stayed in the cubicle for the rest of the set and the ability to breathe gradually came back to me. I unlocked the door, splashed my face and dabbed it dry with a paper towel. As I stepped out of the bathroom, I saw Veronica. A catty smile spread across her face as she approached the door. She leaned towards me, the sour scent of alcohol on her breath. 'You're a little girl,' she hissed. 'Don't ever forget that.'

#

By the time I was in Rory's van, ready to go home, I wanted to cry. I hadn't had a chance to talk to him at all because of Veronica, and he hadn't told her to get lost. And why hadn't he called me yesterday like he promised?

'Man, these mozzie bites,' Rory said as he climbed into the driver's seat, rubbing his knee through his trousers.

I didn't reply.

'It was worth it though, right?'

I stared out the window as we pulled away from the beach.

'Not talking today?'

Part of me just wanted to give him the silent treatment. But I couldn't hold it in anymore. I was sick of him barely noticing the emotional roller coaster he was constantly putting me through. 'You have no idea what you do to me, do you?' I said bitterly.

'What do you mean?'

I dug my fingers into my mosquito bites and bruises. 'I wish I was just like you. I wish I could have sex with someone and walk away without it meaning anything. But I can't.'

Rory looked nonplussed. I slapped the dashboard just above the glove compartment, wishing my hand would ring harder.

'You're not just fucking my body, okay? You're fucking every single hope and fear and insecurity I've ever had. You're fucking the girl who was so worthless that two boys thought it'd be fun to pass her around like a football in the bathroom. You're fucking the girl who needs her best friend to call her when he says he will. To stand up for her when some miserable

183

old hag's taking cheap shots at her like Veronica did today. I'm not your penis receptacle, Rory!'

Rory pulled the van over to the side of the road and stopped the engine.

The stinging silence rang in my ears until he began to speak. 'I'm sorry I didn't call. It's been so crazy at home. Maria's away at the moment. Her mum came over yesterday and said she'd arranged a sitter for the twins coz she wanted me to go shopping with her. I hated every minute of it but she's my kids' grandma and I wanted to keep her happy. But from about five o'clock this morning, I've been getting abusive messages from Maria for going out with her mum.'

I frowned. 'You could've just told me that yesterday instead of leaving me hanging.'

'I know, I'm sorry. And I'm sorry about Veronica. She's a miserable hag, like you said. She wants you to feel small so she can feel better about herself. Just ignore her.'

'It's not that easy.'

'I know. But she'll go away eventually. People always turn up to my gigs for a few weeks in a row and then they find something better to do.'

'I'm still here.'

'You are. You're the only one who's stuck around.' He took my hand, gently caressing it as he studied my eyes. 'You know it wasn't meaningless sex to me, don't you? You're not some random girl. Our friendship is really important to me. And I can't commit to something more than that right now coz I have to put my kids first.' He cupped my face softly in his hand. 'But anything I can give, I'll give to you. Coz I'm like you—I don't have many real friends and you're one of them.'

Under his deep brown gaze, I felt my anger melt away. He looked like he believed every word, and he made me believe it too. 'You're my closest friend,' I said.

'And I love that we're close. I wouldn't take any of it back. You should always feel comfortable talking to me coz that's what I've been trying to make you see. That you can talk to people and resolve things and feel better once you've communicated.'

'Friends aren't forever. They never have been. How do I know you're gonna stick around just coz I have?'

'Because I will. I promise. All I can give you is my word and pray that you'll believe in me.' He unbuckled his seatbelt, leaned over, and placed a warm kiss on my lips. 'I love you. I always have. And I always will.'

It was as close as he'd ever come to saying we'd be in a real, official relationship when he was finally ready. I hoped that day would be soon, but I could wait, because I couldn't love him more.

'I love you too. I believe in you,' I said.

#

'The kids are driving me insane,' Rory said, when he started the car again. 'Ethan saw about five minutes of a documentary on rock climbing and now he's literally trying to scale the walls of our living room. Then Ella told us she could fly coz it's better than climbing and started jumping off the couch. So, Ethan hit her with a toy and they both started crying.' He paused. 'Well, at least it wasn't a documentary on mixed martial arts or something.'

He grinned at me and I smiled back.

'I dropped them off at Faye and Greg's before the gig, so I hope they've settled down by the time I go pick them up,' he said. 'Their fights usually blow over pretty quickly, but you never know. They used to always have their mum home to look after them when I was doing a gig, so it wasn't so disruptive.'

I didn't know why Ethan and Ella had been pretty well behaved around me at the Creek Carnival, but I guess there was a big difference between having kids run around you for a day and being a full-time parent or guardian. I could never be the twins' mother but maybe one day they could love me, like part of me already loved them. They were a piece of Rory, and I could see the adoration in his eyes when he talked about them, even when they were stressing him out.

'I worry about them all the time. I worry about whether I'm doing this right,' he said. 'Am I missing out on seeing them grow up by palming them off to someone else on the weekends? What about when they start school? Are they gonna grow up hating me for breaking up with their mum? I don't have the answers.'

'They won't hate you,' I said. 'Whenever you talk about them, your eyes light up, like you're somewhere else but in a good way. I can see how much you love them. They will too.'

Rory smiled. 'Thanks, babe.' We continued in silence for a moment, then he asked, 'How're things with your mum?'

I shrugged.

'So, that's how it is? I tell you everything and you tell me nothing,' he said, looking amused.

'You don't tell me everything.'

'Maybe not, but I tell you a hell of a lot more than I tell most people.'

'I tell you more than anyone.'

'Well, that's different. You barely talk to anyone so instead of drip-feeding everyone a little of what's on your mind, you just pour it out with me.' He winked at me as we pulled into my driveway.

'I'm all Mum has. I'm supposed to look after her. But I can't stand her,' I said. 'And I'm scared I'm growing up just like her.'

'In what way?'

'Weak. Scared of everything. Can't do anything for myself.'

'You're doing better than you think,' Rory said. 'You stood up to me pretty well just now. No one's ever said the words, "I'm not your penis receptacle" to me before.'

I smiled as his warm chuckle washed over me. He kissed my hand. 'You know, now that you've had sex you enjoy, feel free to use me for booty calls,' he said.

I giggled. 'Where would we go?'

'Car park at the Bluebonnet? You looked pretty good there. Well, you always look good. Why aren't we doing it all the time?'

'Because you have kids at home and I have Mum at mine.'

Rory looked thoughtful for a moment. 'Do hotels do day rates?'

'I don't know.'

'The Creek Hotel's not too far from here. You could even walk there. Can you call them for me tonight and find out? I've gotta get the kids to bed.'

'Call them? On the phone?' I didn't call people except for Rory. I never knew what to say. It was like my brain and vocal cords froze. Rory was the only person who could coax the words out of me.

'Think of it as practice,' Rory said. 'Just breathe and ask them if they do day rates. If they say they do, ask them how much and how long you get the room for. If they don't, then say "thank you" and hang up. If you say something wrong, don't stress about it. They'll never know who you are.' He flashed me an encouraging smile and squeezed my hand. 'Can you manage that?'

I nodded. 'Okay.'

Rory glanced towards my house, then leaned over and gave me a quick kiss. 'Thanks, babe. I'll speak to you soon.'

#

I went into my bedroom and looked up the Creek Hotel to find their contact details. They had a query form on their website that was tempting, but I didn't know if or when they'd reply to me if I sent them a message that way. And Rory was relying on me to call. I had a feeling he was trying to build me into the type of person who could talk to people, and I didn't want to let him down.

I dialled the number, but before it could connect, I hung up. My mouth was too dry. I went into the kitchen to pour myself some water and suck in some deep breaths before returning to my room.

I rang the number again, the washing machine in my stomach tumbling faster and faster.

After four rings, a voice said, 'Creek Hotel, Heather speaking.'

'Hey,' I said, my mind racing to remember what Rory had told me. 'I was just wondering if you do day rates?'

'What do you mean?' Heather asked.

'Um, like if you need a room. But not overnight. Just for a few hours.'

'Oh, right. Yes, we can do that. How many people?'

'Two.' Although we'd done it on a couch and in a car park, so we only needed one bed. 'Or one,' I added hastily.

'It depends on the day of the week but it's usually about one hundred dollars. When do you need the room?'

'I don't know yet,' I stammered.

'Okay, well, I recommend calling ahead to make sure there are rooms available, but there usually are. Our busiest days are Fridays and Saturdays.'

'Thanks.'

There was a long pause.

'Will that be all, ma'am?' Heather prompted.

'Ah, how long do we get the room for?' I remembered.

'You'll need to check in after 10 am and check out before 5 pm. If you stay beyond that you'll be charged for the night.'

'Great. Thank you. Um, bye.' I hung up.

I waited until my face had cooled down before I rang Rory.

'Hey Jade,' he said. 'Nice timing. I just tucked the kids in. I think they've come down with something, so they'll either sleep all night or be up every half hour.'

'I hope they feel better soon.'

'Cheers. Were you able to make the call?'

'Yeah. They do day rates.' I recapped the conversation I'd had with Heather, minus my stuttering.

'That's a good price,' Rory said. 'What're you doing tomorrow?'

'Not much.'

'Give me a call or text in the morning. If the kids are better, I'll drop them at kindy, then come pick you up and … you know, satisfy you. If they're still sick, we'll take a raincheck. Are you down for that?'

'Yes.'

'Great.'

'I love you.'

'I love you,' he said.

My skin tingled with anticipation. I hoped Rory would be touching it tomorrow. And maybe someday soon, we wouldn't have to hide.

Chapter Thirty-Three

I woke up the next morning, brushed my teeth and jumped in the shower before calling Rory. He didn't answer. I was in the middle of texting him when my phone buzzed.

Sorry babe, I'm so sick. Must've come down with what the twins have. Maybe we can meet up later this week or next week?

Hugs. Take care, I replied, adding some Xs and Os. I sank back into bed, disappointed.

He responded with a row of Xs, which made me smile. But my smile faded when Mum rapped on my bedroom door, demanding to be let in. I sighed.

'I must talk to you,' she said, closing the door behind her.

'Why?' I felt trapped.

'What does this Rory say to you?'

'Why?' I repeated.

'Your father made lots of promises to me. Now look at that *ah kwa.*'

'Don't call him that. So what if he's gay?' I snapped.

'You cannot trust those *ang moh*. They will tell you many things and they will lie.'

I could feel my hands trembling with rage. 'In case you hadn't noticed, I'm half white. Is that why you don't trust me?'

'You are my daughter. I only want what is best for you.'

'That doesn't mean you can go around saying all white guys are jerks. That's like me saying all Asians are stupid coz of you.'

I'd grown up always feeling like I didn't quite fit in. Not only was I painfully shy, I was also too Asian for the white kids and too white for the few Asian kids at school. And I'd often walked a few metres ahead or behind Mum, slightly embarrassed by her singsong accent that half the town struggled to understand. But I'd never thrown her race, her culture—which was supposed to be half mine—back at her.

Mum stared back at me, broken and defeated, then turned and left me alone at last. As the door clicked shut, I looked at Deanna and squeezed the rock that was still sitting under my pillow. I wrestled with the impulse to inflict another bruise. No, I had to stay clean. I'd do it for Rory.

At least you'll be with him soon, I told myself. Nothing else mattered when he and I were together. I tried to hold onto the feeling. It was all I had.

#

I didn't see Rory for the rest of the week. He rang me on Wednesday evening to talk about Maria.

'She's impossible,' he fumed. 'She demanded I bring the twins to her mum's house today. So, I did. After an hour, she called me again, saying she couldn't deal with their whining and asked me to come pick them up. So, I did. We were almost home when she called again, saying she'd changed her mind and needed to spend time with them. Naturally, Ethan and Ella were pretty grumpy and irritable when we got back to their grandma's house. And Maria made me stay until it was time for the twins to go home and be put to bed. Didn't get any work done today.' I could hear in his voice that he had some kind of cold or flu.

'Are they asleep now?' I asked.

'Yeah, they dozed off a few minutes ago, hopefully for the night. Maria's just dicking me around. It never ends.'

'I'm sorry.'

'It's not your fault, babe.'

'How're you and the kids feeling?'

'They're a lot better,' he said. 'I'm struggling to shake it, but I'll get there. Might see if Chloe can sing some extra songs this week.'

'Look after yourself,' I said.

'Thanks. Don't worry, I'll be ready to rock your world again in no time.'

I giggled, and he started to laugh with me before coughing.

'Anyway, I don't want to lose my voice, so I'd better hang up,' he said. 'See you Friday?'

'I'll be there.'

#

Faye and Greg were at the Bluebonnet on Friday too. It was the first time I'd seen them since they drove me home—since Faye asked me if I was in love with her brother. But Greg offered me a glass of water and invited me to sit with them, and I didn't think I could say no. And tonight, there were no probing questions from Faye. She just asked me how I was as if nothing had happened, said it was good to see me again, and told me how much her son Lyle was stressing over his assignments. I could relate to that. Where Cedric had been a straight-A student, as well as somehow managing a social life, I'd always hovered around the B-minus range at best. By Year 11 and 12 I was struggling to pass. I did well in English, funnily enough, probably because I sat in the library most lunchtimes reading.

It was the only place left to go once any friends I made moved on to more interesting people.

'I'm so glad you're such a good friend and supporter of the band,' Faye said, after a few minutes of small talk. 'I wasn't sure when I first saw all your pictures.'

'What do you mean?' I asked.

'I wondered what your intentions were. I've seen a lot of girls come and go. But Rory said, "no, Jade's cool, she just loves music". And Alex said the same. And when I met you, I saw that they were right. So, I want you to know I approve of you.'

I blushed. 'Uh, thanks.'

'It's such a mess with Maria,' Faye said. 'I think this is the lowest point their relationship's ever been at. Usually when it looks like it's all over, Rory stays with a friend for a night while things cool down, then goes home and plays happy families again. But they haven't been able to live in peace for over a year. Maria abuses him for hours on end. Then she'll say, "But in spite of everything, I still love you." And all it does is confuse Rory about his feelings. I bet you anything she's doing it on purpose. I wish he'd never met her. The twins are the only good thing they've ever done together.'

Faye looked close to tears. I didn't know what to say. I put an arm on her shoulder and she smiled. And then she looked up, and her smile vanished.

I followed her line of sight. Maria had arrived at the Bluebonnet. She was alone this time, eyeing Rory as he and the band finished setting up for the gig. She flashed him a broad smile. I looked at Rory. He smiled weakly and appeared to let out a long breath.

Rory disappeared into the band room, then emerged through the curtain and walked over to Faye, Greg and me.

'Maria's here,' he said as if we hadn't noticed. He still had the faint rasp of a cold or flu in his voice.

'We're leaving,' Faye said, bolting to her feet. Greg stood up too.

'Oh, come on,' Rory said.

'No. You need to tell her she isn't welcome here.'

'It's a public place. I didn't know she was coming.'

'Who's looking after the kids?'

'She's probably left them with her mum or dad. That's what she usually does when she turns up at gigs. She wouldn't have left them alone or anything. She wouldn't do that.'

'You should've moved to Bali,' Faye said. 'You let her screw you around like this because you think you still love her. So, either stop being stubborn and get back together, or end it once and for all. It'd be better for everyone if she were dead!'

With that, Faye stormed off with Greg following closely behind. My mind was reeling. Rory still loved Maria. And what was that about moving to Bali?

Rory sighed. 'I'm sorry about that. Faye and Maria don't get along.'

'I noticed. What happened between them?'

'Faye and I had a fight a couple of years ago. It started when she asked me how she could make things easier for Greg and Lyle. I suggested she cook dinner for them instead of Greg doing it when he comes home from work. Faye used to love cooking—she did it all the time until the depression hit, so I thought it'd help her too. But she got all offended. Told me I carry on like I've got the perfect family when my family's pretty screwed-up.' Rory rolled his eyes. 'Faye and I didn't speak for a while, but I forgave her coz I knew she'd said it in the heat of the moment. But Maria never forgives or forgets.'

'Can I get a hug?' I said suddenly, remembering that he hadn't given me his usual greeting. I always felt better after his hugs. Then I kicked myself for being so awkward.

Rory laughed, embraced me tightly then disappeared backstage. I still felt empty and wondered if I should follow him. But I stood frozen in front of my seat. Maria was staring at me.

#

I tried to concentrate on the music when the band started. They were playing *Tainted Love* when I risked another glance at Maria. She'd stopped looking at me. Her eyes were fixed on Rory in a way that reminded me of how Veronica had stared at him on Sunday.

Rory spent most of the break talking to Maria near the bar. I tried not to watch, or look like I was watching, as I hung out with the rest of the band. Dom admitted he'd smoked a few times since announcing he was quitting, but he was determined not to tonight.

'Man, she scares the crap out of me,' Tyler said, nodding his head in the direction of Maria and Rory.

'Oh God, remember when I turned up for rehearsal the first time?' Chloe said. 'Rory's like, "say hello to Chloe", and Maria wouldn't even look at me.'

'I haven't even met her yet,' Brad said.

'You will. She's like a boomerang. Always comes back,' Tyler said. 'Band girlfriends are all bad news. That's why we're single.'

Brad laughed. 'Sure, that's the reason.'

'Hey, what about me?' Chloe asked.

'You don't count. You were one of us first,' Tyler said. 'Even if you're a singer.'

Chloe poked her tongue out at him.

'Speaking of women that always come back,' Dom interjected, chewing furiously on a piece of gum. 'I got a really weird message from Veronica Otto this week. Actually, it was more like a sixteen-page essay. Something about how Zayden looks up to me so I shouldn't smoke, even though I never do it in front of my students. And then a heap of really personal questions about Hunter.'

'Why's she asking about Hunter?' Tyler asked.

'She's been going to his solo gigs at Sherlock's,' I blurted out. 'Last time, she called me a little girl and told Rory it's pathetic for teenagers like me to be with grown men.' I blushed as soon as the words came out, wondering what everyone would think of me now. I didn't tell them how sick I felt every time I thought about running into Veronica at a gig.

'Stuff her,' Dom said, giving me a friendly squeeze on the shoulder. 'She's like a schoolyard bully. But unlike in school, you've got us to protect you.' He flexed his ample biceps and kissed them. Everyone else laughed.

I tried to smile. I was standing here now with friends who would never have looked twice at me back in high school. Maybe he was right.

#

After The Lyrebirds had finished playing, Rory left the band to pack up for him. Like he did when he hooked up with me in the bushes, except now he was with Maria. I shook the thought from my head. They were just talking. He loved *me* now.

I said goodbye to Chloe, Dom, Tyler and Brad, and was about to find Rory when he walked through the curtain and into the band room. 'You off?' he asked me.

I nodded.

He hugged me. 'Be safe, beautiful.'

'You too.'

I stopped in the bathroom before I left. That was my mistake. When I opened the door on my way out, I saw Rory and Maria at the other end of the bar. He had his elbow on the counter and was leaning slightly towards her, his eyes locked on hers. He was smiling and so was she.

Then she threw her arms around his neck and pulled him into a long kiss.

I felt like I'd been punched in the gut. My breath caught in my throat and tears prickled in my eyes.

I bolted out the door and ran all the way home.

They hadn't seen me. He thought I'd left.

But what killed me was the way he was looking at her. Because it was the same look I thought he reserved for me.

Chapter Thirty-Four

Mum was usually in bed by the time I got home, but I stood outside the front door for five minutes, making sure my eyes and cheeks were dry before I unlocked the door and went inside. I crept into my bedroom and shut the door.

'What should I do?' I whispered to Deanna. Obviously, she didn't reply. The rock was in my hands before I could think of a reason to stop. I gave myself a fresh bruise and realised I was shaking.

Rory was the person I talked to about the things that made me want to hurt myself. But now he was the cause.

I couldn't confide in The Lyrebirds. They'd all warned me, in their own way, that I should be careful of getting too close to Rory—without even knowing what had gone on between us.

I couldn't talk to Mum. She would just say, 'I told you so', making me hate her even more.

I couldn't talk to Dad. He'd just remind me of my 'personal responsibility' around boys.

I was too embarrassed to talk to Cedric.

Faye. I could talk to Faye. I had to. She already knew how I felt about Rory. Maybe she knew there was more than that too.

I started to dial her number, then hung up before the call went through, my heart pounding. It was late. I decided to text her instead.

Can I talk to you about something? I think I'm going to cry. I hit send and waited, wondering how early Faye went to bed. I didn't think I'd be sleeping tonight.

'Why can't I be enough for Rory?' I asked Deanna. 'I'd never use his kids as weapons to hurt him. I'd never be rude to his family or anyone in his band. How worthless am I if she's a better option than me?'

Shall I call you? Faye replied after what felt like an hour, but was really only six minutes.

I stared at Deanna's frozen black eyes, searching for an answer. I didn't know if I could talk—really talk—to Faye. But who else was there in the world who could actually talk back?

Sure, I sent back. A minute later my phone began to ring.

'What's the matter?' Faye asked.

'Well ...' I stammered, 'Rory and I had sex and I love him.'

There was a long silence at the end of the phone. I was in a state of panic when Faye finally said, 'Go on.'

I tried to gather my thoughts so they'd make sense when they came out of my mouth. 'I guess the story begins when I was sixteen,' I said, thinking about Nathan. 'I lost my virginity and it was kind of a traumatic experience. And no one had ever touched me since then.

'Then Rory took me back to his place and kissed me. And maybe I was supposed to stop him, but I really like him and I'm comfortable with him, and I didn't want some stupid drunken incident from two years ago to stop me from ever having sex again. So, we did it. And he was so gentle.

'But afterwards, he was really distant till I asked him if he'd just used me to get back at Maria. He said he didn't. I wasn't sure we'd ever have sex again, but we did. I thought he loved me. He said he did. But ...' I trailed off.

I couldn't say what I'd just seen because that would make it real. It would make my relationship with Rory over. And Faye already knew anyway. Maybe not that Rory had kissed Maria tonight, but that he would never be over her, and that meant there would never be any room for me, no matter how much I loved him.

All of which became apparent when she said, 'Is this because Maria turned up tonight?'

'I just don't know what to do,' I said. 'It's so messed up. I need to get over him, but I can't lose him as a friend.' That was the most important thing, right? Even if we weren't together? Maybe I could find someone else, and if I looked happy with them, Rory would remember how close I was to being his. And maybe he'd see one day that a loyal, loving friend was better than being with someone who just used him to play games. Maybe I needed to be patient, like he'd said.

'I understand perfectly,' Faye said softly. 'I'm glad you've offloaded this tonight. It must be so hard seeing him so often, never knowing what might happen.'

I sniffed and nodded, even though she couldn't see me.

'I'm sorry I ran off so suddenly tonight,' she said. 'Why don't you come over tomorrow?'

'That'd be good,' I said, and she gave me her address.

#

I put on my sunglasses and caught the bus early on Saturday morning—before anyone could stop me. I was already on the edge of tears and I knew an interrogation from Mum would only make things worse.

Lyle took the bus every day to get to and from school, so Faye had told me which stop to get off and which direction to walk in, and I found the house seven minutes later. Their surname, Cunningham, was etched in curly script on the side of their letterbox.

I walked up the silver cobblestone path to their front door. Taking a deep breath, I tapped the gold-plated knocker against the door.

Greg opened the door and smiled. 'Come in, Jade.'

Maybe it was the hint of sadness or pity in his hazel eyes, but I knew that Greg knew.

I followed him down the hall and into the sun-drenched living room, squinting a little as I entered—I usually kept the curtains drawn in my bedroom and the light hurt my eyes for a few minutes until I got used to it.

Faye was sitting on the couch watching a Midnight Oil concert and altering a pair of navy-blue trousers. 'Hello, sweetie,' she said. 'Come sit with me.'

I placed myself on the soft red leather as Peter Garrett gyrated on the TV screen in front of us. Faye put the pants—which I recognised as part of the Concord Creek High School uniform—to one side. 'I had to shorten these at the start of the year for Lyle,' she explained, 'But he's grown a few inches so I'm letting the hem down.'

I nodded distantly, letting *Power and the Passion* flood my ears.

'How are you?' Faye asked gently.

My lip quivered and she leaned forward to hug me.

'I told Greg what you told me,' she confessed. 'He's my husband. I don't hide things from him. And he can keep a secret, so you don't need to worry.'

'How long have you known how I felt about Rory?' I asked.

'Since the day I met you.'

'And you still approved of me?'

'Lots of girls develop a crush on Rory. He's a singer in a rock band, it's what happens. After I met you, I realised you weren't a skank. You just had that sweet, adoring look in your eye.'

I wondered, not for the first time, just how many 'lots of girls' were.

'What shocked me was when you said you two had slept together,' Faye said. 'Part of me wants to slap you and kick him. But I do understand. He's very charming, isn't he?'

I nodded.

'I've asked him about twenty thousand times if there's any chance he'll get back with Maria. The answer's no. They both play nasty. But he'll never be able to move on until he falls out of love with her, and he can't while he still has to see her all the time. That's why he was thinking of moving away, maybe to Bali where our parents live. But he'd never be able to take the kids with him, so he won't do it.'

Thoughts tumbled around in my head. Why didn't he just tell me how he still felt about Maria? I was his friend, wasn't I? I would've understood. I would've waited. The tears I'd been holding back all day started to slip from my eyes. Faye handed me a box of tissues.

'You said you were afraid of losing him as a friend. I don't think that'll ever happen. I think you're closer to him than anyone.'

If that were true, wouldn't he have confided in me? I wondered, but said nothing.

'It's not like him to have sex with someone like you,' Faye said. 'He usually picks a girl he knows he's not going to see again for months or years. So, I think he does have feelings for you. I don't know why else he'd do it with someone I know he cares very much for. And more than once.'

Or maybe it was because I was always available and he knew it. He knew how I felt. I'd made it clear, and he'd said he felt the same way. I felt sick. I wanted to believe that Rory had feelings for me, but I couldn't shake the thought that I'd fallen for another Nathan.

'I'd love for you and Rory to be together,' Faye said. 'We could go on double dates—you and him with Greg and me. It's been a long time since Greg and I actually went out for dinner as a couple.' Faye put her arm around me again. 'But Rory comes with so much baggage. Much more than most boys your age. Do you really want to deal with that for the rest of your life?'

I would've dealt with anything if it meant Rory loved me for the rest of my life, but the only sounds that came out of my mouth were my strangled sobs.

#

I spent the rest of the day with Faye. Lyle trudged out of his room every now and then to grab a snack, but kept to himself otherwise. Greg dropped me home at night. Mum glared at me when I came through the door and I could see the questions in her eyes, but she didn't speak and neither did I. I went straight to bed and lay in the dark, trying to sleep.

The next day, Faye invited me over again, so I got on the bus to the Cunninghams' house instead of my usual Sunday Sojourn. We watched an INXS concert in the living room before Faye left me sitting under the patio while she did some chores. 'It's a lovely day. You should try to enjoy it,' she said.

I didn't particularly like being outdoors, but I smiled and nodded.

Rory rang me halfway through his gig, when I'd been in my chair for about twenty minutes. I considered rejecting the call, but after five rings, I answered him.

'Where are you today?' he asked.

'At Faye and Greg's.'

'You're not coming?'

'No.'

'I miss you.'

'Yeah, right,' I scoffed.

'What do you mean, "Yeah, right"?'

'I saw you, okay?'

'Saw me what?'

'Kissing Maria!' As soon as the words were spat off my tongue, I started to shake. I hadn't imagined it. It had really happened.

Rory was silent for a long time. 'So, that's what I was doing?' he said at last.

I frowned. 'What?'

'Jade, I was so wasted. I had a couple of scotches … and then she kept giving me drinks and … Honestly, I can barely remember a thing after Faye walked out.'

The fingers on my free hand pinched the bruise I'd given myself after Friday night. Would he not have kissed Maria if he'd been sober? Was it me he wanted after all? But if he really couldn't remember making out with her, and he really couldn't remember his behaviour with Layla … then maybe Chloe, Alex and I had been right to worry, and he did have a drinking problem.

'It's not the first time you've blacked out,' I said.

'Who hasn't forgotten what they did when they were drunk?' Rory replied, a little defensively.

'I haven't.'

'You're different. It's one of the things I love about you.'

I love you too, I almost said, but I bit my lip instead. I could still see him and Maria in my mind, as clear as the sunlight in front of me, and I didn't know if I'd ever be able to erase the image.

'So, what's the situation with you and Maria?'

'Well, we talked a bit yesterday and today. And we were speaking without screaming for once,' he said. 'But the reasons we don't work as a couple are never gonna be resolved. So, I'm just trying to get to a place where we can at least be civil to each other for the sake of our kids.'

I took a deep breath. 'Look, I know she's the mother of your kids. I know she'll always be part of your life. And if you can make peace with her, that's awesome for Ethan and Ella. But where does that leave us?'

'Nothing's changed, Jade. My life was complicated before and it's complicated now. But I love you to bits. You know that. I'm sorry I do stupid things when I'm drunk. Can you forgive me?'

The seconds ticked away. Could I forgive him? He'd been drunk. He had an issue with alcohol. He needed support for that. Maybe I could help him. That's what you did for your friends and people you loved, wasn't it?

'I'll forgive you,' I said.

Chapter Thirty-Five

I spent every day with Faye that week. We spent most of that time sitting in the bed she usually shared with Greg, eating chocolate and watching daytime TV.

'Maybe we can help you find another boy,' she suggested. 'The best way to get over someone you love is to fall in love again.'

But Rory 'loves me to bits', and it didn't stop him kissing his ex. I tried to banish the thought from my mind. I'd told Rory I'd forgiven him, but the image of them together still stung.

'Did I ever tell you about Joey?' Faye asked.

I shook my head.

'I dated him all through high school. I was so convinced he was the one. In our yearbook, we called each other 'hubby' and 'wifey'. And then we graduated and within two weeks, he'd dumped me. I was distraught. I couldn't imagine living a life without Joey.

'And then Greg came along. He's so different to Joey. But by the end of our first date, I knew Greg was someone I could spend the rest of my life with.'

I smiled sadly. If only it were that easy. But there wasn't room in my heart for anyone but Rory, and even if there was, who else would ever love a screw-up like me?

'What about Tyler?' Faye suggested. 'He's single, no baggage, and you're quite comfortable with him, aren't you?'

'But I'd just be using him to get over Rory,' I objected. Besides, even if I knew how to make the first move, there was no way I was going to just ask Tyler out. We were friends, or at least acquaintances, but that's all we were.

'No more than Rory's used you,' Faye said. 'He's a boy. I bet he'll love it, and you'll have someone else to think about.'

I shook my head. 'I can't.'

'Well, if you're not even going to listen to my advice, then why are you here?'

A piece of chocolate fell from my fingers. 'What?'

Faye stood up. 'You called me saying you didn't know what to do. I just told you. And you won't even try.'

'But … I don't like Tyler in that way.' My stomach was starting to wish I hadn't eaten so much chocolate. Why was Faye so mad at me all of a sudden?

Faye squinted at me for a long time. 'Fine, don't go after Tyler. But you have to try with someone else. Okay?'

'Okay,' I whispered.

#

My heart was thumping, but five minutes later it was as if nothing had happened. Shortly afterwards, Faye said she was comfortable enough to tell me about the medication she took.

'I've been close to taking them all at once. I even counted out how many pills it would take to die,' she confessed. 'But then I thought about Lyle. My baby. And I couldn't do it to him. I couldn't do it to Greg. So, I put the pills away and went back to the vacuuming. But I don't think I can function without them.'

My throat tightened. I remembered when I'd found out about Samson and how I'd silently wished I were him. And then Rory had given me something to look forward to. But I didn't have a child or partner to live for. I didn't have anything.

'How long have you been …'

'Depressed?' Faye finished.

I nodded shyly.

'I was diagnosed at twenty. The anxiety came first. I don't know why it started. I was going back to work after lunch with Greg. We'd only been dating a few months. The lift wasn't working so I had to take the stairs. I was about halfway up the first flight of stairs when, all of a sudden, I couldn't move. I couldn't breathe. I thought I was having a heart attack.'

I broke off a row of my chocolate block and let the thick, sweet texture melt on my tongue. I'd never had an anxiety attack in a stairwell before. Maybe I'd just been lucky. But I could sort of prepare myself when I knew I was going to be around a lot of people, or people who stressed me out. I couldn't imagine how much scarier it'd be to start panicking for no obvious reason.

'One of my colleagues found me. She called Greg, who came to take me home. I never went back to work. About six weeks later, Greg went to the office to pick up the things I'd left behind.' Faye placed an arm on my back. 'Greg doesn't always understand what goes on for me,' she said. 'But he married me, just as I am. That's what you deserve. Someone who never makes you feel like you're competing with anyone else.'

I popped the last row of my chocolate block into my mouth, trying to think of something to say. I was competing with Maria. But why did it have to be like that? Why couldn't Rory, Maria, Ethan, Ella and I all get along and be a family? Wasn't that what mature, grown-up people did?

'The worst part about my condition is that I've turned Lyle into me,' Faye continued.

'What do you mean?' I asked after swallowing my mouthful of chocolate.

'I've been like this all his life. And he's just been diagnosed with depression too. It started when his best friend died a few months ago but I can't help wondering how much of it is my fault.'

I put my arm around her and buried my face in her shoulder. 'It's not your fault,' I said. Should I tell her the way I'd been feeling, about the pointlessness of life, about my bruising? She'd been so open with me. But Rory was the only person who knew, and he'd broken my heart after I let him in on my secret.

'You're such a sweet friend,' Faye said. 'I wish you were here all the time.'

'I hate living with Mum. It's like … I don't know, like I'm homesick for something I've never known. But now I know what I've been missing. It's this. Being here with someone to talk to.'

'Why don't you move in?'

The question hung in the air and I wondered if I'd imagined it. 'Are you serious?' I asked.

'We've got a spare room. I just need to clean it up. We know you can't pay board until you get a job, and I'm sure Greg will understand. He likes you. And we can help you look for work.'

I'd applied for jobs but hadn't heard anything back. I'd begun to wonder if I was even employable. I didn't like talking to people before I was comfortable with them. But it was rare for me to ever be comfortable with them. What if the whole town somehow knew that? But Faye seemed to believe that it was possible for me to work, so …

'You can just try it and see if you like staying with us, and if not, you can go back home. We won't be offended,' Faye said.

I searched Faye's clear blue eyes. She seemed genuine. Was this my first step to growing up?

'Okay. Let's do this,' I said.

#

I started packing a wheelie suitcase as soon as Greg dropped me home that night. I wanted to do it before I—or Mum—could change my mind. By the time I told her, I'd already be set to leave.

The suitcase was kept under my bed, even though we didn't travel much. One day I hoped to be brave enough and have the money to go travelling on my own.

I could rotate and mix and match between a few outfits, so I didn't have much to pack. I would take my laptop with me. There was my music collection and all my *Star Trek* stuff, but I could come back for most of it when I'd settled in at the Cunninghams' house. I'd make do with whatever music was on my phone and laptop for now. I looked up at my Bon Jovi poster on the wall, and beside it, the picture of Rory, Alex and me from the Create Tomorrow Ball.

I picked Deanna up. I didn't know how the Cunninghams would react if they walked in on me talking to a plastic toy. I kissed her and placed her back down on the desk. 'I'll come back for you,' I promised.

Then there was my rock. I could leave it under my pillow. I was starting a new chapter in my life, maybe one where I wouldn't need it. But I looked around at all the things I already had to leave behind. 'We all have our vices,' I said, mimicking what Dom had said the day we met for coffee, and slipped the rock into my suitcase.

Now all I had to do was tell my parents.

As I composed the words in my head, I opened my resume document on my laptop and tried to think of ways to make it appealing to someone. I only had one bit of work experience, but it'd been an internship under arguably Concord Creek's most well-known resident. Surely that had to count for something. I didn't want to be leeching off Faye and Greg forever.

#

'Alright, what's this about?' Dad asked, when I opened the front door. I stepped aside and let him and Wayne inside. They were holding coffee cups personalised with their names. I walked them both to the dining room and gestured for them to sit. Mum narrowed her eyes at Dad and scowled at Wayne. On the rare occasions that Mum and Wayne had been in the same room, Mum had never spoken to him.

I took a deep breath and told them the news.

'What?' Dad spluttered, spraying coffee over the dinner table.

'I'm moving in with Faye and Greg,' I repeated as calmly as possible, not quite meeting my parents' eyes.

'You do not know these people,' Mum said in a tight voice.

'I've known them for ages!' I cried. 'They're good to me.' I shoved my hands into my pockets so I wouldn't be tempted to strike the table or myself.

Dad and Wayne exchanged a glance and Wayne whispered something in Dad's ear. I fixed my attention on Dad. He was my way out. If I could convince him, Mum wouldn't be able to do anything.

'Dad, I'm eighteen. Cedric moved to the city at my age. And you told me that's how old you were when you left London, remember? You went to work in another country. On another continent. I'm not as brave as you, so this is just a baby step. But it's really important for me to try this. And I won't be far away.' My heart was pounding. I didn't know where all those words had come from, but I barely stuttered at all. I think even Dad might've been impressed.

'I don't see why we can't let you go on a trial basis,' he said.

Mum whipped her head around to face him. 'You do not even live here anymore,' she snapped. Dad leaned in towards Mum's ear and said something under his breath. I couldn't see her expression, but when she turned back to me, she looked defeated.

'What will you do for money?' Mum demanded.

'I'll figure it out.'

With tears in her eyes, Mum walked over to her bag, picked up her purse and emptied her latest pay into my hands. 'Remember that this is your home,' she whispered.

It was happening. I was moving out.

#

I celebrated by heading out to the Sherlock Arms on Thursday night. Alex and Chloe were making their debut together, filling in for Chloe's old band, the Spencer O'Neill Duo. I'd planned to go with Faye and Greg, but Faye said she was too tired. She sent me a text message telling me to have fun and not be afraid of meeting another boy.

Chloe rushed over to hug me when I walked inside. 'So glad you could make it!'

We headed towards a corner of the pub where Alex was casually playing *Johnny B. Goode* on an acoustic guitar. He stopped to give me his customary fist bump when I walked over to him. 'Hope this gig goes okay,' Alex said with a grin. 'Just got a call yesterday asking if we wanted it. We don't even have a name yet.'

'We were thinking "Fire and Ice",' Chloe said. 'Coz I have red hair and he's a stone-cold fox.'

Alex winked and kissed Chloe. I couldn't help feeling a pang of jealousy. I loved them together but seeing them so happy and relaxed made me think of how complicated things were between Rory and me.

Alex and Chloe kicked off the gig with *Stop Draggin' My Heart Around*. Alex had sung backing vocals for The Lyrebirds, but tonight I heard for the first time how well he could sing. I envied the chemistry between Alex and Chloe and the way their voices blended together.

'Have you ever been a lead singer?' I asked him during their break.

'Not since I was about fourteen in a high school band,' Alex replied, taking his hand sanitiser out of his jeans pocket and squeezing it into his palms. 'It's not my thing. I just want to play guitar.'

'I'm trying to get him to sing more though,' Chloe said, leaning into Alex's neck.

'You're really good,' I told him.

'Cheers,' Alex said. 'Veronica thinks so too.'

'Veronica?' I asked.

'She sent me a message this week asking why I left the band. I ignored it though. It's none of her business.'

I nodded in agreement.

'So, what's new with you?' Alex asked.

'I'm kinda looking for a job,' I said. 'But I don't know what I can do. I'm not that good with people.'

'You're getting better with us,' Chloe said.

'That's different. You … sort of … get me.'

'My parents run a restaurant,' she said. 'I can ask them if they're looking for a waitress or kitchenhand or anything. But keep an eye out for anyone advertising for help.'

I swallowed the lump in my throat. 'I'll try.'

'It's scary, but you've gotta put yourself out there,' she continued. 'Get your resume up the best it can be. Dress well. Smile. No one ever needs to know you're nervous.'

I nodded again. She was right. I had to show the world I wanted to grow up. I just didn't know if I was ready.

#

Mum was crying when I said goodbye on Friday morning. I got on the bus with my suitcase and tried not to think about it.

Faye greeted me with a broad smile when I arrived at the Cunninghams' house and showed me my new room.

It had been a storage area all the other times I'd walked past it, but now it was a bedroom. There wasn't much there—white walls, a lamp and a neat single bed in the corner—but as Faye said, 'It's yours to make your own.' I could see how much work she'd done overnight and I hugged her, excited about my new start.

'You've given me a new lease on life,' Faye told me when we were heating up sausage rolls for lunch.

'How so?'

'It's so lonely here on my own, with Greg at work all day and Lyle at school. But you understand, don't you? You listen. You don't make me feel stupid for the things I go through.'

'They're not stupid. They're real.'

Faye gave me a warm hug. 'You're my gorgeous little ray of light.'

I hugged her back silently. I wasn't a ray of light at all. I was dark and empty inside and bruised on the outside. But I wanted

to be what she thought I was, if only for a moment, so I didn't
say another word.

Chapter Thirty-Six

While Lyle stayed home, Greg, Faye and I went to the Bluebonnet Bar early on Friday for dinner. I wanted a Caesar salad, but I just got a bowl of chips because I could eat those without worrying about making a mess. Eating at home in front of the Cunningham family was still a challenge, but I managed to get my food down eventually—usually after everyone else had finished and I was alone in the kitchen. Greg had joked about me being a slow eater, but it was better than not being able to breathe.

Rory came to chat with us halfway through dinner. I offered him some of my chips, and he chomped down a few before telling me he'd already had dinner and didn't like to eat too much before a gig.

'How did Alex and Chloe's gig go?' he asked me, when Faye and Greg drifted off to talk to the rest of the band.

I hesitated. I hadn't told him I was going because I knew he was still hurt about Alex leaving The Lyrebirds. But then I remembered that Chloe had tagged Alex and me in a post last night, and Rory must've seen it.

'Yeah, not bad,' I said. They were amazing, really, and Alex seemed to have found another gear away from the band, but I wasn't about to rub metaphorical salt into Rory's wounds.

'I haven't seen him since he left,' Rory said. 'I mean, he lives across the street from me and I haven't seen him. He hasn't called. Ella and Ethan have been asking where he is.'

'Have you called him?' I asked.

Rory shook his head. 'He's the one who walked away from me.'

#

I missed Alex. But Brad was a nice guy too. I hoped he didn't pick up on Rory's body language and think he wasn't welcome. It was Brad who drove Rory home when Rory drank too much, which was every Friday. But I didn't know if they talked, or what they talked about.

We all ended up outside, sitting at two tables pushed together, when it got too cramped in the band room.

'Veronica won't stop messaging me,' Dom said. He had a straw dangling from his mouth like a cigarette. 'Sometimes to talk about Zayden, but usually to ask why Hunter's not replying to her messages.' He nudged Rory, who rolled his eyes.

'She's been messaging me too,' Tyler said. 'Not about Zayden obviously, but about Hunter, a lot. Just ignore her, man.'

'I have, but I'm her kid's drum teacher and I wouldn't put it past her to rock up in the middle of a lesson and embarrass Zayden.'

'She messages Alex and me, like every night,' Chloe said.

'What, to tell you to turn on your webcam so she can watch?' Tyler asked cheekily.

Chloe waved her middle finger at him, laughing.

'I haven't gotten anything from her,' Brad said. 'I feel left out.'

'No, you're the lucky one. Enjoy it while it lasts,' Rory said. 'She's been calling and texting me all bloody day. I had to turn my phone off to get some peace. Which means if there's an emergency with the kids right now, I wouldn't even know.'

'Why don't you just tell her to leave you alone?' Faye asked.

Rory sighed. 'Coz she's lonely and depressed and …' He trailed off, looking slightly embarrassed.

'And what?' Faye pressed.

'She and her mates do a lot of events. Corporate stuff. Fundraisers. Parties. Around here and in the city. She said my friendship with her can get us a lot of gigs.'

I stared at him, my mind spinning with contempt for Veronica and disappointment in Rory.

#

Faye didn't seem as shocked as I'd been. 'She's been in contact with me too,' Faye said, when The Lyrebirds returned to the stage with *Every Rose Has Its Thorn*. 'She's told me she's madly in love with Rory and that Zayden would benefit from having a little brother and sister, and that she'd be a great mum to Ethan and Ella. But she knows nothing will come of it.'

'Does she?' I wondered. I looked up at Rory, who was crooning about lying close together with someone but feeling miles apart from them. He hadn't said anything about rescheduling our cancelled hotel date.

I couldn't wait around for him to make the move anymore. Not with Maria and Veronica lurking in the shadows.

Chapter Thirty-Seven

After a week living with the Cunninghams, I'd settled into a rhythm. Spending time with Faye distracted me during the day. The nights were lonelier. I missed Deanna. I missed Rory's body against mine. I missed my own bed and sheets—although I'd never tell Mum that. But eventually the crying exhausted me enough to get some sleep.

I didn't get a chance to be alone with Rory on Friday night. But I decided, before the weekend was over, that I was going to find out where our relationship was going.

I spent Saturday afternoon playing a board game with Lyle and Faye while watching the footy on TV. Footy used to make me pine for Nathan, for the chance to do things over with him, and get them right. Now it was just background noise because all I wanted was Rory.

I couldn't get him off my mind all day. I wished I'd brought Deanna with me. Why did I think I could start a new life without her? She might've been plastic, but she was my friend.

Then there was the matter of whether I'd get the chance to talk to Rory at all. Could I call him? Or should I wait until tomorrow? Would I have any time alone with him? Faye and Greg might be going to the gig with me, and maybe even Lyle. And of course, Veronica might be around, like a blood-sucking parasite.

At half time, I went into my room and called Rory, but I got his voicemail. I hung up. I'd have to bet my luck on tomorrow.

#

I took the bus to the Sherlock Arms on Sunday because Faye wasn't in the mood to go out and Greg was taking care of her. I felt sad for Faye, but the bus ride gave me some time to think of what I was going to say to Rory.

To my relief, Veronica was nowhere to be seen. It was just Rory and me, the way it used to be, the way it was supposed to be. He hugged and kissed me hello. By the time he was singing *End of the Line*, I'd started to believe things would be all right.

'How's life in your new house?' Rory asked.

I nodded. 'Yeah, good.'

'Heard from Veronica?'

'Not recently.'

'She's been pestering me about letting her come over and cook for me and the kids. She's got rocks in her head if she thinks she's gonna be in my family's life.'

We slipped into silence. I wrestled over the words I'd rehearsed on the bus. My neck was prickling with heat and my palms felt clammy. Calm down, Jade. This is your best friend, the one you tell everything to.

'Is something on your mind?' he asked, his chocolate-brown eyes watching me.

I nodded.

He waited, and under his gaze all the perfect sentences I'd composed in my head vanished with the sea breeze.

'Do you still love me?' I blurted out.

He looked startled. 'Of course I love you. You're my best mate.'

'Do you still … want me?'

221

His eyes softened as he reached over and touched my hand. 'You're beautiful, Jade. You don't seem to realise it, but you are. And I've probably told people they're beautiful before when I didn't really mean it, but I do with you. You're physically beautiful and you have a beautiful soul. Any guy would be lucky to have you. You just need to be patient.'

Patient. He kept saying it, and I was willing to wait for him, but I'd come for answers. 'You didn't answer my question.'

He grinned. 'Honestly, I think about being with you all the time,' he said. 'But I can't today … It's been a long week and I'm wiped. We'll do it again soon, I promise.'

When he was driving me to my new home, we talked about nothing in particular, but it was easy and comfortable. I was with the guy I loved and that was all that mattered.

He pulled me into his sister's driveway and we hugged goodbye. 'I know I'm not always easy to be around,' he said. 'So, if you wanted to be with someone else or just on your own, I'd understand.'

'I don't want anyone but you,' I whispered into his ear.

When we broke the hug, he glanced towards the house before kissing me softly on the lips.

#

It was a good start to the week. Rory still wanted me and he'd promised we'd be together again soon. I even helped Lyle write his English essay, since that was the only subject I'd actually done well in during my final year, and I swear I saw the ghost of a smile on his face for once. I felt like I was contributing to my new home at last.

On Wednesday night, I'd been tossing and turning for two hours when I got up for a glass of water. As I started to drink, I became aware of voices. I crept towards them, wondering who could still be up at this time. Sometimes Lyle played video games in his room at night, but the voices were coming from the other direction. There was a slit of light from behind the door of the study. The tiles of the hallway felt like ice on my bare feet.

'Are you seriously going to play dumb with me?' It was Faye. She was probably video calling friends or family overseas, I thought. I decided I should give her some privacy. About to turn back to my room, I heard a familiar voice.

'I have no idea what you're on about,' he said. My stomach leapt into my mouth. His voice sounded far away as it filtered through the speakers, but it was definitely Rory. I'd recognise him anywhere.

'I know, okay?' Faye said. 'I know what's been going on between you two.'

'Okay. You got me,' Rory said. 'What do you think I should tell her?'

Wait, were they talking about me? My hand trembled. I tightened my grip around the glass.

'How about the truth for once?'

What was going on? What truth was he hiding from me?

'I don't even know how it's gonna pan out,' Rory said. 'I should wait till there's something to tell.'

'For God's sake, she's not some little plaything for you to drag home after a gig! Do you even remember what it's like to be with someone who has feelings? I've heard her crying over you in her room when she thinks no one's awake. I've heard her screaming your name in her dreams. Can't you see she's in love with you? Do you even care?'

'Of course I care. But … when you play with fire you're gonna get burnt, aren't you?'

The glass slipped from my grasp and crashed onto the tiles. I heard Faye swear. A second later, the door swung open.

'Oh, Jade …' Faye stared at me with guilt and pity in her eyes.

I stared back at her, then down at the mess of water and broken glass on the floor. 'I'm sorry,' I mumbled, before sprinting into my room.

Chapter Thirty-Eight

I slammed the door. Rummaging for my rock, I gave myself a bruise, but it barely registered. The physical pain wasn't enough to numb the pain inside me anymore. I buried my face in the pillow, crying so hard I couldn't breathe.

I could hear the rest of the house stirring. A few minutes later, Faye knocked on my door.

'Jade?'

I slipped the rock under my pillow and rolled onto my side, trying to catch my breath. Faye walked in and sat on the edge of the bed, looking down at me.

'I mopped up all the glass,' she began.

Of course. I'd broken something in a house that wasn't even mine. I apologised again.

'What did you hear?' Faye asked.

I turned onto my back, facing her through blurry eyes. 'Does it matter?'

'Of course it does. I want to make you feel better.'

I shook my head. There was nothing for me, not in a world where I was a burden on Faye's family and a band slut who played with fire and got burnt. I couldn't talk to Deanna. She wasn't real. None of it was. I was too old to live in a stupid fantasy where my life made any difference. I closed my eyes.

'I don't want to live anymore,' I said. 'I have no reason to. I can't sleep. All I ever do is cry and try to maintain some kind of illusion that I'm not alone.'

'I understand not wanting to live anymore,' Faye said. 'So many times I've thought, "I have enough alcohol and meds to slip quietly away and no one will notice, no one will care." Obviously I never went through with it. And I won't.'

She reached over to touch my hand. I stiffened instinctively, not quite knowing why. She pulled away.

'I know it hurts. Hearts break and yours is broken,' she said. 'But time will pass. Life will change. It'll be good again, and you'll be happy and alive and able to face each day with a smile.

'When you get older, you start seeing the people around you pass away. Greg's parents are both gone. Lyle's best friend had a brain aneurysm. I couldn't face another funeral. Especially yours. I'd feel like I'd let you down. How do you think Rory would react if you ended your life? He'd know and he'd have to carry that with him forever.'

Rory, who thinks I'm too stupid to notice him sticking his tongue down his ex's throat? Rory, who just told his sister that I deserved to get burnt because I was dumb enough to believe in him?

'Oh please,' I spat, turning on her. 'You and Rory would never even know if I walked out of here and killed myself. No one in my family has any form of relationship with either of you, or anyone I'd consider a friend. Mum would be too ashamed of the way I died to tell anyone. I'd just disappear and be a memory. So cut the condescending bullshit and leave me alone, okay? I just want to stop feeling.' I flipped over and sobbed hard into the pillow.

When Faye spoke again, her voice was cold.

'I'm sorry, Jade. I've listened to you cry for hours on end. I have nothing left to give. I have a family. I have a son, whose best friend had no fucking option as to whether he lived or died, but I sure as hell know which option he would've chosen. So think about that.'

Her footsteps faded away.

What now? I couldn't stay here anymore. I wasn't part of this family. I was pathetic to think I ever could be.

I sat up and looked around. I'd barely unpacked, apart from my toiletries that were in the bathroom, my laptop and headphones that were sitting on top of my suitcase, and the pyjamas I was wearing. And the rock under my pillow.

I stuck my head out the door, then tiptoed to the bathroom, got all my things and brought them back to the spare room. I tried to see if I could open the front door, but it was double locked and I knew Faye and Greg kept their keys in the master bedroom.

I was stuck here for the night. I could feel a dark cloud pressing down on my head and chest, even though when I opened my eyes, there was nothing there.

I plugged my headphones into my phone and lay back on the bed. Jon Bon Jovi sang to me about stars that didn't shine and I let the tears roll down my cheeks.

I closed my eyes, but I knew sleep wasn't coming anytime soon.

#

When the sun came up, I pulled my headphones off and heard the voices of the Cunningham family down the hall. I couldn't make out any distinct words.

To my surprise, it was Lyle who came in. 'Get up,' he said.

I scrambled to a sitting position.

'My dad's taking you home now. You're not coming here or speaking to my mum ever again.'

I squinted at him. He was three years younger than me. Why was Faye sending her child in to do her dirty work?

'You're a shit friend,' Lyle said. 'Your relationship with my mum is totally one-sided. You just want her to use all her energy to make you feel better and then you make her feel guilty for letting you down. It's not her job to help you. You're fucked up. Go see a doctor. Or don't. I don't care. Just get out of our lives.'

I dug my fingers into my bruises as he left. I was quietly seething. I'd helped Faye too. She said I'd given her a new lease on life. Our relationship wasn't one-sided.

I changed into a T-shirt and jeans, put everything into my suitcase, and wheeled it out of the room, determined not to give them the satisfaction of another teary breakdown.

Greg was waiting for me at the front door. Faye was nowhere to be seen, but the master bedroom door was closed. I gave it a final glare as I followed Greg outside.

The wheels of my suitcase rolled over the cobblestone path and driveway of the Cunningham house for the last time.

I sat in the backseat of Greg's car, my fingers gripping the handle of my luggage. We drove back to my parents' house in silence.

'Bye Jade,' Greg said softly as I opened the rear door. 'I'm sorry it had to end like this.'

I left the car without a word. I was shaking, but I wasn't going to let him see that. At the front door, I fumbled for my house key and heard Greg's car drive off.

For some reason, I checked my phone before I went inside and saw that Faye had unfriended and unfollowed me on all our social networks.

I turned the key and went inside.

#

Mum was sipping tea and munching on toast in the dining room. She looked up in surprise when I walked in.

'I was not expecting you,' Mum said.

'You said this was my home.' Had she decided she liked not having me in the house? Would she send me back?

'Of course,' Mum said. 'But you did not call or anything.'

I shrugged.

'What happened?' Mum asked.

'I decided to come home,' I said, hoping she wouldn't hear the tremor in my voice. 'Is something wrong with that?'

'Only asking, lah,' Mum said.

I wheeled my suitcase back to my familiar bedroom and closed the door behind me.

Deanna looked at me from the desk, right where I'd left her. 'I'm home,' I squeaked, and the tears started to fall.

Chapter Thirty-Nine

I dried my eyes and bruised myself, trying to find the strength to call Rory. I didn't know what he knew I knew. Faye didn't even know how much I'd overheard of their conversation. Had she told him I'd been lurking on the other side of the door? Rory hadn't tried to contact me, so he either didn't know or he just didn't care.

Rory didn't answer the phone, but I gave him five minutes and dialled again, and this time I heard his voice at the other end of the line.

'Hey,' he said, giving nothing away.

I took a deep breath. 'Are you getting back with Maria?'

He paused for what felt like an eternity. 'The short answer is yes,' he said at last, and my heart splintered all over again. 'But you know there's more to it than that. We're a family, and when we're apart it makes life pretty hard. We don't get on all the time and we don't always agree, but we're generally trying to create peace in our family. I don't know if we can stay peaceful, but we'll see.'

I started to cry again.

'I hope this doesn't change anything between you and me. I cherish your friendship, I really do. And you've become one of the only people who understand me.'

I tried to process his words. He cherished our friendship. He was my closest friend and that's all that mattered. As long as he was straight with me, nothing would change between us.

But he hadn't been straight with me. He was only telling me this because I'd already found out and confronted him with it.

'Rory, I'll always want what's best for you. And that means your family too. If you don't know that, you should,' I began. 'But I think I've earned the right to a little openness and honesty from you without having to fish for it. And if you really cherish our friendship, then why did I have to ask if you were getting back with your ex? You said you loved me! You made me ring hotels for us! How could you not tell me you weren't single anymore, or even thinking about not being single anymore?'

He drew in a sharp breath and exhaled. 'You're right. I should've been more forward about what was happening with me.'

'That's it?' Wasn't he even going to apologise?

'It's really hard work with Maria,' Rory continued. 'That's why we sleep in separate rooms. We have for years. But at least when she's around, I know I've got a babysitter.'

#

I couldn't face seeing Rory that Friday. I was stung by the fact that he thought it was okay to leave me in the dark about his relationship with Maria. Besides, what if Faye turned up to the gig?

The dark cloud—my dark cloud—was sucking the air out of the room. I could feel it all weekend, pressing down on my lungs, turning each breath into an effort. Why was I such a screw-up? What had I done to deserve this? First Nathan, and now Rory. And Faye. I couldn't eat or sleep, so there was no reason to even leave my bedroom.

I found myself researching how to tie knots.

Mum knocked on the door on Saturday morning, trying to find out what had happened.

'Please just go away,' I said.

To my surprise, she did, without any arguments.

#

I couldn't help myself. On Saturday morning, I dragged myself to my laptop to see what Maria had been up to. She'd changed her profile photo to a picture of herself and Rory.

Her latest post read: 'How hard is it to find a decent wedding venue in this town??'

My gut twisted. I could see all her wedding plans on her page. The guests would sign an acoustic guitar instead of a guestbook, there would be activities for the kids, an overabundance of pink flamingos …

A little more digging found a wedding competition she'd entered a year ago—a time that Rory had said they weren't together.

We had our family first so our kids could be part of our big day. But now we've got a gorgeous boy and girl and we're ready to have the best wedding ever!

I rolled my eyes at Deanna. 'More like, "We were too irresponsible to take any precautions so now we have two kids who'll grow up thinking our abusive relationship is normal",' I muttered.

I dug my fingers into my bruises. All this could only mean one thing. Rory was a liar. He was either lying to her or lying to me. Again.

232

Chapter Forty

I couldn't let Rory get away with this anymore. I rang and when he didn't pick up, I kept redialling. Eventually I texted him. *Are you marrying her?!*

When he still hadn't replied by lunchtime, I sent him another message. *So much for cherishing our friendship. I guess your lack of response means I should be grateful that you're not telling me a blatant lie.*

He got back to me a minute later. *Why are you asking me that question? What prompted it?*

I replied: *I may be incompetent in every other aspect of my life but one thing I am good at is stalking people online. And since you've never been straight with me about her, those tidbits are all I have to go on.*

Rory: *She's pretty keen to get married but I think it's just a phase. I don't know how I feel about it. I don't know why she wants to get married. She's never said anything like that before.*

A 'phase'? She'd obviously been thinking about it for a long time if she was entering wedding competitions. Did he really not know that?

I wanted to hear Rory's voice. Even though texting was an easier way for me to communicate, because I could let the words form in my head before I had to send them, listening to his cadence usually made me feel better.

Me: *You claim I'm one of your closest friends so why do I always have to figure out what's going on from other sources? If you think you're protecting me, you're not. It hurts way more hearing things from everyone else. And if you think I simply don't deserve the truth from you, then I have every right to demand better. Sure, your life is complicated. I get that. If you can't love me the way I love you, then just say so. I wouldn't get mad at you for that. I do get mad when you treat me like I'm nothing. If my friendship matters to you, then let me in, dammit!*

I'd written an essay on my keypad, but all he said was, *You're in more than most. :)*

Usually a sweet little text message like that from him made me feel better, but not today.

#

I was woken up on Sunday morning by a call from Alex. The phone rang at least three times before I registered that it was mine and fumbled to answer it.

'Hello?' I said, confused. Alex had sent me the odd text, but he'd never called me before.

'Did I wake you up?' he asked.

'It's okay. What's up?'

'Have you seen Maria's profile today?'

My stomach was doing knots again. 'No …'

'Go have a look.'

Wide awake now, I opened the app on my phone, tapping my hand anxiously as I waited for everything to load, then looked for Maria's profile.

There was nothing there.

'I think she's blocked me,' I said.

I heard mumbles at the other end of the phone, then Alex said, 'I'm at Chloe's place. Come over whenever you can. I think you should see this.'

He texted me the address and I said I'd be there soon. When I was ready, I bolted out of the house before Mum could stop me.

Chloe gave me a long hug when I arrived at her doorstep, which made me even more nervous. What was I going to find on her computer?

#

At the top of Maria's profile was a screenshot of my part of the text conversation I'd had with Rory:

I may be incompetent in every other aspect of my life but one thing I am good at is stalking people online. And since you've never been straight with me about her, those tidbits are all I have to go on.

My name was at the top of the screenshot, with a picture of my face. Maria had captioned the image:

'Get your own man, you fucked up slut.'

Underneath, a bunch of her friends had called me names like 'fugly bitch' and 'slanty-eyed skank'.

The dark cloud was in my face, taunting me. I felt too sick and shocked even to cry.

'Do you know what this is about?' Alex asked.

I wiped my clammy palms on my jeans. 'Rory said he took Maria back in as his babysitter.' My cheeks were warm. 'Then I saw her planning a wedding, so I asked if he was marrying her. But she's just put up the bit where I said I'd stalked her, and not the bit where he said he thought her wanting to get married was just a phase.'

'He can't just let her do that to you,' Chloe said. 'Call him now.'

'No, wait,' Alex said. 'If Maria's got Rory's phone and she sees Jade's name on the caller ID, it could get worse.'

'I'll call,' Chloe offered. She dialled Rory's number. A few moments later, she shook her head. 'No answer.'

'He's got a gig today,' Alex said. 'We'll all go.'

Chapter Forty-One

We took Alex's car to the Sherlock Arms. My stomach churned the whole way. When we got there, Rory was in the car park, halfway through unloading his gear from the van.

'Has Maria contacted you?' Rory asked me, before any of us could say anything.

I shook my head. 'But our messages are on her profile …'

'Yeah, I know,' Rory said. 'She kicked me out. I'm staying at a hotel.'

Oh, the irony. 'I'm sorry,' I said aloud.

'It's not your fault,' Rory said.

'You're right. It's not,' Alex said in a low, menacing tone I barely recognised.

The two men glared at each other until Chloe put her hand on Alex's shoulder and he broke their gaze.

'Has she seen everything we've ever sent each other?' I asked, thinking about the nude photos.

'I don't know. She just told me to pack my things and get out.'

Rory carried his gear into the beer garden and began setting up, without any of our help. Alex turned to his usual crutch, his aloe vera hand sanitiser.

Veronica was already sitting at a table waiting for him. She stood up and beckoned me over with her long index finger. Reluctantly, I approached her.

'I saw what Maria posted and I think if someone has something to say, they shouldn't do it publicly like that,' she said. She leaned in towards me until she was an inch from my face. I could smell her potent blend of floral perfume and wine. I leaned back as far as I could.

'But I don't think you realise how much stress you're putting Rory under by turning up at his gigs,' she continued. 'He doesn't want to deal with this. I love him and if you care about him at all, you'll stay away from him. I hope you're mature enough to understand. It's about respecting him and his family.'

I couldn't take it anymore. Who the hell was she to tell me who I could be with and where I could show my face in public?

'Are you fucking kidding me?' I exploded. 'I'm not the one who bombards him with fifty messages in a row, then harasses his friends about why he's not replying to my messages—that's what you do. I'm not the one who went around telling people what a great stepmum I was going to be for his kids—that would be you. Well, guess what? You're not my boss anymore and you don't get to push me around!'

I was trembling with nervous energy. Veronica looked shocked. With a glance around the beer garden, which was now dead quiet with all eyes on us, she bowed her head and scurried out towards the car park. Suddenly she didn't look so powerful.

It felt good.

I turned to Rory, Alex and Chloe, who were staring at me with shock and maybe even a hint of admiration. I had a voice and it was louder and stronger than I'd ever known it could be.

Then Rory's phone began to ring and he moved towards the beach to answer it.

'Way to go, dude!' Alex whooped, when he finally spoke.

'That was amazing. I wish I'd filmed it,' Chloe added.

I grinned. But my elation was short-lived.

Rory jogged back towards us, his eyes on me. 'Maria's on her way here with her mum,' he said. 'You have to go home.'

My face fell. 'Did you show her my messages?' I had to know.

'Of course not! She went through my phone. She reckons she's been doing it for years.'

'Like she wouldn't've seen way worse than that before if she's been going through your phone all this time,' I said. Layla came to mind. Not to mention all the messages Veronica had sent him.

Rory sighed. 'I don't know. I'll try to get her to take that post down. But you need to go, okay? I'm trying to get my house back.'

'Oh, cry me a river,' Alex snapped. 'How many times have you kicked each other out? If you had any balls, you'd tell her it was your house before she ever came along and change the locks. What's the difference between her and all the other Summit girls you took home? Nothing, except that she conveniently got pregnant when you wouldn't commit to her!'

Rory turned on him. 'Grow the hell up. What do you know about life? You think this fairy-tale romance of yours is gonna feel like this forever? You think any other band in Concord Creek's gonna take you when you get bored of playing with yourself at home? Not with you washing your hands for an hour!'

Alex launched himself at Rory. Rory caught him. They grunted and grappled with each other's collars, neither of them quite landing a blow.

'Stop it!' Chloe screamed.

Her words pierced through before a real brawl could begin. The two men disentangled themselves, still scowling at each other. Alex's hand hovered over the pocket containing his hand sanitiser.

I looked from Rory to Chloe to Alex, and finally back to Rory. 'Let's go,' I said quietly to no one in particular. Chloe squeezed my hand and interlaced her fingers in Alex's. I stole one last glance back at Rory on our way out. He locked eyes with me and his mouth twitched before he turned away.

#

Maria's post about me was still there for the world to see when Alex dropped me home that night, and on Monday morning. I wondered how Rory's talk with her had gone. Not well, by the looks of things. What were Ethan and Ella thinking? That their dad had abandoned them? I tried ringing him three times at lunchtime but he didn't answer.

He called me back a few hours later.

'Are you okay? I've been freaking out,' I said.

'I'm fine,' he said in a terse voice. Why did he sound so exasperated? I cared about him … Didn't that count for anything?

'Did she come yesterday?' I asked.

'No, she didn't turn up.'

So he'd kicked me out for nothing. 'Are you back home?'

'Yes, I am.'

The irritation in his voice was too much now. I wanted to ask about the twins, but I started to cry instead.

'I don't know what you want me to say. Do I love her? Yes, I do. Do I hate her? Yes, I do. It's not as easy as breaking up coz then I'll lose half my property and assets.'

Property and assets? He was going to stay in a stuffed-up relationship and throw away the love and promises we'd made—for a bunch of material things?

'So, this is what adult relationships are about,' I said bitterly.

He laughed mirthlessly. 'Take a look around. How many people do you think have built their whole lives on relationships like this?'

I thought about what Veronica had said, about how you stayed with someone because you were used to them and not because you loved them anymore. I thought about my parents, and how they'd spent almost three decades in an unhappy relationship and probably would've died that way if Dad hadn't met Wayne.

'Most of them,' I said, defeated.

'Most of them,' Rory agreed.

I was an idiot to ever think love was enough, or that it even counted for anything. But it wasn't just romantic love. He was my best friend. He said I was one of the only people who understood him. Didn't I deserve better treatment, or was I stupid to believe that too?

'Babe, you know things about me that other people don't,' Rory said, his voice softening. 'Nothing has to change between us. You're still my closest friend.'

I sniffed, struggling to find the words or even the ability to speak.

'Are we okay?' he asked.

I didn't reply.

'Will I see you on Friday?'

I didn't know if I wanted to see him. I didn't know if I could handle that. But what I did know is that I needed some kind of closure. We couldn't end like this, could we?

'Okay,' I whispered.

Chapter Forty-Two

Apart from meals and showers, I spent the rest of the week in my room. I knew Mum wanted to interrogate me about what had happened when I was living with the Cunninghams and I had no desire to talk about it. At all.

Chloe had promised to keep me updated on anything Maria posted about me, but I didn't hear from her, so I hoped that was good news.

There was nothing I could do but crank up my comfort music and hold onto my rock. Wailing electric guitars and melancholy piano keys filled my bedroom as I tried not to think about the dark cloud choking me.

At least I still had Rory's friendship, I tried to tell myself. And as long as I had that, I could get through the pain of losing his love.

#

Before leaving the house on Friday, I slammed my rock violently against my forearm. I needed the pain relief. I didn't bother to conceal the warm, swollen bruises that formed. They were a part of me. I'd wasted so much energy trying to hide them. What was the point? I hadn't managed to get Rory to stay in love with me. And the Cunninghams would've tossed me aside sooner if they knew what I did to myself.

I tried jogging to the Bluebonnet Bar to try to run off my nervous energy, but all it did was show me how unfit I was. By the time I got there, I was still shaking—not enough for anyone to see, but enough for my arms and legs to feel like jelly. The stitch cut into my side like a razorblade.

I asked the bartender for a glass of water, then closed my eyes, took a deep breath, and walked into the band room. Rory came over to me right away and pulled me into a tight hug. In the warmth of his body and his scent, I started to feel like we really could beat the dark cloud.

I watched the first set from backstage. When Chloe sang *Rolling in the Deep*, I caught Rory studying me as if he wanted to say something, but his guitar strums never missed a beat.

'Let's go outside,' Dom said as soon as the band left the stage for their break. We all knew his latest attempt to quit smoking had been unsuccessful and he needed a cigarette. The others nodded and started to file out behind him.

I looked at Rory, inclining my head towards the door to ask if we were following them.

'Actually, could you stay for a minute?' Rory looked nervous, unsure—things I usually associated with me, not him. I nodded. He sat down in the corner and I took a seat next to him.

'I wanted to explain this in person,' he said. 'I want you to understand that I've never set out to try to hurt you. It's just …' He trailed off, opening his mouth for a moment, then closing it as if the words had slipped away from him.

I placed my hand on his, trying to encourage him. 'It's just …?' I prompted.

'Maria and I have a lot of history,' he said. 'Not all of it good and not all of it bad. It is what it is. But—'

Rory suddenly jerked his hand out from under mine. Standing in front of the black curtain was Maria. She was with a friend, who I recognised from my online stalking. Both of them were holding identical drinks.

Maria marched over to us, throwing her free arm around Rory's neck and pulling him into a deep kiss that was clearly for my benefit. Then she turned to me.

Chapter Forty-Three

Her eyes blazed with blue ice. 'You better get out!'

I turned to Rory, but he quietly got up and moved to another corner of the room. He refused to meet my gaze.

'Grab your drink and fuck off,' Maria said in a slow staccato, as if I didn't speak English. 'Go sleep with someone your own age, you little slut.'

'Look who's talking,' I managed to say.

She raised her glass as if to smash it in my face. Her friend tugged at the waist of her dress. With a final glare at me, Maria stormed out of the band room, her friend by her side.

'I think you'd better leave,' Rory said, finally speaking up.

'No way.'

Rory's eyes widened. 'How much grief is this gonna cause me?'

'Well, you should've thought of that before.'

'Are you kidding me?'

I stared at him, my lip shaking. How could he kick me out? Again? He said I was his closest friend. He knows how much I need these gigs. He knows I don't have anyone else. I felt hot tears prickling in my eyes and wished I'd gone outside with the rest of the band. I would've been safer with them. But I'd bet all my chips on Rory.

'I have a job to do,' Rory said. 'I can't do it with you two fighting.'

'So make your babysitter leave. She's the one trying to pick a fight.'

'She's my partner, Jade.'

'You said it was over with her! You said she was a terrible mother! Alex told me he wanted to take the kids in to protect them from her, and you stopped him. Great fucking father you are.' Rory's mouth tightened but I couldn't be silent any longer. 'What's her problem, anyway? She knows she could fly to Bali and murder your parents and you'd still welcome her back with open arms. I'm not a threat to her. I was never a threat to her. She was the threat to me, only I didn't know it coz I believed every lie you told me to get me into bed with you!'

Rory paled. I realised he was looking somewhere over my shoulder and I spun around.

The rest of the band looked back at us, looked away, tried to look busy.

I didn't know how much they'd heard. For a moment, I hoped they would back me up, but I couldn't ask that of them, even as Chloe stepped forward to hug me. Rory was their boss. I choked back tears as I wrested myself from Chloe's arms and sprinted out of the band room and out of the Bluebonnet Bar for the last time.

The dark cloud had finally won.

My eyes stung. The streets were a blur. My legs carried me to the Creek Hotel where Rory had promised we would meet. I knew what I had to do. I'd check in like we'd planned.

They would find my body in the morning.

Chapter Forty-Four

The yellow-tinged lights in the lobby seared into my eyes as I walked into the hotel. Its brightness mocked me. I craved the eternal darkness I was about to throw myself into.

I checked in with cash. The man at the front desk told me I was on the second floor and handed over the key card with a vacant smile.

My legs felt stiff and heavy as I walked towards the lift and pushed the button. My heart kept time with the churning of my stomach. I glanced at the front desk again, wondering if the man had seen the death in my eyes. Not that he would've cared anyway. Not even my best friend cared.

The doors opened with a sharp ping that made me jump. I stepped inside, pressing the button for Level Two. The doors sleeked shut, sealing me inside. The lift hummed up to the second floor.

It was quiet when the lift doors opened. I walked down the corridor, my shoes whispering against the carpet as my eyes scanned the numbers on each door. The whole floor smelled vaguely of bleach.

I found my room and swiped the key card. The little light above the lock flashed green with a feeble beep. I pushed open the door and went inside. The lights flickered on.

There was a pen and a pad with the hotel's letterhead on the table in front of me. I could leave a note, but I didn't know if it'd ever find its way to the intended recipient.

Jon Bon Jovi once sang about a guy whose heroes had all died. I updated my status with the lyric and switched off my phone.

I pulled the tightly-made milk-coloured sheets off the bed, sweating with the effort until I couldn't tell where my tears ended and the sweat began. My arms trembled and ached as I tied them around the door, forming a noose.

There were two glasses next to the bathroom sink. I picked one up. Before I could lose my nerve, I squeezed my eyes shut and shattered it against the wall. With the largest of the shards, I sliced through the bruises on the inside of my forearm. An angry red river leaked from the cracks in my stinging skin. I bit my lip against the pain. It was backup, in case the next part of my plan didn't work.

I tried to think of something nice, like the Bon Jovi songs that had made me smile before I knew how soul-destroying love and friendship could be, but as the necklace of sheets tightened around me, my mind filled with Rory and Maria and Faye and Lyle and the band and my parents and how the people I loved the most would never even know I was choking to death.

But I couldn't even get that right.

My body flailed wildly, fighting my decision. The knots loosened and my chin crashed to the floor. My teeth shuddered with the impact. I lay on my stomach, catching my breath. My arms throbbed and ached and stung.

Then I got to my knees. I'd checked in for the night and there was blood streaming from my arm so there was no point going anywhere. I found my feet and crawled into the stripped bed, numb and alone, with cold tears staining my face. I closed my eyes and waited to bleed out.

Chapter Forty-Five

I woke up. Alive.

My eyes snapped open when I felt the sun pierce through the curtains. My arms prickled. I looked down and saw the dried blood that had started to cake over my wounds. For God's sake, how hard is it to die?

The display on the digital clock in my room was blank. I tapped the screen uselessly. It must be broken. I found my phone and turned it on. As soon as it powered to life, it began to ping and vibrate repeatedly.

I had a dozen voicemail messages from Mum, two from Dad, two from my brother Cedric, and one each from Rory, Alex and Chloe, as well as text messages from Mum asking when I was coming home, where I was, and if I could call when I got the messages.

It was seven-forty in the morning.

Cedric had tagged me in a post asking if any of my friends had seen me because my family couldn't get a hold of me and they were all panicking. I blushed, even though no one could see me. Mum would normally be in bed by the time I got home from the Bluebonnet. I hadn't thought about what would happen if she wasn't asleep yet, or if she'd gotten up in the middle of the night or early in the morning and noticed I wasn't home.

I was about to start calling them back when my phone rang. It was Rory. Usually I'd answer in a heartbeat. But he'd abandoned me when I needed him.

I deliberated over whether or not to pick up, letting it ring half a dozen times before finally accepting the call.

'Jade, where the hell are you?' he asked.

'Creek Hotel,' I replied, wondering if he'd understand.

'What? Why?'

'Because promises mean something to me.'

He paused, and I could almost hear the cogs in his brain turning to produce the words that would make me melt. 'I'm sorry about last night. I didn't know she was gonna be there.'

'Don't you talk to each other? You live in the same house, remember?'

'Like I said, it's hard work.'

'You know what else is hard?' I said in a dark tone I didn't recognise. 'Trying to hang yourself with a bed sheet.'

There was a long silence at the other end. 'Is that what you were doing last night?' he asked, his voice suddenly sounding small.

'Yeah.'

'Am I responsible for what you're going through?'

'I don't want you to be.'

'Well, if I am then I am.'

'I think you might be, yes.'

'I'm probably responsible for everything Maria's going through, and everything Faye goes through too. At least you have the guts to tell me,' he said. 'Would it help if I said I was really sorry?'

'Not if you don't mean it.'

'I do mean it. I just can't fix it.'

I felt a tear roll down my nose and into the crease of my mouth. I wiped it away. 'Maybe some things aren't meant to be fixed.'

Chapter Forty-Six

When I got off the phone with Rory, I texted Cedric to let him know I was fine and that I was about to call Mum and Dad. I was nervous about what would happen when her relief melted into anger, but I knew I'd just have to suck it up. I'd gotten myself into this mess.

Just as I'd psyched myself up to talk to her, my phone rang again. Chloe.

'Hey, Rory just called me,' she said. 'Are you still at the hotel?'

I froze. 'Yeah. Why, what'd he say?'

'That's he's gonna go talk to your mum and I should come pick you up.'

My throat felt dry. Rory was going to see my mother? He'd never even met her before. He'd never come to the door when dropping me home. What was he going to say to her? What was she going to say to him?

'Jade? You there?'

'Mm-hmm. Did Rory say anything about …'

'Hang on, I shouldn't really be on the phone. I'm driving. I'm like fifteen minutes away. We'll talk when I get there. Just stay at the hotel, okay?'

'Okay. Should I check out?' I stared dubiously at the bloodstains and the sheets I'd strewn onto the floor. 'It's kind of a mess in here.'

'Yeah, check out if you want.'

When we hung up, I cleaned up the glass and tried to remake the bed as best I could. I came to the conclusion that I would never have a housekeeping job at a hotel. I ran my arms under the shower, yelping as the water stung my cuts, and dabbed them dry with a towel. With my aching hands, I scribbled an apology to whoever would be forced to clean up after me. Then I went downstairs.

I handed my key card to the front desk, trying to keep my hands facing downwards so the clerk wouldn't see my wounds. Chloe arrived as I was checking out. Her eyes flickered over my cuts but instead of gaping, she gave me a hug and led me to her car.

'I should call my parents,' I said when we were inside.

'Okay, but I'm taking you to the hospital,' Chloe replied.

'What?'

'Boss's orders.'

'So, everyone knows?' I felt the shame of my inability to cope burning from the pit of my stomach.

'No, I think he just told me so I could get you.' She squeezed my shoulder and smiled.

I tried to return to the smile, but I don't think I succeeded. I called our home phone.

'Hello?' It was Dad's voice that answered the phone. I wondered when he'd gone to be with Mum.

'Dad, it's me.'

'Where've you been? Are you okay?'

I guessed that meant Rory hadn't been to my house yet. 'I'm fine. I'm with Chloe—the singer in Rory's band. I'm sorry for making you worry.'

Mum must've snatched the phone from Dad when she realised it was me on the other end because the next thing I heard was her voice crackling in my ears. 'Last night I cannot sleep,' she said. 'You did not call or message.'

'I … forgot. Look, I'll be home soon, okay?' I hung up, not wanting to pre-empt Rory's visit.

#

Concord Creek Hospital smelled like disinfectant and the walls and floors were uncomfortably white. I tried to breathe slowly and deeply to choke down what I feared was the start of a panic attack. The cries and wheezing coughs of small children cut through the fog in my brain. I was going to get sicker here than if I'd just gone straight to my bedroom and talked to Deanna.

'I want to go home,' I told Chloe.

'You need to get assessed,' she said gently, taking my hand and leading me to the triage desk. Chloe looked at me, as if waiting for me to speak, before she said to the nurse, 'This is my friend. She, um, has some cuts on her arm.'

Chloe spoke in a quiet voice, just loud enough for the nurse to hear, but it felt like the whole room stopped when she said it.

I was ushered away from Chloe and into a smaller room where another nurse cleaned my arm. 'You should've come in sooner. It's too late for stitches,' she said, clicking her tongue.

'Sorry,' I said, gritting my teeth against the stinging sensation in my arm. My eyes began to water.

'What're you crying for? I thought you liked pain.'

'What?'

'You're just another attention seeker, aren't you?'

I tried to open my mouth, but I couldn't think of anything to say.

'I see at least one of you every few weeks. I could show you where to cut if you're actually serious about wanting to die.'

She finished bandaging me as I sat in shock. 'Stay here. Doctor's coming,' she said abruptly. She left the room and I was once again as alone as I'd been in the hotel room. How could a nurse say that to me? Did she speak that way to the other 'attention seekers' she saw? I burned with anger and shame. I couldn't believe she was working in a hospital, or anywhere where people's lives were in her hands.

Doctor Eden was a stocky man who looked to be in his forties, with a short beard peppered with grey and a thinning head of hair. I felt his blue-grey eyes studying my body and the bandage on my arm before finally resting on my face.

'You attempted suicide last night?' he asked.

I nodded and stared at my shoes.

'What happened?'

I tried to meet his gaze, but his eyes reminded me too much of Maria's and Veronica's and Faye's, and my head dropped again. 'I checked into a hotel and cut my wrists and tried to hang myself.'

'I see. Have you attempted suicide before?'

I shook my head.

'What about suicidal ideation?'

I thought about what I'd told Faye on my last night at her house, and about how I'd envied Samson when I found out he was dead, and how Rory had been the one to give me hope until he didn't anymore. 'A little,' I murmured. 'But nothing serious,' I added quickly. 'Can I go home?'

'Not yet. Do you take any drugs or alcohol?'

I shook my head.

'Really?' He looked like he didn't believe me. 'What's been going on in your life that triggered the suicide attempt?'

'I … I was in a relationship that ended.'

'A relationship breakup?' Doctor Eden tiredly arched an eyebrow, and in that moment I knew he wasn't going to help me.

'I'm okay, really. I just had a bad moment yesterday but I'm totally fine now,' I said.

'Do you believe you'll be safe if I let you go?'

'Yes.' I didn't want to spend another minute with Doctor Eden and his sceptical eyebrow or in this hospital with nurses who wanted me dead. When he kept staring at me, I added, 'My friend's here. I just need to be with my loved ones.'

Doctor Eden finally let me go. I found Chloe in a rush. 'Let's get out of here,' I said.

She nodded and drove me home.

#

'Do you want me to come in?' Chloe asked as we pulled into my driveway. I shook my head, still feeling numb.

Dad was pacing in the family room when I went inside, while Mum was sitting in a chair. She'd obviously been crying. They both looked up and stared at me when I walked in. I didn't see Wayne anywhere, and figured Dad had told him to stay home so that Mum wouldn't throw around any homophobic slurs that Wayne didn't understand but could guess the meaning of.

'Has Rory been here?' I asked.

Dad nodded, staring at my bandage. I folded my arms behind my back, out of his sight.

'What'd he say?'

'Something about you being in a bad place at the moment and running out of his gig and trying to commit fucking suicide!'

I assumed Rory hadn't told them why I was so upset that I'd run out in the first place. 'It's fine. Chloe took me to the hospital. They assessed me. I'm fine.'

'It's not bloody fine!' Dad roared, jabbing his fist against the wall.

'Why don't you talk to us?' Mum demanded.

'Because I didn't trust you to listen!'

Mum and Dad looked at each other, then back at me.

'We're your family,' Dad said.

'Yeah? Well, you're never around anymore unless it's to try to show Mum up in some way. And Mum, you're too busy trying to control me and stop me from doing the things that make me happy. It's my life to live and learn from, but you just want to make it yours. So why the hell would I talk to either of you?'

My parents were still and silent for a moment. Dad's face was red, though from anger or embarrassment, I couldn't be sure. Then surprisingly, it was Mum who spoke up.

'We will try to listen better next time.'

Chapter Forty-Seven

For the next few days, I stayed at home in my *Star Trek* pyjamas, listened to music and scoured the job ads for something I thought I could do. I was almost nineteen, and it seemed I was too old for most employers to want to train me from scratch for a job I could've been doing when I was in high school. If I got into uni, I could move to the city and hopefully find work there. But there was still a lot to figure out about my life.

On Wednesday afternoon, Chloe and Alex came to visit on their way to a gig. I was surprised Mum let them in after everything that had happened, but maybe this was her trying to listen better and let me choose my friends.

'We wanted to bring you a little present,' Chloe said.

'It was Chloe's idea,' Alex said, carrying his acoustic guitar into my room.

'But I haven't warmed up my voice so it might be awful,' Chloe added.

I felt self-conscious having them in my bedroom. This was my space, where I talked to Deanna, where I bruised myself. And I didn't exactly make an effort to keep the floor tidy. I worried that Alex would have a heart attack. But neither he nor Chloe said anything.

Alex quickly tuned up his guitar. 'We listened to some videos of this on the way here, so hopefully it's not too bad.'

I recognised the opening chords of *Livin' on a Prayer* as soon as Alex started playing. Chloe's full, rich voice made me tear up, and Alex's harmonies were perfect. I wondered, not for the first time, why he hadn't sung more in The Lyrebirds.

'You guys are the best,' I said. 'I'm sorry I never appreciated that before.'

Chloe blew me a kiss as Alex propped his guitar up against the wall and smiled, popping open his trusty bottle of hand sanitiser.

'Chloe told me about what happened at the hospital,' Alex said.

I burned red.

'Hey, I know it can be hard sometimes. I mean, I can't pretend I know how you feel. But I've dealt with medical professionals who made me feel like I was wasting their time. I don't know, maybe it's coz they see so much messed-up shit every day that they need to stop caring about it as a way to cope.'

I'd never considered that, I thought, as Chloe reached over to squeeze Alex's hand. But it didn't change how ashamed I'd been made to feel in the hospital.

'Anyway, what I really wanted to say is that it took a while, but I found a great doctor.' Alex slipped his hand into his pocket and pulled out a card for the GP clinic on the outskirts of Concord Creek. 'Her name's Lisa Riviera. She's awesome, and she might be a good fit for you.'

'Thanks.'

'Don't mention it,' Alex said, reaching over for a fist bump. 'Has Rory come to visit you?'

I shook my head and tried to look like I didn't care, but I think they could see that I wanted him to. Alex and Chloe exchanged glances.

'He will,' Chloe said firmly. 'He has something he has to tell you.'

'Like what?' I demanded, thinking of the conversation with Faye and wondering what else Rory could be keeping from me.

Chloe exchanged another glance with Alex. 'We think it's really better if he tells you himself.'

Alex quickly peeked at his phone. 'We need to hit the road if we want to start on time,' he said. 'We're playing in Easton Rock.'

Chloe nodded. 'Talk soon,' she said giving me a hurried hug. Alex nodded towards me as they left me alone with my thoughts once more.

I turned the card over in my hands. Maybe Alex's doctor was worth a try.

#

Rory came over the next morning. I'd moved from my bedroom to the dining room, though not out of my pyjamas, and I was the one to answer the door.

'Hey,' he said.

'Hey.'

He looked over my shoulder and waved hesitantly. I followed his gaze to where Mum was standing in the hall, watching us.

'Do you want to talk outside?' I asked.

He nodded, looking relieved. I stepped out and closed the door behind us, thinking about how, after everything that had happened between us, he still hadn't seen my room and probably never would.

We sat on the front step in silence for a minute before he asked how I was.

'Fine,' I replied.

'Nice PJs.'

'Thanks.'

'I heard Alex and Chloe were here yesterday.'

'Yeah.'

'How are they?'

I lifted an eyebrow. 'Chloe's in your band. Alex lives across the road from you. Don't you communicate with anyone?'

He flashed me a wry smile. 'I never said I was perfect.'

'No, you just made me believe you loved me and that I could trust you.'

We slipped into another silence as I tried to think of what Rory was supposed to be telling me. 'How's the family?' I asked.

'Good. We just finished reading every Dr. Seuss book we could find, so now Ethan and Ella won't stop reciting them. And Maria hasn't picked any new fights with the neighbours yet.'

'So, are you two okay?'

Rory sighed. 'That's number one on the list of things people ask me, "Are we okay." And the truth is, I don't know. I don't know that we'll always live together. We've always been up and down and in and out. But I love the woman.'

I thought about all the things he'd told me about her and tried to think of one nice thing he'd said. But I couldn't.

'I don't think you love her at all,' I replied. 'Just like you never loved me, even though you said you did.'

'What makes you say that?'

'You don't talk about people you love the way you talk about Maria. And you don't treat people you love the way you treated me.'

'You can love someone without loving everything about them,' Rory countered.

'Even if the only thing you love about them is their ability to give birth to your kids?'

Rory stared at the ground, then out towards the street before finally turning back to me.

'She's pregnant,' he said, not quite meeting my gaze.

I closed my eyes. So much for just being his babysitter. But he'd lied about everything else, so why wouldn't he lie about that too?

'Is it yours?' I asked.

'Yep.'

'Are you sure? Given the way you two got together, it seems like she's quite happy to drop her pants for random guys she's only just met.'

I waited for him to defend the woman he supposedly loved, the mother of his children, the person he was probably going to spend the rest of his life with. But all he said was, 'It's mine. The dates match up.'

It was over. My best friend, my lifeline, was gone. He'd betrayed me. He'd promised me a future, and then ripped it out from under me when my eyes were on the stars.

But it was my fault too. I'd latched onto the first sign of light I came across. I'd put all my eggs into the basket labelled 'Rory'. And now every one of those eggs had shattered on the ground around us.

'Are you excited?' I asked.

'Sure. I think so,' he said. 'I mean, whatever happens with Maria, I'll always love the kids we make.'

But will they still love you when they're old enough to see your relationship for what it is? I wondered. I shook my head. It wasn't my problem anymore. Ella and Ethan and their new sibling wouldn't be the first kids to grow up in an uncertain environment, and they wouldn't be the last. But their parents' relationship didn't have to define them. And who knows, maybe the third time around, Rory and Maria would actually be able to sort their shit out for the sake of their kids.

'If you're happy, I'm happy for you,' I said. 'But I think you should go now.'

He stared at me. His eyes still held the same sweet, chocolate-brown gaze that had drawn me to him the day we met. And the truth was, I still wanted to dive into them. But I'd seen the reality behind the fairy-tale I'd dreamed up about us. And surely Maria had too. But if she still wanted to make believe, then who was I to stop her?

'I don't want to lose you, Jade,' Rory pleaded. 'And I get the impression you don't want to lose me either.'

'I never wanted to lose you! We could've been happy together. I would've loved Ethan and Ella as if they were my own. But you made a choice, and that choice obviously wasn't me.'

Rory looked wounded. 'It's not like we planned this. It's not like I wanted to hurt you.'

'Well, it happened, and I'm hurt.' I stood up. 'Just go, Hunter.'

He got to his feet, slowly. 'I'm sorry. I mean that. And it was good to see you again. You look well.'

I flashed him a sad smile. 'Thanks for coming,' I replied softly.

Chapter Forty-Eight

On Friday morning, I took the bus to the other side of town. I'd made an appointment at the GP clinic after looking up Doctor Lisa Riviera on their website, which described her as a mother of two who enjoyed all areas of family medicine and had a special interest in mental health.

I spent a nervous twenty minutes in the waiting room, watching cheesy infomercials until she called me in.

'I'm Lisa,' she said with a smile, inviting me to sit. 'What can I do for you today?'

My eyes floated over the pale green walls in her office, the bed, the scales, the computer on her desk and the poster that read Children Should Be Seen and Heard.

'I guess I feel really depressed,' I said at last.

She nodded, her face revealing nothing. 'How long have you been feeling like this?'

'A couple of years. But it's been worse in the past couple of weeks.'

'Did something happen to make it worse?'

I told Lisa the story of how I became friends and then more than friends with Rory, the rise and fall of my relationships with him and Faye, and what ultimately happened with Maria. Lisa handed me a box of tissues and tapped some notes into her computer.

'That must have really hurt you,' she said.

I nodded, dabbing at my nose and face.

'Is there a time of the day when you usually feel more depressed? Or is it about the same all the time?'

I was about to say it was always the same, but I remembered Faye had told Rory about me crying over him at night, so I tried to think harder about my answer. 'It's always there,' I said. 'But it's worse at night.'

Lisa nodded. 'During the day, it's easier to find something to distract you, which can make things a bit easier. Is that right?'

'Yeah.'

'What do you do for fun? Or to relax?'

'I like listening to music.'

'Do you exercise?'

I shook my head.

'It's not a bad idea to try maybe going for a walk each day if you can. You might find it lifts your mood, maybe even helps you sleep better so you're not thinking about things for so long at night.'

I didn't know if she was expecting a reply, so I said nothing.

'Have you had suicidal thoughts? Or made a suicide attempt?' she asked.

I stared at her poster and nodded. It was hard to say aloud but I knew I had to. That's why I was here. Because I couldn't rely on Rory or Faye or anyone else for my happiness. If I was ever going to get better or look forward to tomorrow, I would have to take care of it myself.

I took a deep breath. 'I checked into a hotel after Rory kicked me out of the gig. I tried to slash my wrists and hang myself with a sheet, but it didn't work.'

'And how did you feel when it didn't work?'

I shrugged. 'Empty.'

'Were you disappointed? Relieved? A bit of both?'

I considered her question for a moment. 'Maybe a bit of both.'

Lisa nodded. 'Had you ever self-harmed before you slashed your wrists?'

I bit my lip. I'd told Rory what I'd been doing and he'd let me down. Had anyone else ever seen the bruises? Had they quietly wondered how I got them, or had I been clever enough to make them look like they weren't there, or like the kind of bruises you got from bumping into furniture? I squinted at Lisa's computer, wondering what she'd typed, but the angle of the screen meant I couldn't read it, no matter how hard I looked.

'Yes,' I whispered at last.

'What sort of self-harming?'

'I hit myself.' I watched Lisa's reaction, wondering if she would think I was just an attention seeker too. 'I mean, it's just bruising. I know it's not like cutting or burning or something that leaves a scar,' I added.

'You're still hurting yourself,' Lisa replied. 'And bruising is internal bleeding.'

I looked down at my shoes.

'But it's not something to be embarrassed about,' she added. 'It's a way of coping that you've found works for you. I'd just like to help you find other ways that can work too, so that eventually you won't need to hit yourself anymore.'

I tried to remember how I'd been before I started hitting. But my rock had stayed with me when my real, living, breathing friends had thrown me away. Could I really give it up?

'What do you want me to do?' I asked.

'Do you want to try some things that might make you feel better?'

I nodded.

'Well, we basically have three options. One is just continued self-care. So, for you, that could be listening to your favourite songs, or going for a half-hour walk around the neighbourhood every day to see how you feel. Maybe even joining a social group or sporting team so you can meet new friends.'

There was a big difference between meeting new people and making friends—as in real friendships, that would continue even when you weren't useful to that person anymore, or after you stopped seeing each other all the time. Lisa was probably a people person and didn't know how hard it was to have a conversation with someone who wasn't paid to listen to you.

'The second option is medication.'

'I'm not taking drugs,' I said flatly. The thought of being dependent on a substance to function, like Faye, terrified me.

'It's not "drugs", it's medication,' she said. 'There's no shame in taking medicine to help correct an imbalance or to feel better. That kind of shame that people carry with them is what drives them to think they have no options left.'

I wondered if she'd lost someone to suicide that set her on the mission she was now on, but it didn't feel like my place to ask. 'What's the third option?' I asked.

'I can refer you to a counsellor,' Lisa said. 'I think that's a good place for you to start, especially since you're not keen on medication. You can have a few sessions, talk through what you're experiencing and then come back to see me. If you feel like it's working, you can continue, and if it's not, we'll try something else.'

I thought about Deanna. After all this time, I was going to talk to a real counsellor in the real world?

'Let's try the counselling,' I said.

Chapter Forty-Nine

My heart thumped in my ears as I stepped into the psychology practice for the first time. Lisa had given me a referral and I'd managed to book an appointment over the phone without passing out. Although I felt like I might pass out now.

I drew in a deep breath. The receptionist looked up and smiled.

'Hi, how can I help you today?' she asked.

I cleared my throat. 'Um, I have an appointment with Eleanor.'

The receptionist glanced down at her computer. 'Jade?'

I nodded.

'Take a seat, she'll be with you soon.'

There was a bottle of hand sanitiser at the front desk. I pumped some into my palms and sat down. The waiting room was decorated in soft pastel shades. There was a fish tank in my line of sight. I watched the fish swim gracefully around their home. They looked so calm, free of the fear and sadness that ruled my life.

'Jade?' a woman's gentle voice interrupted my thoughts. 'I'm Eleanor, it's nice to meet you. Would you like some tea, coffee, water?'

'Water, please.'

I followed her into a room. She gestured towards one of two couches. 'Make yourself comfortable. Let me just get your water.'

I sank into a couch cushion and looked around. Eleanor reappeared a moment later with a glass of water. I took it from her hands – trying not to tremble – and took a sip before setting it down on the table next to me.

Eleanor sat on the opposite couch with an iPad in her hand. 'So, how are you today, Jade?'

I shrugged. 'I'm okay.'

'I know it can be really daunting coming to a place like this and sitting in front of a stranger,' Eleanor said. 'A lot of people wouldn't do it. So, I think it's very courageous of you to take that step.'

I smiled nervously.

'And I want you to know that this is a safe space,' Eleanor continued. 'Anything you share with me is confidential unless I need to tell someone else in order to keep you safe. If you're at risk of causing serious harm to yourself or others. But I'll always let you know before I talk to anyone about anything you say in here. Does that sound okay?'

I nodded.

'Now, I'm going to ask you some questions. I know it's difficult but be as open and honest as you can be. Do you think you can try to do that?'

'Yes.'

'Great. I've seen your GP's referral but I'd like to hear this from you. What brings you here today?'

My mind started to scramble, trying to collect all the reasons that had led me to this room with Eleanor. I looked at her. She had warm, dark eyes and a kind smile. So had Rory, but Eleanor felt different somehow. I paused, started then stopped.

Focussing on Eleanor, I realised her face held no judgement. Perhaps, if I took it slowly, there might be a way through the darkness. I took a long, shaky breath and cleared my throat.

'I knew something was wrong with me when I found out Samson Otto was dead and all I could feel was dull envy…'

END

Acknowledgements

Before you close this book, I have a few people I wish to thank for their part in my first novel.

The first draft of Black and Blue was completed while I was enrolled in the Australian Writers' Centre's Write Your Novel program. Thanks to Pamela Freeman for her guidance and to all the talented authors who took that ride with me and helped workshop my manuscript in its infancy.

Thank you to Melissa-Jane Nguyen for giving my manuscript its first edit and believing this story was worth telling.

Thank you to Ian Andrew (a writing/editing/publishing triple threat!) for going above and beyond to turn my dream into a reality. It's a privilege to have you in my corner.

Thank you to all the musicians (way too many to name) who made a weirdo like me feel welcome and acted like it was perfectly normal when I started taking notes. I'm releasing this book during a pandemic that's been really tough on your industry and I'm thinking of you.

Thank you to my friends, family, colleagues and everyone who's had my back.

Thank you to my doctor and psychologist for helping me find my way.

Thank you to Marina Sirtis for bringing Jade's first counsellor to life on screen.

Thank you to the past and present members of Bon Jovi for their role in my soundtrack – and Jade's.

Thank you to my parents for their lifelong support. Thanks for taking me to the library. Thanks for reading to me. Thanks for making sure I had everything I needed. I love you and hope I make you proud.

Thank you to my big brothers for always looking out for their baby sister, even when I was being a little brat.

And last, but certainly not least – thank you, dear reader, for taking the chance on my little book.

About the Author

Lee-Ann Khoh is a self-confessed socially awkward butterfly who prefers writing to talking but has been known to sing in front of an audience on occasion. Hailing from Perth, she studied journalism at Curtin University before deciding she was better at making up her own stories. She is now a library technician who fantasises about the day someone asks if there are any Lee-Ann Khoh books in the library.

If you meet Lee-Ann, she probably won't say much, but you can read some of her thoughts at leeannkhoh.com.

Need to talk to someone?

Australia:

Lifeline - http://www.lifeline.org.au

Kids Helpline - https://kidshelpline.com.au/

Beyond Blue - https://www.beyondblue.org.au/

Suicide Call Back Service
https://www.suicidecallbackservice.org.au/

1800RESPECT - https://www.1800respect.org.au/

United Kingdom:

Samaritans - https://www.samaritans.org/

National Suicide Prevention Helpline UK
https://www.spbristol.org/nsphuk

Shout 85258 - https://giveusashout.org/

United States:

National Suicide Prevention Lifeline
https://suicidepreventionlifeline.org/

Crisis Text Line - https://www.crisistextline.org/
RAINN - https://www.rainn.org/
New Zealand:

Lifeline Aotearoa - https://www.lifeline.org.nz/
Youthline - https://www.youthline.co.nz/
The Lowdown - https://www.thelowdown.co.nz/
1737 - https://1737.org.nz/
Ireland:

Samaritans - https://www.samaritans.org/
Pieta - https://www.pieta.ie/
50808 - https://text50808.ie/
Canada:

Canada Suicide Prevention Service
https://www.crisisservicescanada.ca/en/

Kids Help Phone - https://kidshelpphone.ca/
Crisis Text Line - https://www.crisistextline.ca/